The Visitor by Dennis Holt

And Enoch walked with God; and he was not; for God took him – Genesis 5:24

CORNELIUS' HOUSE MINISTRIES
3115 Pyburn Extended
Pocahontas, Arkansas 72455

This book is gratefully dedicated to everyone who has
enjoyed the adventures of Father Rex Macon

CHAPTER ONE

Strange Medicine

"All right, let's vote," John Burns announced. "All those in favor of moving bingo to Monday nights so that it doesn't conflict with the basketball schedule at the high school, please say aye."

Father Macon looked around the table as each parish council member voiced their vote. In all the years he had been a parish priest this was the one thing that he could not get used to. Parish administration was the last thing on his list of favorite things.

"All those opposed?" John continued. He was president of the Parish Council. "Looks like it's unanimous." He looked at Father with a smile. "Is that okay with you, Father?"

"Sure," Father smiled. "I think we need to do all we can to support the public school system. Besides, I don't think it will make the people of the parish much difference when the bingo is."

"As long as it is," Wilma Taylor quickly added. "I know a lot of the older people really enjoy it and for some it's about the only time they get out."

Father nodded his head in agreement. He was amazed how important entertainment was to the people of the parish. He wished they cared as much for spiritual things. But that seemed to be the way of the times. He inhaled slowly then let his mind drift. He was glad that the meetings were only once a month.

"Excuse me, Father," a voice interrupted from the corner of the room.

Everyone sitting at the table turned toward the voice. It was Molly Hampton, Father's secretary.

"I'm sorry. I didn't mean to interrupt. But Father, you have a long distance call from Albuquerque, New Mexico."

Father frowned as if to tell Molly that he didn't need to be disturbed. She read his expression.

"I told him you were in a meeting, but he said it was important." She shrugged her shoulders. "He says his name is Chief Walking Cloud."

The eyes of every parish council member quickly turned from Molly and focused on Father.

Father pushed back his chair and got up. "John, go ahead with the meeting. There's nothing on the agenda that really needs my attention." He nodded to the other members seated around the table as he made his way over to Molly. He knew they were waiting for an explanation but he thought it better just to leave them wondering. When he reached Molly she turned and led him out of the room and down the hall to his office. She waited for him to enter then she pulled the door almost closed.

"Call me if you need me," she whispered, as Father reached to pick up the phone.

He nodded and smiled, placing the phone to his ear. Molly pushed the door shut.

"Hey, Chief, how's my favorite medicine man?"

"I'm fine, Father. How are you?"

His old friend sounded the same as he remembered. It had been at least five years since he had seen the old warrior.

6

"Molly says you're calling from Albuquerque. Is that where you're staying?"

"Yes, I've been here for about two years. I've been living among the Pueblo outside Albuquerque. They are a good people. They remind me of myself in my younger days."

Father laughed. "You mean full of the old ways?"

"Yeah. They still have a lot of bitterness towards the whites and also the white man's God. Many have clung to the ways of their fathers. Some have accepted Christ but it is certainly slow going."

"Is everything all right? You sound worried."

The old Indian laughed. "You haven't lost your gift of discernment. I didn't realize I was wearing my heart on my sleeve. But you're right. I am concerned."

"What's going on?"

"The people are calling it strange medicine. Do you remember this past summer when we had all the forest fires out here?"

"Yes, I remember. I saw it on TV. It seemed like the entire western half of the country was on fire."

"Well, it certainly was out here. It took firefighters two months to get the fires under control. It burned almost 300,000 acres, and most of it was land that belonged to the Pueblo. The old medicine men said it was a sign of the return of the gods. The earth was purified by fire in anticipation of the god's return. They may have been right."

"Why is that?"

"The fire burned a lot of the land and scorched a lot more. In the process it brought to light some of the older sites that had been overlooked because of the overgrowth."

"You mean archaeological sites?"

"Yeah, that's right. Some of the findings were pretty remarkable. But, the greatest find seems to be in a place called the Chaco Canyon. It's a national park, but since the fire it has been closed, not because of the fire, but because of something that the fire revealed. Apparently the heat caused an area of the canyon wall to collapse, exposing an entrance to a large cave. Some of the fire fighters entered the cave, but the government was quickly called in and the area sealed off to everyone except government personnel."

"What did they find? Do you have any idea?"

"Ben Running Deer's son, Gabe, was on the fire line when they found the cave-in. He was one of the first ones inside. He was told by the Feds to say nothing. He obeyed except he did speak to his father, Ben, who is a Tesuque Pueblo medicine man. What Ben shared with me was pretty amazing."

"Can you share it with me?" Father asked, anxious to hear what had been discovered that was so protected by the federal government.

"I can," the old chief replied, "but not over the phone. Believe me it would be better. Things are very much on edge around here. Whatever was in that cave has caused the realm of the spirit to become very active. All of the medicine men are aware that something is going on. There is a lot of concern. That's why I'm calling. I was hoping I could get you to come out and stay with me for a couple of weeks."

Father respected the old chief's abilities in dealing with things of the spiritual realm. He was a Cherokee medicine man who knew his trade very well. Father had prayed with him to accept Jesus as Lord about five years before and that had only enhanced the old man's spiritual prowess. If the Chief was concerned, something very powerful was going on.

"Gosh, Chief, I don't know. I'll have to check my schedule and also see if I can find a replacement for that length of time."

"I know it's short notice, Father. I wouldn't have called you if I hadn't thought it was important. I would certainly appreciate it if you'd pray about it and see if the Lord thinks it is as important as I do for you to be out here."

Father wished his old friend would elaborate more. He wondered why he was so reluctant to discuss anything over the phone. He needed to know more. "Is the strange medicine caused by demonic activity?" he boldly asked.

The old Chief was silent for a few seconds. "I don't know," he finally answered. "Whatever it is, it is building. Just recently some of the families have reported their children lost."

"What?" Father exclaimed.

"The last I heard five children, all below the age of five, had suddenly vanished. It has most of the people around here pretty antsy."

"I guess so. And you think there is a connection between the cave and the missing children?"

"I think so. The sheriff's office has investigated the missing children but…"

The old man stopped suddenly.

"But what?"

"It's like they don't care," the old man whispered. "They come out and look around. They ask questions. But, it's as if finding the children isn't a priority."

"The Feds?"

"I think so. But I can't prove it."

"Boy, this is heavy."

"A lot more than you realize. Like I said, I wouldn't have called you if I didn't need you."

Father looked up at the ceiling. Two weeks was a long time away from his parish. "Maybe I could come out for a couple of days."

"I would certainly appreciate it, Father. If we could sit down and talk in private, I think you, too, might see the urgency here. Pray about it and call me in the morning. I'll pray on this end, too."

"I will. In fact, I'll go into prayer as soon as we hang up. I'll call you back about 10:30 tomorrow morning. Do you have a number where I can reach you?"

The chief gave Father Macon a number where he could be reached then wished him a good night. Father hung up the phone and looked at the number he had written on the note pad. He wondered what was going on. What did the Feds find in the cave? What did the missing children have to do with the whole thing? He got up from the desk, shut off the light to the office, and stepped out into the hallway. He walked a few steps, then stopped and peered into Molly's office. She looked up at him from her desk and smiled.

"Was that a real Chief or was it a practical joke? I thought it might be one of your priest friends."

"No," Father laughed. "It was a real Indian Chief. I met him about five or six years ago in the northern part of the state. He's a real Cherokee medicine man."

Molly could see the concern develop in Father's face as he talked about his old friend.

"Is everything okay?"

Father shook his head. "I'm not sure." He pointed down at the day planner on Molly's desk. "Would it be possible for me to take a couple of days off?"

Molly took her finger and traced it across the entire week. "You don't have anything really pressing until the weekend. Today's Monday. You could probably sneak off until Saturday. Confessions are at four o'clock and Mass is at five-thirty. Want me to mark you off?"

"Not yet. Let me wait until the morning. I'll let you know then."

Father turned and started out of the room.

"Are you going back to the meeting?"

Father had forgotten about the meeting. He stopped and scratched his head. He looked back at Molly. "No, I don't think so. I believe I'll go over to the rectory and pray."

"Sounds good. I'll see you in the morning. Have a nice night."

"You, too."

Father left and walked out the back way of the office building and over to the rectory. He knew that if he went back to the meeting he would have to explain about the Chief. That was something he would rather not do at the moment. He would explain later.

It was almost dark as Father unlocked the rectory and walked into his living room. He sat down on the couch and immediately began to pray in the Spirit. After about thirty minutes, he had received nothing. He took one of the pillows on the couch and placed it behind his head as he stretched out. He shut his eyes but continued to pray.

Suddenly he was standing on the moon, looking down at the

11

earth. It was a beautiful blue hue with white clouds swirling all around. As he watched a small black cloud began to form off the eastern side of the tip of Florida. It grew in size and intensity. Quickly it covered most of the United States and South America. The cloud seemed to swallow the earth and after only a short time the earth was completely covered.

"And darkness was on the face of the deep," a voice shouted.

Father looked around to see where the voice came from but there was no one. When he turned back to the earth a huge wind was blowing the dark cloud off the earth. It took what seemed a long time, but the blue orb was finally free from the darkness. When the wind stopped, the earth was no longer covered. It was beautiful and pristine once more.

Like a silent rocket, Father began to lift off the moon and move toward the earth. As he got closer he recognized he was heading toward the southwestern United States. He could see it clearly. Suddenly the black cloud began to re-appear over the area. Small at first, it continued to grow as he got closer and closer. By the time he reached the cloud it was much thicker and completely blocked his view of the earth. He could smell the cloud. It was strangling in nature. It was heavy with the odor of sulfur. He began to cough as the smell penetrated his nostrils and his lungs.

"Lord Jesus, help me," he screamed. But it was not his voice that he heard coming out of his mouth. It was the voice of the old Chief. He coughed, trying to breathe. He felt like he was drowning. He could feel the life leaving his body. With all the strength he could gather, he again called out. "Lord Jesus, save me." To his amazement, his voice was like the sound of many waters. But as he listened, it was no longer the sound of flowing water at all. It was the sound of children's voices. The voices echoed over and over again as he spiraled toward the earth. With a great thud he hit the earth and dust flew. He was in no pain but was unable to move. Lying on his back he saw a billboard off to his right. There was a picture of an Indian in full dress doing a ceremonial dance. Off to the side were some words. They read: Welcome to New Mexico, the land of enchantment.

Father opened his eyes and looked at the ceiling. He took a deep breath. His lungs still ached. He could still smell the sulfur. It had been a dream. He knew that. But, it was also an answer to his prayer.

He quickly got up and picked up a notebook from the end table beside the couch. He took a pen out of his pocket and wrote down the dream as completely and precisely as he could remember. He included every minute detail, for he knew that every tiny thing mattered in the dream.

As soon as he finished, he read the dream twice, trying to figure out its meaning. What did the cloud represent and why did it come from off the east coast of Florida?

"New Mexico, the land of enchantment," he read aloud. He knew in his heart that this part was the answer to his prayers. He was definitely supposed to go. He laughed as he remembered hitting the ground with a loud thud and the dust cloud that was produced. He looked up as if looking into heaven. "Lord, this doesn't sound like a good entrance."

He looked at his watch. Molly had already left for the day. He would have to tell her the first thing tomorrow morning that he would be going to New Mexico for the week. He picked up the phone book and found the number for the airport in Little Rock.

The Visitor

It took little time to make the travel arrangements. He found a flight that connected to Albuquerque by way of Dallas. It departed Little Rock the next day at 4:10 in the afternoon. That would be plenty of time, he thought. He would also call the Chief tomorrow morning and tell him the time the plane would be arriving in Albuquerque.

His mind went back to the dream and the sound of the children's voices. It was strange how, at first, it had sounded like a huge waterfall cascading over a large drop off. Then quickly it had become the voices of small children crying out to God in their distress. Did this have something to do with the missing children that the Chief had mentioned? His curiosity was further enhanced as he thought of the cave and what was contained there. He would find out tomorrow.

The rest of the evening was spent getting his things ready for the trip. He decided to skip supper and fast as preparation for the spiritual guidance he would need for the week ahead.

By bedtime, he had everything packed and ready to go. He would say Mass in the morning, call the Chief, then head to Little Rock. His prayers before bed consisted mainly of petitions for protection and guidance for himself and the old Chief.

"They have murdered me!"

Father opened his eyes. He lay quietly listening. The voice had been that of a young man. He wondered whether it was a dream or whether it was demonic tomfoolery. Nothing else came. Father got up and sat on the edge of his bed. He looked at his watch. It was almost time for him to get up anyway. He got up and headed toward the bathroom. As he stepped into the shower, he could still

14

hear the voice in his mind. What did it mean? He could hear both frustration and desperation in it. "They have murdered me," he repeated as he stuck his head under the shower.

Father informed Molly of his trip plans and told her he would be leaving right after Mass. He gave her the old Chief's number where he could be reached in case of an emergency.

After Mass he walked back to the rectory and called the Chief. He knew something was up as soon as his old friend answered.

"Chief, this is Father Macon. What's wrong?"

The old Chief took a deep breath. "My heart is heavy, my friend. Gabe Running Deer was killed last night."

"What!" Father exclaimed. "How?"

"He ran off the road and down an embankment. He was pronounced dead at the scene. Funny thing though, he's been driving those roads for years. He was a good man. He will be missed."

As the old Chief talked, Father remembered the voice he had heard that morning. Were they connected? He started to share it with the Chief but decided to wait. "Will there be an autopsy?" he asked.

"I'm not sure, Father. The family will have to decide that. I would guess not, however. With things the way they are around here Ben will probably elect to keep the burial as simple as possible."

"Do you think it's connected to the cave?"

"I don't know. Gabe was a baby Christian. Only recently did he make Jesus Lord of his life, so he did not understand the protection he had against Satan nor his demons. Who knows what could have happened out there on the road? It's secluded. It was dark. The

15

road is steep and made of loose rock. He could have seen anything. He might have even swerved to miss a deer. Only God knows. But, it is interesting that he's the only one who could tell us what was in that cave."

"Man, things are strange out there."

"Oh Father, that is an understatement. Strange can't describe it. The old timers say it is much worse than with the Roswell incident."

"Roswell?"

"Yeah, you know. Back in the forties a flying saucer was supposed to have crashed in the desert around Roswell. That's only a few miles south of where we are. The government came in then, too, and tried to squelch all the information and cover up the incident. They said it was a weather balloon that the government was using at the time. Those around here who know say it was no weather balloon."

"I remember now," Father replied. "Didn't they find some bodies from the crash site, small little creatures that ended up in a place called Area 51?"

"That's right. But the government denied everything. Not one piece of the craft was left on the desert floor. They had the military scour every inch. Sounds strange for a weather balloon, doesn't it?"

"Is it a big operation out there now?"

"Oh, man! No one can get within two miles of the cave. The military is everywhere. It's big, and mum is the word with every solider out here. There are some members of the press here, too, but they've come up empty also. The military has set up a base camp northwest of Albuquerque. Whatever they're pulling out of the cave, they are taking it there first. No one but the military is allowed even close to the base. You need to see it for yourself."

"I guess I will. I'll be in Albuquerque this afternoon."

"Fantastic," the old Chief laughed. "That's the best news I've heard in a long time."

Father filled the Chief in on his travel plans. His flight was scheduled to arrive around 7:45. The chief agreed to meet him at the airport.

After hanging up, Father's mind returned to Gabe Running Deer. He prayed for the soul of the young man. He was glad he was saved. "Thank you, Father, that Your mercy endures forever." As he prayed, the voice from the early-morning dream returned. Were they connected? If they were, who would be so cold as to murder an innocent young man? And why? Was it to keep him silent? What was that important?

Father loaded his jeep and locked the door to the rectory. He walked back over to the office complex and to Molly's office to say good-bye. She told him to have a good time and that things would be okay while he was gone. As he started to leave, he turned back to Molly.

"Molly, what do you know about Roswell, New Mexico?"

Molly laughed and shook her head. "Just what I've read and seen on TV. Supposedly some type of spaceship crashed out there and the government tried to cover it up. They found some little spacemen at the crash site who were all dead." She laughed again and shrugged her shoulders. "That's about it."

"Do you think it's real?"

Molly looked at Father and frowned. "I don't know. I guess I've never really thought about it. If it were real, how would it fit into our Christian belief system?"

"That's a good question. I've wondered that myself."

Molly laughed. "You're not going out to New Mexico to chase little green men, are you?"

Father smiled and shook his head. "I hope not."

Molly's facial expression revealed that she was not expecting his answer. She wondered why he was going. But, she knew that if he wanted her to know, he would tell her.

Father told Molly good-bye and left the office complex. He walked to his jeep.

The trip to Little Rock went by quickly. Father's mind was so full of thoughts that time was forgotten. It was only as he pulled into the airport entrance that he became aware of how fast the trip had been. He parked and made his way to the terminal. The lines were short and checking in was simple. It had been a while since he had been in the terminal. He enjoyed studying the people as they hurried along. He prayed for some as the Spirit prompted. His mind, however, kept drifting back to the conversation with Chief Walking Cloud. What had the cave contained that caused the government so much concern?

The plane was on time and soon he was on board and in his seat. He watched as other people came aboard and found their seat assignments. The noise of the overhead compartments closing slowly diminished with time, indicating that departure was near. The plane was only about half full and the seat next to him remained empty. After the flight attendant finished her pre-flight ritual, he watched out the window as the plane taxied out to the runway. They had to wait only a few minutes. With a soft roar the plane raced down the runway and leaped into the air. He prayed in the Spirit as he looked out the window toward the horizon. It caused him to remember his dream. He could still see, in his mind, the dark cloud coming out of an area in the southwest. It smelled like hell.

"Would you care for a soft drink?"

The voice brought him back to the present. He turned and looked up at the flight attendant. "No thanks. Maybe later."

"Just call if you change your mind."

"I will, thank you."

She smiled then continued up the aisle. He looked out the window again as his mind returned to the dream. Suddenly he reached under his seat and pulled out his carry-on. He unzipped the pocket and took out his Bible. "And darkness was on the face of the deep," he said quietly to himself as he thumbed the Book's pages. That's what the voice had said in the dream. He knew where those words were found. It was Genesis chapter one, verse two. Finding the scripture, he read: *And the earth was without form, and void; and darkness was upon the face of the deep. And the Spirit of God moved upon the face of the waters.*

He closed his Bible and leaned back in his seat. He knew where this darkness had come from which made the earth void. Satan had brought it about. He was the author of darkness. Was he responsible for the cloud that he had seen in his dream? Father Macon knew that this fallen angel was unrelenting in his attempt to destroy mankind. He'd had many encounters with the prince of darkness, and each one had been severe. What did satan or his demon hoard have to do with the cave?

Father placed his Bible back in his carry-on as the pilot came on the intercom and announced that Dallas was only a few minutes away. They would be on the ground for about a half-hour, then on to Albuquerque.

The western sky radiated a red hue as the plane touched down and slowly pulled into its docking position. After a few minutes some people got out of their seats, recovered their carry-ons and made their way off the plane.

For a while, Father thought that no one was going to board. They had waited more than thirty minutes and he figured that soon they would be getting under way. Suddenly a large chain of people appeared and began to fill the aisle. The ear-shattering litany of the overhead compartments began again as the newcomers stowed their bags.

A young woman stopped at his seat and looked at the letter on the overhead. "Twenty-two B," she said. "I believe this is mine."

Father Macon smiled and watched as she stored her bags then sat down and fastened her seat belt. She bent over and placed a bag under her seat then rose up and looked over at him.

"I'm Denise Cameron."

"Rex Macon," he returned with a smile.

"You from Texas, Rex?"

"No, ma'am. I'm from Arkansas."

She smiled and shook her head. "I thought Rex sounded like a Texas name."

Father laughed. "I guess it does. I never thought of it that way."

"What line of work you in, Rex?"

"I'm a Catholic priest."

The look in Denise's eyes revealed her surprise. "I thought you guys wore a white collar?"

"We do most of the time but I'm kind of on vacation."

Denise laughed. "I didn't know that you guys ever took a vacation."

"I can see you are not a Catholic."

She laughed again but was interrupted by the flight attendant who once again repeated the proper use of the seat belt. She and Father listened attentively then sat in silence as the plane backed out and began to taxi.

"What line of work are you in?" Father asked as the plane stopped on the runway.

"I'm a reporter with the *Dallas Herald*," she answered, looking past Father to the outside.

Father Macon frowned and studied her face as she watched the plane prepare for takeoff. He guessed her to be about thirty-five. She had short brown hair that just covered her ears. Her green eyes were large and beautiful. She wore little makeup but her complexion was flawless. Everything indicated that she was a woman who was used to frequent travel. He noticed a small pendant on a gold chain which accented her long neck. It was the symbol of the yin and yang. He looked down at her left hand. There was no ring.

She looked at him and smiled as the plane began its race down the runway. "Exciting, isn't it?"

Father nodded.

"I fly a lot with my job and it never gets dull. I love it. Oh," she giggled, as the plane left the runway. "That tickles."

Father laughed. It did tickle in the pit of his stomach. He had forgotten to notice.

Denise settled back in her seat as the plane continued to climb.

21

"You heading to Albuquerque?" Father asked.

"Yeah. I'm supposed to check out some type of military activity going on out there."

"You must mean the cave."

She turned and squinted her green eyes at him. "What do you know about the cave?"

"I know that the brush fires that ravaged the land out there caused one of the canyons to cave in and expose some type of archaeological site that the government has all but quarantined."

"Do you know what they found?"

Father shook his head. "I don't have a clue. Do you?"

"Not really. It's all hush-hush. That's why I'm going. Something that secretive has to have a story in it."

Father could sense that she knew more than she was sharing. "Do you think it might be related to the Roswell incident?"

She looked over at him and grinned. "For a priest you sure are in the know, aren't you?"

Father shrugged his shoulders. "Just speculating."

Denise turned her head and looked around the plane then ducked her head behind the seat in front of her and looked at him. "You may be more correct than you realize," she whispered. "It is *very similar* to the Roswell incident. Some think that whatever was found in the cave is what the aliens were looking for when they crashed."

"You mean they buried something in the cave then came back to get it?"

"Yeah, but what was buried had been there a long time, maybe since the beginning of this planet. Some think that it sent out a signal of some kind that attracted the alien spacecraft. But, they crashed coming into our atmosphere before they could recover it."

"So you think it might be some kind of alien spacecraft?"

"I don't know what it is. But whatever it is, the military thinks it's pretty important. According to those who are out there now, they have the place sealed off like an outbreak of Ebola."

"Have you heard about the missing children?"

Denise frowned. "Is it connected?"

"I don't know but by the last count there were five children missing in the same general area."

Denise bit her lip as she again shook her head. "Man, this thing just keeps getting stranger by the minute."

"Do you think the government will ever make any kind of announcement?"

"They'll have to with as much exposure as this thing has given them. But," she shook her head in disgust, "you know the government, they'll come up with some smoke and mirrors excuse that has nothing to do with the truth. I feel we will never know what's going on unless we find out for ourselves."

Father was impressed with her tenacity. "Are you concerned that the process of finding information may be dangerous?"

Denise smiled. "I've found many times that the truth threatens a lot of people. But, usually there is someone who knows, who cannot keep quiet. It's my job to find that individual. That's what makes a good reporter. It's as much instinct as it is talent."

Their conversation was interrupted long enough for both of them to receive a soft drink from the flight attendant who was making her way up the aisle of the plane with her refreshment cart. Denise sipped her drink then looked at Father.

"Are you going to Albuquerque, too?"

Father nodded, taking the time to swallow. "Yes. I have a friend who lives just north of Albuquerque. He invited me out for a couple of days."

He took another drink. He felt that it was best not to mention the Chief. Something had happened to Gabe Running Deer and until he knew more, he thought it best to remain silent.

They had just finished their drinks when the intercom came alive and announced that the plane would be landing very shortly. They had already been given permission to land.

"That didn't take very long," Denise smiled. She reached under her seat, recovered her carry-on and placed it on her lap. She looked again at Father. "I've certainly enjoyed talking to you. Maybe I'll see you again in Albuquerque."

"I hope so," Father smiled. "I don't know that we'll get back into town. But, if we do we may run into each other. How long will you be here?"

Denise shrugged. "I guess as long as it takes." She reached into her carry-on and pulled out a card and handed it to Father. "I'll be staying at the Marriott. If you hear anything that you think is important, give me a call."

Father took the card and looked at it. Denise Cameron, Reporter was in the center of the card. Dallas Herald was in bold blue letters across the top. At the bottom was her phone and fax numbers. He put the card in his shirt pocket.

The plane landed with little effort and quickly made its way to the terminal docking bay. People were already in the aisle before the plane stopped completely. Once again the overhead compartments came alive. Denise followed the crowd and removed her bags from the compartment over her seat. Father had decided

24

to let the crowd thin out somewhat before he attempted an exit.

"Rex, I'll see you," Denise said, then turned and jumped into the fast moving line up the aisle.

Father waved but Denise didn't see him. It only took a matter of minutes until the number of passengers on the plane had thinned to just a few. Father gathered his bags and made his way to the front of the plane. He thanked the plane's crew then walked to the terminal.

As he walked into the main lobby he spotted the old Chief. The five years had been kind to the old man. He looked almost the same as he had the last time Father had seen him. His white hair hung in braids on either side of his dark and wrinkled face. His six foot frame hadn't changed its countenance one bit. He stood tall and proud.

The Chief had spotted Father about the same time. He waved and smiled. Father made his way to his old friend. When they met Father set his bags down and embraced the Indian. "It is very good to see you, my friend."

"Our brother the wind has been kind to us today," he said as he hugged Father Macon. "He has brought us together again."

"Amen," Father replied, then turned and picked up his bags.

"Need some help with those?" the Chief asked.

"No thanks. Just lead the way."

Father followed the Chief through the terminal. The crowd was heavy for a small airport. Father noticed some of the men wearing Army fatigues. He said nothing. They walked to the baggage area, reclaimed Father's luggage, then made their way to the parking area.

"It doesn't look like much," the Chief laughed as they found his old truck. "But it will get us around. The desert is harsh on mechanical equipment."

"It looks great to me," Father encouraged. "This is just like home."

The Chief laughed. "That's right. I forgot." He pointed to the bed of the pickup. "Just throw your gear in there. It'll ride fine."

Father put his bags in the bed of the truck against the cab and opened the door. The Chief was already behind the wheel. He smiled as he started the truck's engine.

"Looks rough, but runs like a horse."

Father smiled as the old Indian put the truck in gear and headed out of the parking lot. Once they were on the highway, Father could wait no longer. "What did Gabe Running Deer say they found in the cave?"

The Chief took a deep breath then looked over at Father. "I don't want to play games with you. But, before I tell you I want to show you something."

Father frowned. He knew his old friend well enough to know that he was a wise man. As much as Father wanted to know, he respected the Chief's wisdom. "Where are we going?"

"We are going to one of the canyons near Chaco. I want to show you some pictographs, you know, prehistoric rock drawings."

Father nodded.

"We've got about an hour's sunlight left and I think it's important that I show you these pictographs before we go home. I think you'll find them interesting." The old man looked over at Father and smiled, revealing his white teeth. "This group of pictographs is called the Holy Ghost panel."

CHAPTER TWO

The Cave

"What?" Father asked, thinking that the Chief was kidding.

The old man laughed. "I'm not fooling. What I want you to see is a set of rock drawings that have some very odd looking characters."

Father frowned. "Why do they call it Holy Ghost?"

The Chief didn't answer for a few seconds. He started to speak but stopped. "I'd rather wait and let you see for yourself. There are about eighteen panels. They are all very strange."

Father nodded. He knew what the Chief was trying to do. Rock pictographs were like Rorschach ink drawings. One could read about anything into them. The Chief, knowing that, didn't want to influence Father's opinion with his own.

The western sky was turning a bright orange when the old Indian pulled the truck to a stop. He turned off the key and opened his door. He looked back at Father. "Let's go."

Father opened the door and followed the Chief toward a large rock bluff. The shadows were growing rapidly in length as they made their way along the rock wall. Even in the dimming light he could see the deep red color of the rocks.

"Here we are," the Chief suddenly announced.

The Visitor

Father Macon walked to where the old man was standing. He looked at the rock face. "Anasazi."

The Chief turned and looked at Father in surprise, then slapped his leg. "I forgot. You've got a degree in archaeology."

"An old degree," Father laughed. "I remember seeing some of these drawings years ago. I know they were attributed to the Anasazi, but I don't remember anything being mentioned about the Holy Ghost."

"That's the name of this set of pictographs. I'm not sure when it was given that name." The old man leaned forward and put his finger on one of the drawings. "I think this figure…"

"Is the Holy Ghost," Father interrupted, finishing the sentence.

"Yeah, that's right. Notice how he appears at different places on the rock face."

Father scanned the other drawings. "Some of the figures are wearing robes like we do during Mass."

"Yeah, or lab coats."

Now it was Father Rex's turn to look in surprise at the Chief.

The old man smiled. "Look here," he said, pointing again. "This figure shows up three times on this set of drawings. It is always with the Holy Ghost figure."

Father turned and again studied the drawings. "It looks like a man in a bull's headdress."

"That's right," the Chief agreed. "But notice how he seems to always be in front of the Holy Ghost figure."

"You mean like he was protecting him?"

"Yeah, possibly."

Father turned his head to one side. "Or it could be that the guy with the horns is a shaman calling forth the spirit. Maybe these fellows in the robes around them are the assisting medicine men."

"That, too, is a possibility, but," the Chief grinned. "I wanted you to see these drawings in light of what Gabe Running Deer saw while in the cave."

Father looked at the Chief. "What did he see?"

The Chief took a deep breath. "He said that there were two large canisters, each one about twice the size of a large coffin. They were metallic in color with half of the canister covered by a clear glass-like material that allowed him to see inside. He said that one of the canisters had been broken into at an earlier time because it contained only a skeleton. But the skeleton was not that of a man. Or at least part of the skeleton didn't look human. The bottom half had the torso and legs of a man. But the skull looked like a bull or some type of animal with horns."

"You mean like a minotaur?"

The Chief pointed to the horned figure painted on the rock. "Like that right there."

"I didn't think of it before," Father said, staring at the drawing, "but that figure represents a minotaur, a half-man, half-bull creature found in Greek mythology."

"Were they real?" the Chief asked, shaking his head.

"No. They weren't supposed to be."

"Well, Gabe said that was what was in the first canister."

Father nodded. "What was in the other one?"

The old Chief turned and looked Father in the eyes. "He said it was a man. But the man was in some type of clear sack or plastic bag."

Father pointed to the Holy Ghost figure. "Like this guy right here?"

"Exactly," the Chief nodded.

"Was that all there was in the cave?"

"Gabe said there were a lot of cave pictographs like these here and a round metallic container about the size of a garbage can."

Father Macon stood studying the pictographs. The light was almost gone.

"Let's head back to the truck," the Chief suggested. "It'll be dark soon."

Father nodded, then turned and followed the Chief. Neither of them spoke as they carefully made their way back to the truck. Both were deep in thought.

Once inside the truck, the Chief started the engine, turned on the lights, then looked at Father. "I've been trying to figure out where those canisters could have come from."

Father nodded. "I was wondering the same thing. Did Gabe say anything more about the canister that contained the man?"

"Only that there was a fog inside the glass that prevented a good look at him. He said he could tell the figure was a man, but his features were blurred because of the fog."

"Cryonic suspension."

"What's that?" the Chief frowned.

"It's a process of preserving human tissue for an extended period of time by using extremely low temperatures. The fog that Gabe saw was what they call the cryoprotective agent or the chemical that keeps the body in a suspended state."

"I didn't know we had that technology."

Father looked at the Chief. "We don't."

The Chief laughed then put the truck in gear. "No wonder the government was so excited about the cave."

The headlights of the truck cut through the thick darkness like a knife. The stars shone like miniature diamonds in the sky above them. The Chief pointed to the horizon ahead of them. "Did they come from out there?"

Father shook his head. "I don't know. If those things were really cryonic suspension chambers then they are not from earth. We don't have the technology. And there is no telling how long those containers have been in the cave. What little we do know about cryonic suspension has just been learned since the early sixties. Whoever put those chambers in the cave was way ahead of where we are now."

The old truck rattled as it bumped across the desert floor. The Chief, at times, seemed to fight the wheel as if struggling with an unseen force. It failed, however, to distract him from the issue. He looked over at Father Macon. "That's the only explanation though, isn't it?"

Father forced a frown that seemed to come from deep within him. "I just can't believe that an alien civilization exists with this degree of technology. Or maybe I should say I don't want to believe it."

"Why is that?" the Chief asked, again fighting the wheel.

"Because everything that has been made was made through Jesus Christ. If there was a group of people or beings from another planet would Jesus be their Savior, too?"

"Oh, boy!" the Chief replied, gritting his teeth. "I see your point. I never thought of that. It would certainly cloud the picture for a lot of people, wouldn't it?"

Father nodded. "I'm afraid it would. Christianity as we know it would suddenly be faced with questions that it could not answer.

The Visitor

Many people would lose their faith. It would be hard to believe that the God of Abraham was the same as the God of Zorba the alien from Uranus."

"Unless the canisters contained references to a deity."

"That's true. But, even then, how would the story of Adam and Eve and the sacrifice of Jesus Christ fit into their civilization history?" Father shook his head. "There's got to be another explanation."

The Chief looked over at Father and grinned. Even in the dim light emitted from the speedometer he could see the frustration in the face of his friend. "Could it be some kind of trick from Satan?"

"I thought of that. But Satan does not have the power to do something of this magnitude in the natural realm. He is a spirit. He exists and works within the realm of the Spirit. This is something in the natural, governed and controlled by natural laws." Father looked at the old Indian and squinted his eyes. "Satan may have had something to do with this, but he did not build the metal chambers nor produce the rock pictographs."

"Then what does that leave us?"

Father laughed. "Not much. There's only one other possibility."

The Chief waited, expecting Father to continue. When he didn't, the old Indian slapped the steering wheel. "Well, don't keep me hanging. What's the other possibility?"

Father took a deep breath then exhaled. "Maybe the chambers are from a time on this earth when a group of people had the technology."

"Man, that's farfetched."

"About as farfetched as aliens," Father laughed.

"That's true," the Chief nodded. "But, at least with the aliens they could have dropped the containers off from a spaceship. How would an earlier civilization get the chambers to the desert of New Mexico?"

"Maybe it wasn't desert when the containers were placed in the cave. And if they had the technology to perform cryonics maybe they had the technology of flight."

"How long ago are you talking about?"

"Pre-flood," Father replied quickly.

"Whoa! You mean before Noah?"

"Exactly."

"But all of that happened over in the Middle East. Man was fairly primitive, wasn't he?"

"That's the image we have of the time before Noah. But, think about it. During this time people supposedly lived to be really old. Think of the knowledge that could have been accumulated during those long life-spans." Father cleared his throat. "Have you ever heard of the Oronteus Finaeus Map?"

The Chief looked at Father and shook his head.

"The Oronteus Finaeus Map is a map of the land mass of Antarctica without the ice and snow. It shows in minute detail the mountain ranges, both internal and coastal. It also shows the rivers that meander their way to the sea. The map was apparently made before the land was covered with ice. Modern science has proven it to be very accurate."

"But hasn't Antarctica been covered with ice for a long time?"

Father nodded. "That's my point. It has been covered for millions of years and yet we have an accurate map of when the land was dry and ice-free. The strangest part is that the map is so accurate in its depiction of the coastline that it looks as if it was drawn from the air."

"You mean from an airplane?"

"Yeah, or something like an airplane."

"So, you're saying that if man was that advanced in times past, then maybe he tried to make himself immortal through the use of cryonics?"

Father shrugged. "That's what we're trying to do today. The people who are put in cryonic suspension are dying from some disease, for which we presently have no cure. Their hope is that sometime in the future man will discover the cure, wake them back up, and use the new technology to prolong their life."

The Chief paused in their conversation long enough to pull the truck onto the highway. He then turned again to Father Macon. "That still sounds farfetched, but I will be the first to admit that we must keep our minds open to every possibility."

"I agree. And there is one other thing that might help us. Is there anyone around here that is well-versed in legend and folklore?"

The Chief smiled and nodded. "Old Ben Running Deer is very knowledgeable. Like I told you, he is a Pueblo medicine man and he has lived in this area all of his life. If anyone would know anything about its history, he would. The only thing is, he may be tied up for a while with Gabe's funeral."

"What is his interpretation of the pictographs that you just showed me?"

"I've never heard him say. He's not real outgoing." The Chief laughed. "He doesn't have much use for the white man."

Father smiled. "I can understand that. Do you think he'll talk with us?"

"I can't say. He's upset about losing his son."

"I can understand that, also. But we need someone who knows this area well. If someone from earth put those chambers in that cave, there's got to be an old legend or story that might give us just a tidbit of insight into who and how."

"Even if it's been millions of years?"

"Do not most of the Indian tribes have a story of a time when there was a great flood which covered the entire earth?"

The Chief nodded. "Yeah. They differ from tribe to tribe, but all have the same basic theme."

"Well, that was millions of years ago."

"That's true. Maybe we'll get lucky."

Father saw a lone light ahead of them. He watched as the Chief turned the truck off the highway and headed toward the light. "Is that your house?"

"That's it. It's not much but it's home."

The house became more discernible as they drew nearer. It was modest in size but very much southwestern in design. The adobe walls reminded Father of some of the old churches that dotted the southwest. Red tiles lined the roof and a single utility pole stood nearby with an electrical transformer providing a single wire that ran to the house. That wire was the source of power that fed the beacon of light in the desert darkness.

The Chief pulled the truck to a stop in front of the house. There was no driveway. Everything around the house was the same red dirt that they had experienced in the canyon.

Shutting off the engine, the old Indian looked over at Father. "I'm glad you're here. You are a good friend to the Great Spirit. I can feel Him with us. He will guide our path."

35

Father smiled. The Chief opened the door and Father followed. He reached into the bed of the truck and removed his bags. The Chief held the door, allowing Father to enter. He smiled again as he looked around the room. The house consisted of one large room which housed the living room and kitchen. Two large windows adorned the back wall allowing them a view of the desert. The house was neatly decorated and very well kept. Two bedrooms and one bathroom finished the rest of the building. The Chief walked around Father and motioned with his hand.

"Come on. I'll show you your room."

"This is a five-star, isn't it?"

"You bet," the Chief laughed.

The bedroom was small but adequate. Father put his bags down on the bed. "This will work. Very nice."

The Chief smiled as he accepted the compliment. "You ready for bed or would you like something to drink?"

Father looked at his watch. "I'm a little tired but something to drink sounds good."

"Good. Let's go back to the kitchen and I'll see what we have."

The two men walked back to the large room. Father took a seat at the dining table as the Chief opened the door to the small refrigerator. He turned, still bent over, and looked at Father. "Cola sound okay?"

"Sounds good. It may be my imagination but just the little time we spent in the canyon really dried me out."

"It's not your imagination," the Chief replied, opening the two bottles of cola. "You're not used to this dry heat. It takes a few days to get used to it. I'll make sure we keep a container of water in the truck when we go out."

Father nodded his thanks.

Chief Walking Cloud set the drinks on the table and sat down across from Father. He took a sip of his drink then set the bottle down.

"Tell me more about this cryonic suspension."

Father Macon swallowed a mouthful of soda. "I don't know a lot. I became involved when a parishioner asked me the moral implications of "being frozen" as she called it. I couldn't answer her, so I found a few books on the subject. That's been some time ago, however."

"But, you think that's what the chambers were that they found in the cave?"

Father took another drink then nodded his head. "Chief, I really don't know. That was just the first thing that came to me when you described the chambers. Cryonic suspension involves taking a deceased human and preserving him or her in a solution of liquid nitrogen at a temperature of −196 degrees Celsius."

The Chief frowned. "Man, that's cold!"

"Yes, it is. But, the idea is to preserve cellular integrity because the cells begin to break down very soon after the body dies."

"So, if the chamber was punctured or the nitrogen was lost, the body would decay just like normal?"

"That's correct."

The Chief rubbed his chin. "That would explain why there were only bones of the minotaur, or whatever you called it, in one of the chambers."

Father took another drink of soda and nodded his head as he took time to swallow. "That's right. Rocks falling from the ceiling of the cave could have broken the glass-like material and allowed

37

the cryoprotectant to escape. Without it, the flesh would have deteriorated quickly in this desert heat."

Both men sat quietly, their minds racing, searching for ideas. Father Macon was the first to break the stillness.

"You know, if Gabe was right and what he saw in the canister was for real, then the scientific community is going to have a rude awakening."

The Chief nodded. "I was thinking the same thing. The bones of an animal, half-man and half-bull, would be a remarkable discovery any day. But, if you combine that with the man in the canister and the technology to keep him suspended, then we may have to re-think a lot of things."

Father Macon squinted his eyes as a thought shot through his mind. He stood up and looked down at the old man. "Let me get my notebook. I want to read you something."

The Chief watched as Father walked back to his bedroom then returned with a small notebook. He sat down again at the table and thumbed through the notebook's pages. He found what he was looking for and looked up.

"This is a dream I had the night before I decided to come out here. Some of it I think I understand, but the rest... Well, just listen."

Father read the dream, pausing at times to allow the Chief time to digest his words. As he finished reading he looked up at the old Indian.

"You say there were three voices?"

"Yes. One voice was loud and distinct. It said: 'And darkness was on the face of the deep.' The second was your voice. The third was the strangest. It started out like the sound of a waterfall then changed into the voices of children."

The Chief shook his head. "I don't know. I'm drawing a blank. I think it's very significant that you're the one crying out to the Lord but it is not your voice. First it is mine, then the voices of children. All three of us are crying out to God for help. I admit that this has been my prayer to God. That's why I called you, but, the children..." He looked across the table at Father. "Could that be the voices of the children who are missing?"

Father smiled. "I thought that, too. But what really puzzles me is the black smoke that covered the earth, then disappeared, then returned. When I woke up I could still smell it. It was bad."

"You said it started off the East Coast of Florida?"

"That's right. But there is nothing there but ocean."

The Chief shook his head again. "We need more information to fill in the gaps." He laughed. "How many days you got?"

"Only until the weekend."

"Oh, Lord. We need a big break."

"Amen to that. I say that tomorrow morning we hit the ground running and find out as much as we can."

The Chief frowned. "But where do we start?"

"I would say Ben Running Deer. That is, if he will see us."

The Chief's frown grew more pronounced, forcing more crevasses into his already wrinkled face. "If he is in mourning, he will not speak to us."

"How long will he be in mourning?"

"Hard to say, three days, three weeks, three months."

Father exhaled then rubbed his face. "We don't have that much time."

"I know," the old man shrugged, "but honoring the dead is very

39

important to our people. And on top of that, this is Ben's son. So that only complicates the situation. Is there any other place we could start our search?"

Father laughed. "We could break into the military compound and ask them what they found."

They again sat across the table looking at each other, both trying to discern their next move. This time the ringing of the phone broke the silence.

The Chief got up slowly and made his way to the phone that hung on the wall of the kitchen. The Chief's disappointment was reflected in his voice as he picked up the receiver. That changed immediately, however, as the conversation grew. Father could tell that whoever was on the other end was very upset. The conversation lasted only about four to five minutes with the Chief promising to see them first thing the next morning. Father watched his old friend hang up the phone then walk back to the table and sit down.

"That was Susie Running Deer, Ben's daughter. The government came tonight and took Gabe's body."

"What for?" Father frowned.

"She said they were wearing bubble suits and driving a large lab-like truck. They told her father that the body was being confiscated because of possible contamination."

"What kind of contamination?"

"They wouldn't tell her. They said it would all be explained at a press conference tomorrow morning in town."

Father Macon leaned back in his chair. "Well, I guess that solves the problem of our next step."

The Chief nodded. "Remember, watch out what you pray for,

you just may get it."

Father laughed. "Isn't that the truth?"

"That's not all. Susie said that Ben wanted to see me tomorrow as soon as I could get around."

"Does he live far away from here?"

"Not far. But I think we would do well to be at that press conference tomorrow. Then we can drive out to Ben's afterwards. Apparently this thing is growing in magnitude to the point that the government is having to offer some explanation."

"You're right there," Father agreed. "I met a reporter on the plane who was from the *Dallas Herald*. She was coming here to investigate the situation because of the military's strong presence."

"Did she have any ideas?"

Father shook his head slowly. "She seemed convinced that whatever was in the cave was alien in origin. Roswell came up."

The Chief laughed. "Boy! This should be good. It's going to be interesting to hear the government's side of the story."

"Do you think they'll tell the truth?"

"What do you think? My people are convinced that the government *always* speaks with a forked tongue. They've forgotten how to tell the truth. I am definitely biased in my opinion, but the press conference will probably be a waste of time on our part."

"You're probably right. But, I think we still need to be there. Did Susie say what time and where the press conference would be?"

The Chief nodded. "It's at 10:00 on the steps of the court house."

Father looked at his watch. "It's getting late. I say we hit the sack and get some sleep. Tomorrow may be a long day."

The Chief got up and pushed his chair against the table. He looked at Father. "Is God in this or have I gotten you out here on a wild-goose chase?"

"He's in it all right. I've got the how. I just don't know the why." Father got up and also pushed his chair against the table. He pointed at the Chief. "You and I being together again is the how. If I could fully interpret the dream, I would tell you the why."

"Then we must trust the Great Spirit."

Father smiled. "That's all we can do. In His own time He will bring the pieces together. But we must be sensitive to His prompting. I sense that we could be in very grave danger for what we already know."

"I have felt that, too. That is why I believe the government will not tell the truth tomorrow. Whatever they found in that cave is too valuable to them."

"Valuable enough to kill Gabe Running Deer to keep him quiet?"

The Chief nodded sadly. "I'm afraid you are correct. Taking his body away from the family will be part of the cover-up plan. Just wait and see."

"Then how safe is Ben?"

"Ben is like us. He is safe as long as they don't know that we know. The second they find out that Gabe shared what he saw in the cave, well…"

Father looked down at the floor. He didn't want to believe that his own government would kill innocent people to keep them quiet, but…

The Chief interrupted Father's thoughts. "If you knew what I know it would not be so hard to believe." he said, almost reading Father's mind. "My past and the past of my people are full of the callousness and brutality of the government. To lie is nothing to them; to deceive is gain. Nothing is too immoral. The end always justifies the means. Gabe Running Deer became a victim because he happened to be in the wrong place at the wrong time." The old man's eyes narrowed as he continued. "And never doubt for a minute, my friend, that they would not do the same thing to a Catholic priest if they thought that is what it would take to silence him."

Father smiled, trying to lighten the seriousness of the old man's words but in his heart he knew that the Chief was right. That was the reason for the sense of caution that he was feeling in his spirit. "One way or another, we will know more after the press conference tomorrow."

The Chief finished a yawn then nodded his head. "That we will, my friend."

CHAPTER THREE

The Otlancho

Father heard the Chief's alarm go off in the next room. He opened his eyes and silently prayed for their day. He had slept well. He was amazed at how quiet the night had been, void even of the sound of traffic on the highway. The Chief certainly lived out in the middle of nowhere.

He heard the Chief stirring but stayed in bed until he smelled the odor of coffee invading his room. He threw off the light blanket and climbed out of bed. He pulled on his clothes and followed the smell of the coffee to the kitchen.

"Good morning," the Chief offered with a smile as he saw Father Macon round the corner.

"Good morning."

"Sleep well?"

Father made his way over to the table and sat down before answering. "Yes. I didn't realize how tired I was. Man, it sure is quiet out here."

The Chief laughed. "Noticed that, huh?" He set a cup in front of Father then filled it full of the black liquid. "Wait until the coyotes start. They have a great harmony that will sing you to sleep."

"Well, I didn't hear anything last night," Father said as he brought the cup to his lips.

The Visitor

The Chief looked at his watch. "It's seven forty-five. I thought we'd have coffee then eat breakfast in town. It might give us some time to scope things out before the press conference."

"Sounds good." Father took another sip from his cup then looked at the Chief. "I wonder if there will be very many people at the conference?"

"I look for it to be fairly crowded. A lot of people are upset about the military being here and others are just plain curious. It's been the talk of the town since the beginning and I think folks will welcome an explanation."

The two men finished their coffee, got things together and headed for town. The Chief had been right. The town was alive with people. They had trouble finding a place to park but finally found a spot on a back street about two blocks from the restaurant.

The traffic in the restaurant was normal, however, and by nine o'clock they had finished breakfast and were out on the street walking around, waiting for the appointed time. A lot of other townsfolk were doing the same thing. They had just crossed the street and were heading for the courthouse when they heard a lady's voice.

"Hey, Rex."

Both men turned to see a woman, with a large smile, approaching them. It was Denise Cameron.

Father smiled as he recognized her and stuck out his hand to her as she reached them.

"You wouldn't be on your way to the press conference, would you, Father?" she asked, taking his hand.

"Seems like the right thing to do," he laughed.

"Are you sure you're not a reporter?" she frowned.

"No way," he laughed again, then turned to the Chief. "Denise Cameron, this is Chief Walking Cloud."

Denise let go of Father's hand and took the Chief's. "You're a real chief, aren't you?"

The old man laughed, dropping her hand. "As real as they get. But to be honest I'm really a medicine man."

Denise turned her head to the side and laughed again. "A Catholic priest and an Indian medicine man; are you guys sure you're not reporters?"

They all laughed. Father shook his head. "Just good friends who want to know what's going on."

"Boy! You can say that again. This whole town is abuzz with this thing; something about a strange virus?"

Father Macon frowned. "What was that?"

"Yeah," Denise continued. "We've already received some preliminaries and whatever was found in the cave was carrying a virus. They believe it killed the two men that first entered the cave."

Father looked at the Chief then back at Denise. "Both men are dead?"

"Yeah," she nodded. "The young Indian man that they thought was killed in an automobile accident? They now think it was the virus that caused him to pass out and run off the road. The other man, he was from some firefighting crew in Arizona. They found him dead in his motel room yesterday afternoon. If I'm not mistaken, that's what they'll tell us at the press conference." She looked at her watch. "We'd better hurry. It's almost time."

Denise led the way as the two men followed close behind.

46

Father looked at the Chief and shook his head. "You may be right."

"I told you last night, they would use Gabe's death in the cover-up."

Denise didn't stop walking but turned back over her shoulder. "What cover-up?"

"Nothing, Denise, just a theory," Father answered, again looking at the Chief with a frown.

The Chief nodded his head that he understood. It was vital that they not draw any attention to themselves. All they needed was a reporter, like Denise, exposing them to the military.

They found the courthouse. It wasn't hard. A large group of people had gathered in front of the steps, which also afforded a podium with a microphone attached to its side. There were numerous individuals with badges on their shirts like Denise's. Father figured them all to be reporters from different news agencies around the area.

Exactly at ten o'clock, four people exited the courthouse and made their way to the podium. Three were dressed in lab coats. One was a woman. The last was an army general. The four were accompanied by two army soldiers who each supported M-16's. The four speakers came to rest side by side directly behind the podium.

One of the men walked to the podium and adjusted the microphone. "Good morning. I am Dr. Melvin Laird." He then pointed with his hand. "To my left are General James Sears and Dr. Bernard Tobin. To my right is Dr. Angela LePage."

Each of the people bowed to the crowd as they were introduced. Dr. Laird continued.

The Visitor

"Approximately ten days ago a group of firefighters were fighting a fire near Chaco Canyon. Because of the intense heat, a side of the canyon collapsed, revealing a large cavern. Two men entered that cavern. They were..." Dr. Laird paused to read from a paper he had placed on the podium. "They were Thomas A. Camp from Tucson, Arizona, and Gabe Running Deer from here in Albuquerque." Dr. Laird removed his reading glasses and again faced the crowd. "These men experienced immediate effects from their time in the cavern. Their fire group commander was notified and the military was brought in to examine the contents of the cavern. What we found was astounding. Inside the cavern were three ideally preserved mummies. We believe them to be from the time of the Anasazi. The only problem is that the mummies are carrying a strange virus that the medical community has never encountered before. Both of the men who first entered the cavern are dead." Father could hear mumbling throughout the crowd. Dr. Laird paused until the mumbling subsided, then continued. "Both men were killed, we believe, by the virus carried by the mummies. Their bodies have been confiscated by this medical team and are under strict quarantine. They will undergo thorough autopsies to ascertain the cause of death. But, at this time we are reasonably sure that both of the men were contaminated by their time in the cavern. That is why the military is here and most of Chaco Canyon is off limits to the public. I will now take your questions.

The crowd began to yell and raise their hands until Dr. Laird pointed to a man in front of the crowd.

"Dr. Laird, have the mummies been taken from the cavern?"

Dr. Laird again adjusted the microphone. "Yes. The mummies have been taken, under the greatest care, to the temporary

48

compound that we have established about twenty-five miles from town."

The crowd again came alive. Dr. Laird once again pointed to one of the reporters.

"How long will the military be here?"

Dr. Laid turned to the general and gestured with his hand. The General walked to the podium and bent down to the microphone.

"We will be here as long as Dr. Laird's team needs us. We are here to make sure that the public's safety is upheld at all cost. When Dr. Laird says it is safe, we will leave."

The general smiled at Dr. Laird then walked back to his place.

The crowd continued to ask questions for more than an hour. Father and the Chief listened as Denise wrote frantically in her note pad.

"This is a snow job of the greatest magnitude," the Chief whispered.

"You can say that again," Father replied.

Denise looked at Father and frowned. "Do you guys know something I don't? No, let me rephrase that. Do you guys know something I should know?"

Father looked at the Chief then back at Denise. "Ask them if the cavern has anything to do with the missing children."

Denise again frowned but quickly stuck her hand into the air, waving it back and forth.

"Yes, ma'am, the young lady toward the back."

It took Denise a few seconds to realize that Dr. Laird was pointing to her.

"Yes," she stammered. "I was wondering if anything from the cavern has anything to do with the missing children in the area?"

Denise's question caused the crowd to again mumble loudly. Apparently this was new knowledge to most of them.

Father watched the four behind the podium as they heard Denise's question. He could tell that it had struck a chord, a very sensitive chord. Father noticed that Dr. LePage was especially moved. She bit her lip and brushed the hair out of her face. Dr. Laird shook his head as he turned and looked at the others behind him. They, too, joined Dr. Laird in shaking their heads in the denial of any connection. Dr. Laird turned again to the microphone.

"We are unaware of any missing children in the area. In no way is this connected to the mummies or the cavern." Dr. Laird turned toward Denise. "Are you with the local paper?"

"No, I'm with the Dallas Herald."

Dr. Laird nodded. "I see. And your name is?"

Denise held up her badge as if the doctor could read it over the crowd. "I'm Denise Cameron."

"Thank you, Ms. Cameron." Dr. Laird then scanned the crowd. "Ladies and gentlemen that concludes this press conference. We will do our best to keep you updated on our progress. I want to assure everyone, however, that there is no immediate danger to anyone in the area. You are all safe. Thank you and good day."

The four turned and walked back into the courthouse, followed by the two soldiers.

"Well, I guess that is that," Denise sighed. "All this fuss over a couple of old Indian mummies." She looked up at Chief Walking Cloud. "No offense, Chief."

The Chief smiled. "None taken."

They watched as the crowd began to thin. A small man with

glasses came up to Denise. "Ms. Cameron, what is this about missing children in the area?"

Denise shook her head. "Don't ask me. Ask these guys." She pointed to Father and the Chief.

"Five children have been reported missing since the cave was discovered," the Chief offered.

"Are you sure they were reported *after* the cavern was discovered?"

The Chief nodded. "I'm certain."

The little man smiled. "I'm Bill Staples. I'm with the New Mexico Star, a weekly magazine based in Santa Fe. I used to work as a police investigator and I've seen the impact certain questions have on people." He turned to Denise. "Your question made them squirm."

"What do you mean?" Denise frowned.

"He means they were lying about the children," Father added.

Bill nodded. "He's right. I thought there was more to this when I drove up here. If you want a story young lady, that is it. They know about the children and somehow they are connected."

"But what would missing children have to do with a couple of old Indian mummies?" Denise objected.

Bill laughed. "If I knew that I would have the story. I don't have the time or the physical stamina to follow up on this but I'm telling you that somewhere behind this simple façade is a great story."

Father looked at the Chief. He knew Bill was right but he wasn't sure that Denise needed to get involved.

"You mean," Denise interjected, "that this whole story is fabricated. In reality there are no mummies? It's the Roswell weather balloon thing all over again?

"I don't know," Bill shrugged. "All I know is that your question caused those people more concern than all the other questions put together. I could see it on their faces. Whether they are directly or indirectly involved in the missing children, it's hard to say. But I can assure you that they know about it."

Denise looked at Father Macon. "What do you think?"

"I'm neither a reporter nor an investigator but I think Bill is right." Father Macon felt the old Chief grab his arm. "But a story like this could be very dangerous to pursue."

Bill nodded. "He's right, Ms. Cameron. It might be a great story but it might not be worth the price."

Denise laughed. "You guys make it sound like I might have to wrestle alligators."

"It would be nice if it were that easy," Bill replied. He reached into his pocket and handed Denise a card. "I will be around town for a while. My hotel and room number are on the back. If I can help you in any way let me know. My advice, however, is to be careful. Those guys with the guns were not there by accident."

Bill turned to Father and the Chief. "Gentlemen," he said, then turned and walked away.

They watched him until he turned a corner, taking the little man out of their sight.

"You guys had lunch?" Denise asked, breaking their trance.

Father looked at the Chief then shrugged his shoulders. "No."

"Good. Let's walk back to my motel and I'll buy us all lunch."

"Can't beat a deal like that," the Chief laughed. "Madame, lead the way."

The three walked to Denise's hotel. The restaurant was crowded but they managed to find a seat. As soon as the maître d' walked away, Denise looked across the table at the two men.

"What do you guys know that you're not telling me?"

Father looked over at the Chief who sat quietly for a few seconds then nodded his head. Father turned and faced Denise.

"First off, I think you are in danger."

Denise's eyes grew wide. "What?"

"Didn't it strike you as strange that Dr. Laird asked you for your name and where you worked? Did he ask anyone else in the crowd for that information?"

Denise picked up a spoon and lightly tapped it against the tabletop. She looked back up at Father. "I never thought of that. But it's not that uncommon. But why would I be in danger?"

"Because you know about the missing children and they don't know how much you know. They will attempt to find out."

Denise laughed nervously. "You make it sound like the Gestapo."

"It's worse than that," the Chief added. "One of the men killed by the so called 'virus' was a good friend of mine. I know what he saw in that cavern and it was not Indian mummies. He was not killed by a virus. He was murdered."

Denise's eyes grew wide again. "They wouldn't do that!" She turned and looked at Father. "Would they?"

Father reached across the table and took Denise's hand. He could feel it trembling. "I think they are capable of anything. They are convinced that what was found in the cavern must be protected, at all cost."

Denise pulled her hand away, trying to hide her fear. She looked at the Chief. "What was in that cavern?"

The Chief looked at Father then back to Denise. "We can't tell you because it would put you in extreme danger. But I can assure you that it was not Indian mummies."

Denise laughed, again trying to hide her fear. "I thought I was already in danger because of my question about the missing children?"

Father nodded. "You are. But when they find out that you know nothing, they'll leave you alone."

Denise frowned and shook her head. "This is all a little much. How do I know that you guys aren't the real problem?"

Father laughed. "I can understand your concern. That is good. But if I'm right, they will have to make contact with you and find out how much you know about the children."

"And where she got the information," the Chief added.

"That's right," Father agreed, then turned back to Denise. "And you must not tell them, please. Just tell them that you had heard about it second hand from folks around the area."

Denise again frowned. "And if no one shows up?"

"Then we are wrong, and you can forget about us and this conversation."

"Fair enough," Denise smiled.

They ate their meal with very little dialogue. Father could tell from Denise's silence that she did not believe nor trust them. The Chief could feel it too. They quickly finished eating.

Father took a pen from his pocket and placed it on a napkin then pushed them both toward the Chief. "Write down your address and phone number."

The Chief followed his instructions then pushed the napkin toward Denise.

"If need be," Father instructed, "this is where we can be reached."

Denise smiled, took the napkin and placed it in her shirt pocket.

Father stood up and extended his hand. "Thank you for lunch. It was great."

The Chief followed Father's lead and also extended his hand. "Thank you."

Denise forced a smile as she shook the men's hands. "It was interesting."

Father turned to the Chief. "Ready?"

"I'm ready."

Father nodded his head toward Denise then walked to the restaurant entrance. He held the door for the Chief. Neither spoke until they were well away from the restaurant.

"She didn't believe us," the Chief offered as they waited for a stoplight to change.

"I know. But she will. I just pray that nothing happens to her."

The Chief frowned. "I don't understand."

"You and I both know that they will check her out. They have to. But, if they *assume* she knows too much already, then..."

"Then they would kill her," the Chief interrupted.

Father looked at the Chief and nodded.

The two walked to the truck. "Are we ready to talk to Ben?" the Chief asked, starting the engine.

"Not yet. Do you know the place where Gabe Running Deer was killed?"

"Yeah, it's on the way to Ben's place."

"Good. Let's go take a look."

The Chief nodded then pulled the truck out into the flow of

traffic. They made their way through town and onto a highway that took them out into the desert toward Ben Running Deer's place. They followed the blacktop for only a few miles then turned off onto a half dirt, half gravel road. The old truck bounced and jumped which caused the Chief to fight the wheel again. As it leveled out he turned to Father.

"What are you thinking?"

Father laughed. "I guess it's doubt. We have assumed that Gabe was murdered because they lied about what was in the cavern. But, I think it would do us good to look over the scene, unless they have moved everything."

The Chief shook his head. "No, Gabe's truck is still out here. At least it was two days ago."

"Let's hope it still is."

They drove for a good while. The terrain changed as the road carried them up a large canyon. The Chief pointed as they started down the other side.

"See the blue over there in the canyon floor?"

Father rose up and looked in the direction the old Indian was pointing.

"Oh yeah, I see it. Man! That was quite a drop."

The blue spot turned into the shape of an old truck as they drew closer. As they started down the canyon, they lost sight of the truck due to the angle of the grade. Father turned and looked at the road behind them as the Chief pulled the truck off onto the shoulder. He shut off the engine and opened his door.

The two men stood looking down at the blue truck about a hundred feet below them. Father again turned and looked up the road.

"I take it Gabe was coming down the hill and just ran off the road?"

"That's what they said. He's driven this road thousands of times and this once just missed it."

Father pointed back up the road. "That's a pretty steep grade. If he was traveling too fast, it could happen."

"I don't think so," the Chief frowned.

"Well, let's check it out."

The two men made their way carefully down the steep embankment. The truck was a crumpled piece of steel. It would have been a miracle for anyone to have survived a fall of such magnitude.

"I wouldn't touch anything," the Chief said, as they reached the vehicle.

The hood was up and all the windows had been knocked out. The truck had managed to land upright. Father peered at the engine. He then got down on his hands and knees and looked under the front of the vehicle.

"Look at this," he said, looking up at the Chief.

The old man carefully bent down and looked to where Father Macon was pointing. "What is it?"

"Look at the brake line on this side."

The Chief studied the area then compared it to the opposite side. "I'll be! It's been cut. But that could have happened during the crash."

Father stood up. "That's true, but look up there." He pointed back up at the road. "If the brakes went out while the truck was coming down that canyon road, there's no way Gabe could have controlled the truck. This is where he would have ended up."

"But how can we prove this?" the Chief challenged. "They'll just say that the brake line was ruptured some time during the crash."

"Unless..." Father paused. "How far does Gabe live from here?"

"About a mile back the way we came then a quarter mile from there. Why?"

"It's a long shot, but let's go take a look."

Father started his climb back up the ravine wall, followed by the Chief. They were both breathing hard after they reached the top. It didn't take long for the Chief to turn the truck around and head back toward Gabe Running Deer's house. Father watched as he turned off the main road and started toward a house in the distance.

"This is it," the Chief announced as he pulled the truck to a stop. "What are we looking for?"

Father didn't answer but got out of the truck and began looking around on the ground. He stopped, bent down, dragged his finger through the dirt, then put his finger to his nose. He finally stood up and motioned for the Chief to join him.

The Chief made his way over to Father and looked down at a brown oily spot on the ground. "You mean they cut it right here?"

"That's right," Father nodded. "Look here."

Father pointed to a small trail of the same oily dirt leading away from the main puddle. "See how it was still leaking as he pulled the truck out of its resting place?"

They both followed the trail for about twenty feet until it became faint and splotchy.

"This is crazy. Whoever did this was determined."

"And calculated," Father added. "They figured that there was just enough brake fluid left in the line to get him to the top of the canyon. Pretty slick."

"Pretty sick, you mean," the Chief snarled.

"Definitely. But to them it's all done for a purpose that justifies even the killing of their own citizens. It makes me sad to be an American when stuff like this happens."

The Chief frowned. "Now you know a little of what we as Indians have felt for a long time. They've been doing this to us from the start."

Father nodded. He understood. He could see the sadness in the old man's eyes. "I cannot even comprehend the mentality that thinks any discovery could be worth the lives of good people."

"But to them Indians are not good people. We are just a life form that has always been in the way. Our ideas, our pride, our masculinity, our traditions, and even our lives mean nothing to them. Gabe Running Deer was a good man. He laughed and cried, loved and worked hard. He joined the fire fighters because he was concerned about his people's safety and their homes. That concern cost him his life, snuffed out by a government sworn to protect *his* safety."

"I know. There have been many times when I have not understood the mindset of the government. Why does everything have to be such a secret?"

The Chief frowned. "I'll tell you what I think. It is because sometimes the project is so morally objectionable that if the public found out they would raise holy hell."

"That may have been true years ago, but the public today is so apathetic that as long as it doesn't affect them personally, they don't seem to care what the government does."

"Then why such savagery? Someone had to sneak out here under the cover of darkness and cut Gabe's brake line, knowing that without brakes, these canyon roads would be a death trap. What kind of a mind could conceive such a plan then give the orders to carry it out?"

"The kind of mind that will apparently destroy anything that stands in the way of this discovery."

"Do you think that the four individuals at the press meeting this morning are the ones really in charge of this thing?"

Father nodded. "That's a good question. I've been thinking about that myself. Bill Stapes was right about Denise's question causing them a problem. They were uncomfortable for sure. They are scientists, however, except of course for the general. He would be the only one, in my opinion, who could actually give the orders for such a deed. I cannot imagine those scientists being that cold hearted and blood thirsty, regardless of the magnitude of the discovery." Father laughed and shook his head. "At least I sure hope not."

The Chief looked at his watch. "If we are going to go see Ben, we ought to be heading that way."

"I'm ready. I sure hate to tell him that his son was murdered."

"He already knows. He knew it from the start."

Father looked at the Chief as they walked back to the truck. "How did he know?"

The Chief smiled. "He is a medicine man, and he knows the heart of the white man."

Father smiled, then frowned suddenly as a thought shot through his brain.

The Chief noticed Father's change in facial expression. "What's wrong?"

"I had forgotten about it. But the night before I flew out here I was dreaming or about to dream when I heard a voice cry out. 'They have murdered me.' I didn't know what it meant at the time. But I think I do now."

The Chief nodded and smiled. "You and I know that the realm of the Spirit is alive and very active. We know that the blood of Abel cried out from the earth to God. For those who are sensitive, the ears and eyes hear and see a lot more."

Father opened the door to the truck, climbed in, and slammed the door. He looked over at the Chief. "That's how Ben knew?"

The Chief started the truck then nodded. "That's how we all knew."

Father looked at the old man, not really understanding what he meant. He watched as the Chief turned the truck around and headed back down the dirt road. "You heard it too?"

Without looking at him, the old man nodded.

"But why?"

The old man looked at Father and frowned. "Why did the blood of Abel cry out to God?"

Father studied the question. "Because it was the shedding of innocent blood and God was the only one who could do something about it."

The Chief took his eyes off the road and looked at Father, waiting.

Father's eyes widened. "The Holy Spirit is concerned. He has allowed us to hear because we have been appointed to do something about it."

The old man smiled and nodded. "For those who have ears, let them hear what the Spirit is saying."

"This means that God, too, is very concerned about what was found in the cave."

The Chief nodded. "Absolutely. Remember your dream, the black cloud that smelled like sulfur. The Spirit is guiding us and, with time and patience, He will show us the path we must take."

Father Macon laughed. "Chief, you'd make a good priest."

The Chief looked at Father and winked. "I had a good teacher."

Father smiled. Coming from the old Chief, that was quite a compliment. They drove the rest of the way without speaking. Even as they drove past the wrecked truck down in the ravine neither of them said anything.

Ben Running Deer's place was very picturesque. There were two hogan-like dwellings built of logs and adobe bricks. Four dogs ran out to meet their truck as the Chief pulled it to a stop. As he shut off the motor he pointed to one of the hogans.

"That one is Ben's daughter, Susie's."

Father nodded, then opened the door slightly. "These dogs okay?"

The old man laughed. "Yeah, they won't bother you."

The two men exited the truck, slammed the doors and walked toward Ben's hogan. The dogs followed, barking and wagging their tails. They were almost to the hut when the front door opened and Ben appeared. He was wearing blue jeans but the upper half of his body was covered by a blanket. His face was wrinkled even more so than Chief Walking Cloud's. He wore his long white hair loose with no braids. His eyes narrowed as the two men approached.

"Ben," the Chief greeted.

The old man smiled at the sound of the Chief's voice. "How is George this day?"

"I am doing well. I have brought you my friend, Rex Macon."

The old man turned to face Father, squinting even more. He extended his hand. "Welcome, Rex Macon."

Father took the old man's hand and shook it. "Thank you. I am glad to meet you."

The old man nodded. "Come in. My house is honored by your presence."

Father looked at the Chief and smiled, then followed the old man into the hogan. Father was immediately fascinated by the hogan's interior. It was very simple. The walls were mud bricks and the ceiling was covered with different sized logs. A small cook stove stood over in one corner. Ben invited them over to another corner where a large couch and chair were resting.

"Please have a seat."

Father and the Chief sat on the sofa as the old man took a seat in the chair.

"Our hearts are saddened from the loss of your son," the Chief offered.

The old man nodded his head deeply. "A father is never prepared for his son to precede him in death. It is something the heart should never have to face."

"Did you hear about the press meeting this morning?"

Again the old man nodded. "I heard. Susie told me. It was not enough for them to kill my son. They had to dishonor him in death also. If I had been younger, I would have fought them. They would not have taken my son's body. But, I am old and weak, like an old woman. They said that he was killed in a wreck. That was a lie. They said he passed out and ran off the mountain. That was a lie. They said he was sick with a strange virus. That was a lie. They said he was a threat to those around him. That was a lie. The night he was killed I sat with him all night. There is no so-called virus. It is all a lie." He turned to the Chief. "George, you told me that the white man's Bible says that the Great Spirit hates a lying tongue?"

The Chief nodded. "That's right, Ben."

"Then tell me, why does the Great Spirit continue to honor the white man? He is full of lies and yet he continues to possess the land."

The Chief looked at Father as if passing the question on to him. Father shook his head and shrugged his shoulders.

"My father and my grandfather fought the blue coats when they came to take our land," Ben continued. "My grandfather said that the white man would never survive because of the way he abused the earth and its bounty. I have waited many years for my eyes to see the fulfillment of my grandfather's words. But still it does not happen. The blue coats have changed their clothing but their hearts are still the same. They came with guns just like in the old days to take something from the Indian. Once they took our land and now they have taken my son. They said it was for the good of all people. They still use the same lie as before. My son was not a threat to anyone. He was a good son who looked after his father in his old age." Ben looked up at the Chief. Father could see the tears running down his wrinkled cheeks. "My son was not killed in a wreck. My son was murdered by the white man. I have heard his death cry in my sleep. It was not the cry of one who dies in peace."

The Chief nodded. "I know Ben. I have heard it too." He then

64

turned to Father. "Rex has heard it also."

Ben turned to Father and again squinted his eyes. "Is this true?"

Father swallowed hard as he nodded. "I heard it the night before I came out here. I did not know who it was or its meaning."

A grin came slowly to the old man's face. "It is a sign that your heart is right. The Great Spirit made you aware for a reason."

"What reason is that?" Father asked.

The smile faded from Ben's face. He shook his head slowly. "I do not know. I would like to think that the Great Spirit is saddened by my son's murder and that you are part of the retribution. But I do not know."

Father frowned. He wondered what Ben meant by retribution but did not ask.

"We know he was murdered, Ben," the Chief shared. "Rex and I have just come from the wreck site and Gabe's hogan. Someone cut the brake line on his truck."

Ben wiped his face with his hand but he could not wipe away the sadness. He looked up at the Chief. "It is because of what Gabe saw in the cave. Once more the white man cannot stand the truth."

The Chief nodded. "We believe you are right. The other man who was in the cave first with Gabe is dead also."

Ben's eyes widened then squinted again showing his anger. He looked at Father. "What is so important that it requires the lives of so many?"

Father Macon was compelled to answer. "George told me what you shared with him about what Gabe saw in the cavern. A discovery of that magnitude would be of great significance to many in the government. So significant, in fact, that they are willing to kill innocent people to protect it."

"Protect it from whom? The white man says that this is a nation of the people, and yet it cannot trust those people? My grandfather saw that in the leaders of the white man many years ago. They could not trust the word of the Indian because they could not trust themselves. They thought everyone was a liar because in their hearts they knew *they themselves were liars*. They assumed that all men were like themselves. They have not changed. Their hearts are still bad."

Father looked at the Chief then back at Ben. "What they found in that cave has the potential to change society as a whole, and maybe even the world. That knowledge is what they are trying to safeguard. Those in power are not ready to subject the scientific community to this new discovery. It is wrong, I agree. But, I believe there is something happening here that is even much bigger than they can imagine. I believe it is significant that I heard the death cry, as you call it, of Gabe. The Great Spirit drew me here at the request of the Chief." He nodded his head toward the old Chief. "I don't know why, but I believe it is important that we find out what was in that cave and why the government is willing to kill to protect it. You are right; they are liars. They proved that today at the press conference. But if we are going to find answers we are going to have to work together."

"I agree," the Chief added.

"But we must be cautious," Father continued. "We know they will stop at nothing to protect what was found. Until we are sure, we must not trust anyone. Our lives could depend on that."

Father was still speaking when the door opened. The three men turned and watched as Susie, Ben's daughter, entered then slowly closed the door. She looked at the Chief and nodded but then her dark eyes came to rest on Father Macon. They remained fixed on him as she walked to where they were seated. She sat on the arm of her father's chair. She continued to stare at Father Macon, her concern very apparent in her eyes.

The Chief was the first to speak. "Susie, this is Rex Macon. He is a very good friend of mine. He is here to help me find out what is going on out at the cave."

Father smiled and nodded. Susie only nodded. Father guessed her to be in her late twenties. She was very beautiful. Her long black hair hung down past her shoulders. Her dark skin was challenged in beauty only by her dark eyes and right now they were piercing through him. Before she arrived they had been talking about trust and it was very apparent that Susie held none for this white man in her father's hogan.

Father Macon turned and looked at Ben. "Ben, tell us what Gabe told you about the cavern."

Susie grabbed her father's arm.

"It's okay, Susie," the Chief smiled. "I have known Rex for a long time and I would trust him with my life. He is here to help us."

She released her hold on Ben's arm as if giving him permission to answer Father's question.

Ben started slowly but after a long while he related to Father what he had previously shared with the old Chief. They all sat quietly, listening to every detail. Father could see Susie watching him out of the corner of his eye. She was studying his response to her father's story.

When Ben had finished, Father began to share what he had shared with the Chief about cryogenics and how science did not possess the technology to imitate what Gabe had seen in the cavern. As Father talked, he could see Susie's countenance changing. The way she looked at him even changed. He could actually see the anger for him leave her eyes. He didn't blame her, however. She had just lost her brother to a bunch of mysterious white men, and to her, he was no different. By the time Father had finished, he could tell that he had won her confidence. In fact, she was the first one to respond.

"So you're saying that whatever Gabe saw in that cavern was not of this world?"

Father smiled and shook his head. "Not necessarily. I'm saying that what was in that cavern was either not of this world or not of our time."

Susie frowned. "What do you mean not of our time?"

"That's why we came to see your father. Yesterday we went to what you call Holy Spirit Rock. We were hoping that Ben might have heard his father or grandfather talk of the rock and what they believed it meant."

Ben nodded.

Susie turned to Ben. "You do know, don't you, daddy? I've heard you speak about it before."

Ben again nodded. "I've heard my grandfather speak of it many times. It is the story of the Otlancho, the people of the white eagle."

"Otlancho?" Father repeated.

"Yes," Ben confirmed. "My grandfather said that they came to the land long before the red man. When they came, the land was not a desert. It was like a garden. The great white eagle came and built her nest here. She laid her eggs and waited for them to hatch.

When they did, it was the Otlancho. But not all of the Otlancho looked the same. Some had great horns that grew out from their heads."

Father looked at the old chief and smiled.

Ben continued. "A great conflict arose between the Otlancho. Those with the horns were considered outcasts. The great white eagle, sad that her children could not get along, began to beat her wings against the ground, causing the land to sink. The great sea then rushed into the hole, destroying all but a few of the Otlancho. As the water receded, it left deep canyons and the land parched. What was once a garden had now become a desert. The Otlancho that survived lost all their knowledge of their greatness. They became so despondent that they cried out to the great white eagle. In her pity she gave them grains of maize and taught them how to grow it. But it was not enough. The Otlancho had been used to extravagance and now they were paupers. In their sorrow, they moved away."

"How about the rock drawings?" Father asked.

"It is said that the great white eagle had the Otlancho make the drawings so that they would never forget what had caused them to lose their way of life."

Father nodded slowly. "So the beings with the horns represented on the rocks, they were considered real?"

"Very much so," Ben replied.

"They were strong and powerful but lacked intelligence. Their brothers who had no horns were weak in body but very mentally adept." Ben laughed. "It was a case of brains over brawns. In this case the brains won."

"But in their victory, they lost the care of their mother, the great white eagle," the Chief added.

Ben nodded.

"How about the red man?" Father asked.

"Years passed and the maize grew so tall that it cried out to the great white eagle for someone to care for it and eat of its fruit. The great white eagle fanned the red dirt of the desert with her wings until the maize became disoriented and began to produce multicolored kernels. The eagle ate only the red ones and laid her eggs again. When they hatched, they were the Pendentro, the father of the red man. Because they had their origin from the maize they considered the maize their brother. They became one with the maize and learned to reap its bounty."

Father looked at Susie and smiled. He wondered how much of Ben's story had to do with the cavern and the capsules that Gabe had seen. He again turned to Ben. "Where does the Anasazi fit in?"

"What you call the Anasazi, we call the children of the Pendentro. Because the maize was one with the earth, it taught the Pendentro the secrets of the earth. With that knowledge, they became a great people. The great white eagle, now content with her children and confident in their abilities, flew back toward the rising sun. Before she left she took the chiefs to the rock and told them the story of the Otlancho. She warned them that if they could not get along, she would return and destroy their prosperity, just like before."

Father sat looking at Ben. His mind was searching for anything of value from the old Indian's story, anything that might offer some assistance as to why *he* was in the desert of New Mexico.

Susie could tell he was studying her father's story. There was something about this man that intrigued her. He seemed to have a genuine concern for her brother's death and for finding out the truth about the cave's contents. "Do you glean anything of value from that story?" she asked, interrupting his concentration.

"I'm not sure," Father answered. "I thought it was worth a try. Most of the time these old stories have a way of harboring the truth." He looked at Ben. "I think it's fascinating that your story says the men with the horns are real."

"But they were born from eggs," Susie objected. "How real can that be?"

Father laughed. "What do you think the capsules would look like to a primitive mind?"

Susie thought for a moment then smiled. "I'll be. The way Gabe described them, they would resemble giant eggs."

"Hey, Rex, that's good," the Chief added. "The removal of a man from the capsule would, to a primitive mind, look like an egg hatching."

Father nodded. "And how would a primitive man describe an airplane?"

"Like a great white eagle," Susie quickly added, then frowned. "Are you saying that there might have been airplanes in the past?"

"Susie," Father laughed. "Again, I'm not really saying anything. I'm just looking for answers. Those capsules came from somewhere and I don't want to believe that it's outer space. Your father's story has quite a few elements that give cause for study. The facts are that Holy Spirit Rock has a man with horns drawn on it. Ben's story has a man with horns. And one of the capsules has a man with horns. Is that coincidental? I don't know. But it sure seems like a very strong coincidence to me. That makes me want to believe your father's story more than I want to believe that the capsules were left in the cavern by little gray men from another planet."

"But if that is true," Ben replied, "this would have taken place a very long time ago. Probably even before recorded history."

Father nodded.

Susie shook her head. "That means that those capsules have been lying in that cavern for thousands of years. Even while my grandfather was walking these canyon trails, they were there."

"That's true. He probably walked to the Holy Spirit rock many times and wondered at the images painted there, and buried only five miles away was the real thing. It took the heat of the brush fires to reveal them."

"But I still don't understand how they got there," the Chief frowned. "Even if they had airplanes where did they come from? And why did they decide on this place?"

"That's a good question," Susie agreed, looking at Father, waiting for an answer.

Father laughed. "I don't know. All of this is just conjecture. Until we can get some more information about that cave and those capsules, we are all just guessing."

Susie leaned forward from her perch on the arm of the chair. "How do we do that, Mr. Macon? Personally, I'd like to blow the lid on this thing so high that the whole world would know. It would serve them right for killing my brother."

Father looked at Susie and shook his head. "I understand your anger, Susie. But that kind of talk can get you into a lot of trouble really fast around here. Exposure is these people's greatest fear. They don't want this out in any form or fashion. That's why we must keep as silent as possible. Mum is definitely the word, at least the safest word for now."

"Then what do we do now?" Susie asked.

Father looked at the Chief and then at Ben. "Susie, I think it would be better if you stayed out of this. It could be very dangerous."

"But they killed my brother."

"I understand that. But don't think for a moment that they wouldn't do the same to you to keep you quiet. We must make them think that what Gabe knew, he took with him. If they think, even for a second, that you or Ben know anything, then..." he paused, "well, you know."

"I am old but I will help in any way I can," Ben offered.

Father smiled at the old man. "Thanks, Ben. You've already been a lot of help. Thanks for trusting this white man."

Ben laughed and nodded.

Father looked at the Chief. "Ready?"

"If you are."

Father stood up and offered his hand to Ben. "Thanks again, Ben."

The old man didn't get up but extended his hand.

"I'll walk with you to your truck," Susie said, standing up.

The Chief shook hands with Ben, then together with Father, followed Susie out of the hogan and toward the truck. The sun was getting low in the sky. The familiar orange hue was beginning to form on the horizon.

When Susie got to the Chief's truck, she turned around. She looked at Father. "I am not afraid. I want to help. I hope you'll let me."

Father smiled. "We must first find out what to do. Right now, we don't have any plan. We are going to have to wait until something comes to light. When it does, if we can use your help, we will call."

She smiled and nodded her okay.

She followed Father around to the passenger side of the truck and watched as he climbed in. He slammed the door then rolled down the window.

"Will something come to light?" she asked as Father looked out at her.

"I'm positive it will. But we must be patient."

She stood silent and watched as the Chief backed the truck out and started it back toward town. Father waved then rolled his window back up.

CHAPTER FOUR

Roswell

"You seem very sure, my friend," the old Chief said, not taking his eyes off of the road.

Father took a deep breath then slowly exhaled. He looked at the Chief. "I've been here before. The Scriptures say that the steps of a righteous man are well ordered. I think that is very true in this case. I'm here because I'm supposed to be. You're here because you're supposed to be. We know a lot about what's going on around here but not enough to know why we're part of this thing. That's going to have to come from the Holy Spirit. I have never known Him to let me down when I have come this far. He will let us know when it's time. I assure you, He *will* let us know. Somewhere, someone within the structure of this hidden organization is a vessel that will be used by God. Whoever he or she is will be the key to this whole thing. It is for that person that we need to pray."

The shadows were getting long as they passed Gabe's truck off in the ravine. They could barely make out its outline from their position on the road. Father made the sign of the cross and prayed quietly for the soul of Gabe. As he finished, a smile came to his face. He looked over at the old Chief.

"You know, as long as I've known you, I didn't know your first name was George."

The old Chief laughed. "It's really not my first name. It's my middle name. William is my first name."

"William George Walking Cloud," Father repeated. "Sounds regal."

The Chief laughed again. "I am, man. I am prophet, priest and *king* made possible by the Blood of Christ."

"Amen," Father laughed.

By the time they reached the Chief's house it was dark. The stars had appeared and were twinkling their message from their position high above. Father stood alongside the truck, enjoying the performance.

"What do you think, Chief? Think there is life out there?"

The Chief walked around to where Father was standing and looked up. "I really don't know. I don't know which is easier to believe: that there's some intelligent life form out there that dropped off the capsules, or that some intelligent race here on earth put them in the cavern long before time, as we know it, existed. They're both pretty far-fetched if you really think about it."

"But isn't it interesting that Ben had an explanation for the Holy Spirit rock and that the explanation included men who were half man and half bull?"

"Yes, that is exciting, but…"

Father looked at the Chief. "But what?"

"It's going to take a miracle for us to get any information from that government compound. It's like we are stuck."

Father laughed. "In the natural it may look like we're up against impossible odds, but let's give God time. He makes a way where there is no way. Remember the Holy Spirit is working on someone right now." He slapped the old Chief on the shoulder. "You got anything to eat in there? I'm starved."

"How about a TV dinner?" the Chief laughed.

"Now you're talking," Father replied, as he followed his old friend into the house.

The Chief was as good as his word and soon had a couple of TV dinners on the table.

"You know, these are not half bad," Father said as he savored a large mouthful.

The Chief smiled. "I've eaten enough of these things to fill my truck bed a few times over."

Father laughed and nodded. "That's twice today you've sounded like a priest. How to fix TV dinners was one of our courses in the seminary."

"Really?" the Chief laughed.

"No, not really. But it should have been. Without a woman around the rectory, meals can be quick and skimpy, to say the least."

They were both hungry. It had been a long day and both of them knew that unless the Lord opened a door, they were done with any more investigation. Father had grown accustomed to waiting on the Lord. It was part of the job description. The problem was, he only had until the weekend, unless something broke. But he knew that God was aware of that, also. He prayed silently as he helped the Chief clean up the table. They had just finished when the phone rang. The old Chief looked at Father.

"I wonder who that could be?"

77

Father shrugged, then watched as old Chief walked over and picked up the phone.

"Yes, he's here. Want to speak to him?"

The Chief handed the phone to Father. "It's Denise," he said with a big grin.

Father took the phone. "Hello. Yes. When? Do you have a car? Let me give the phone back to the Chief. He can tell you how to get here. Okay, be careful. We'll see you in a little while."

The Chief again took the phone and gave Denise the directions for getting to his house. He told her it would take about forty minutes. He also told her to be careful then hung up the phone. He frowned as he looked at Father.

"She was pretty upset. What happened?"

"She said that Dr. Laird and Dr. LePage had paid her a visit."

The Chief's eyes widened. "So soon? What did they want?"

"She just said they asked a lot of questions that all centered around her knowledge of the missing children. She was scared. She knows now that we are real and that we were right. She said she had to talk to us so I thought it was best if she came out here. I hope that was okay."

The Chief nodded. "That's fine. Do you think she might be followed?"

"I don't know. It depends on how convincing she was with her answers."

"There's one way to find out. You can see someone coming down the road for miles from here. He looked at his watch. "When it gets close to the time for her to be here, we'll go outside and wait. We should be able to see if there is an extra set of car lights."

"Good idea."

Both men spent the minutes getting cleaned up from the day's activities. The old Chief was ready first and when Father walked back into the kitchen, the Chief motioned that it was time.

"She should be here in a few minutes."

"Good. Let's go."

Together the two men walked back outside and leaned against the side of the truck. They both looked down the road. They saw only darkness. Father prayed quietly for Denise. After a while the Chief again looked at his watch.

"She's late."

Father continued to watch down the road. "Maybe she didn't leave right when she finished talking with us."

"I hope not. If she's not here in a few minutes, maybe we ought to go look for her."

Fear tried to rise within Father Macon but he bound it in the Name of Jesus and continued to pray in the Spirit. They waited another ten minutes.

"What do you think, Father?"

"If they were following her, they may have tried to intercept her before she had the opportunity to leave town."

The Chief turned and looked at Father. "You don't think they would hurt her, do you?"

Father started to answer but suddenly pointed back down the road. "Is that car lights?"

The old Chief turned and looked to where Father was pointing. He waited. It did look like it was getting lighter at the horizon. Suddenly two lights came into view. The old Chief laughed then turned to Father.

"Alleluia!"

"Let's hope it's her," Father added.

"Amen."

They continued to watch the car's head lights as the vehicle made its way closer through the desert night. The car was still miles away but could easily be seen.

"So far there's no one following her," the old Chief said.

"You're right. We could certainly see if anyone was tailing her."

They stood silently watching the lights, waiting, hoping it was Denise. They were relieved when the car's turn signal came on.

"It's her," the old Chief laughed.

Father put his hands to his eyes as the car's headlights bathed them in brightness. The car pulled alongside the Chief's truck and came to a halt. The two men walked around to the driver's side just as the door opened.

"You had us worried," Father greeted.

"Yeah, you're late," the Chief added.

"I know. I'm sorry," Denise apologized as she shut the car door.

"Did you have any trouble?" Father asked.

"No. But I was on the elevator when I thought it might be safer for me if I stayed with you guys. So I went back to my room and got my things." She looked at the Chief. "Chief, you got room for me?"

The Chief looked at Father.

Even in the dim light Father could see the concern in the old man's face. "She can have my room," he quickly offered. "I can sleep on the couch."

"I appreciate that, Father. I apologize for putting you guys out. But, I'm scared to death and you guys have some answers that I need to hear."

The Chief took one last look down the road. Convinced that it was indeed clear, he motioned with his hand. "Let's get your things and get into the house."

Denise nodded then opened the back door of the car and withdrew a large suitcase.

"Here, let me have that," Father said, taking the bag.

He followed Denise as she followed the Chief into the house. He held the door until Father set the large bag on the floor beside the couch.

He shut the door then looked at Denise. "Have a seat. Care for something to drink?"

"No thanks," Denise replied, taking a seat on the couch.

Father sat down on the other end. The Chief pulled a chair from the kitchen, placed it close to Denise and sat down facing her. "Tell us what happened."

She looked at Father Macon and smiled. "First of all, I owe you an apology."

Father laughed. "Why is that?"

"When I left the restaurant, I was pretty upset with you guys. I didn't know what to make of you two. So," she laughed, "I called the Little Rock Diocese and asked if they knew of a Father Rex Macon. The woman said that she did, and she gave me your parish phone number. I called the number and your secretary said you were out of state. Sorry, I didn't trust you."

Father nodded. "That's okay. Apology accepted. But to be fair to you, I know we must have seemed pretty weird."

"You certainly were. I thought you had set me up at the press conference. Then when you started telling me I was in danger…Well, let's just say I had gotten my fill of you guys."

"Tell us what changed your mind," the Chief urged.

"After I left the restaurant I went to my room to go over my notes from the press conference. I lay down on the bed and I must have fallen asleep. I was awakened by a knock at the door. When I got up to answer it, Dr. Laird and Dr. LePage wanted to know if they could come in and talk to me. I must have turned three shades of pale because I remembered what you had said. I stumbled around, trying to think up a good excuse to turn them down but my brain deserted me. So, I invited them in. They started off by telling me that they needed someone to serve as a public relations person and they had been impressed by me at the press conference. They used that to interview me, but I could tell that in reality they were on a fact-finding mission. They asked a lot of questions about the missing children. They wanted to know where I had gotten my information. When I told them I had heard people talking, they wanted to know who. I felt like a prisoner being interrogated."

"How long did they stay?" Father asked.

"About an hour and a half. Dr. Laird asked most of the questions. Dr. LePage seemed very nervous. She kept asking me really weird questions."

Father frowned. "Like what?"

"She wanted to know if I thought I could die for my country. I told her I thought I could if it was something worth dying for. She seemed satisfied with that. She wanted to know if I had children. I told her, no. Then she asked that if I did, could I give them up for the good of mankind. I didn't really know what she meant and when I asked her to clarify her question, Dr. Laird changed the subject."

Father looked at the Chief, his mind searching. What were they after with this type of questioning? He turned back to Denise.

"Did they mention the mummies?"

Denise shook her head. "Not one time. They were there for one reason; to find out how much I knew about the missing children. I think I finally convinced them that I truly knew nothing." She looked at Father. "Which is the truth. I know nothing. You guys are the ones with all the knowledge. And I think it's time that you let me in on what you know. After all, it was you guys that got me in this mess. The least you can do is let me in on what you know."

Father looked at the old Chief who nodded his head.

"What about the public relations position? Father asked, looking at Denise.

"They said they would get back to me."

"Sure," Father laughed. "When pigs fly."

"I agree," Denise smiled. "But, you were right about them coming to see me. That means you were right about them knowing about the missing children. I'm convinced now that they know. What I want to know is why. What was in that cave? When we were walking to the press conference I heard you say something about a cover-up. I've told you everything I know. I think it's time that you guys leveled with me."

"I agree," Father nodded. "But ours is a long story. It began with a phone call from the Chief."

For the next two hours, Father and the Chief shared with Denise everything that they knew about the cavern. Her eyes grew wide when Father described the skeleton of the half man, half bull that was in the broken capsule. He went into great detail about cryogenics and how it worked. They told her about Gabe Running Deer and how he had been killed because of what *he* had seen in the cave. The old Chief described the broken brake line and the fluid in the dirt outside Gabe's house and how the wreck had been by design and not by accident. They shared with her their trip to Ben's and his story of the Otlancho. When they finished, Denise sat looking at Father as if in a daze.

"Man," she said. "That is some story. If this is for real, this is the story of the century."

"It's real all right," the Chief sighed. "Oh, how I wish it wasn't."

"But you still haven't explained how the missing children fit in."

"We don't know," Father shrugged. "We just know that they started disappearing *after* the cavern was discovered."

Denise looked at the old Chief. "You think that the capsules and the creatures in them came from a time long, long ago?"

The Chief laughed. "No, that's Father's theory. I don't know. We've decided it's either that or the capsules are the work of extraterrestrials."

"Little gray men?"

"Maybe. Father told you that we don't have the technology to do what was in those capsules."

Denise looked at Father. "I could believe little gray men before I could believe that those capsules came from a time in our past."

Father nodded. "I understand that. But think of Greek mythology. They have a creature that was half man, half bull."

"I know," Denise interrupted. "It was called a minotaur. But that was just mythology."

"Maybe," Father smiled, "and maybe not. Ben's story about the Otlancho also had a minotaur like creature."

"That may be so, but I still like the Chief's idea about the capsules somehow being connected to the space ship that crashed near Roswell. It might be worth our time to find out more about that."

"You mean go to Roswell?" the Chief frowned.

Denise nodded. "Yes, it's not that far from here and someone might know something that could shed some light on this whole thing."

"What do you think, Father?" the Chief asked.

"It's either that or storm the military compound and get a look at those capsules ourselves."

Denise laughed. "No thanks. I've had enough of those people to last me for a while. There is a Pulitzer prize story in this and I intend to get it, but not posthumously."

"What do you think Roswell has to offer that we don't already know?" the Chief asked.

Denise laughed. "We know what they want us to know. I'm a reporter. When it comes to matters like this, there is always a lot of the truth that is left out. Why? I don't know. But, there is someone in Roswell who knows a lot more than has been printed in the newspapers. If we can find that person, we may be able to fill in a few more of the pieces."

Father looked at the Chief and smiled. "I think it's worth a try. I don't know of any other option we have right now."

The Chief shrugged his shoulders. "Any idea as to how to find this certain person?"

Denise smiled. "I've got a good idea." She looked at Father. "You need to wear your clergy collar if you have one with you."

"I do," Father answered, "but what will that do?"

"As long as I've been a reporter I've noticed hesitancy in the people to share what they know. There is a genuine fear that it may get them in trouble or cause them a lot of public abuse. So they keep what they know to themselves. But if they trust you and they know you're not from the government, then most of them will share." She laughed. "A priest is someone that people naturally trust. If we find the person, trust me, the collar will make a difference."

"Okay," Father agreed. "I see your point."

The Chief turned and looked at the clock above the refrigerator. "If we're going to get an early start tomorrow, we ought to hit the sack."

Father nodded then got up from the couch. He turned and walked to his room then returned carrying his suitcase. "You can move your things into my room."

"Thanks," Denise smiled. "I hate to put you guys out."

"No problem. This couch will make a fine bed. I've certainly slept on worse."

"Father, I'll get you some bedclothes," the old Chief added, walking to a hall closet.

Denise walked over and picked up her suitcase then carried it back to the room Father had vacated. Father covered the couch cushions with the sheets.

The Chief watched, satisfied that Father needed no help. "Rex, I'll see you in the morning."

Father looked up. "Okay Chief, good night. God bless."

The Chief smiled then slowly walked toward his room. "Good night, Denise," he said as he passed her room.

"Good night, Chief, and thanks again."

Father sat down on his makeshift bed and began taking off his shoes. He thought of what Denise had shared about her "interrogation" with the government officials. He sat staring, his mind trying to reason. His thoughts were interrupted by Denise making her way to the bathroom.

"Denise," Father called.

She turned and looked at him.

"What do you think Dr. LePage was getting at with her question about giving up children for the good of mankind?"

Denise shook her head. "I don't have a clue, but it sure was weird. She seemed like she was trying to convince herself of something by the way I answered her questions."

Father frowned, not understanding her.

Denise could tell that he did not understand what she was trying to say. "I know it sounds crazy, but it was as if she was doing something that she wasn't quite sure of and she needed support from me to convince her that it was okay."

"You mean that it was okay to sacrifice children for the good of mankind?"

Denise nodded. "Yeah, something like that."

"How about Dr. Laird? Did he show the same attitude?"

"No way. He was as cool as a cucumber. He was the one who really made me nervous."

Father nodded and Denise turned and walked to the bathroom. Father heard the door close. He removed his shirt, walked over and turned off the light. He returned to the couch and lay down. He stared at the ceiling, his mind still seeking, searching. After a while he heard the bathroom door open and Denise quietly going back to her room.

"Rex?" she said quietly, stopping at the doorway.

"Yeah?"

"If they are responsible for the missing children, what do you think they are doing with them?"

"I'm not sure but it scares me to think about it."

"I know what you mean. It is scary." She paused, looking toward the couch, her eyes still unaccustomed to the darkness. "Well, I'll see you in the morning."

"Okay, goodnight."

He heard Denise close the bedroom door. He quietly prayed in the Spirit for the missing children and their parents. The more he thought about it the more he realized that Dr. LePage also needed prayer. Whether it was the Spirit's urging or just his heart's concern, in obedience, he prayed for her.

Father opened his eyes. The room was barely coming alive with the first rays of light. He looked past the kitchen, through the large windows to the desert sky beyond. Above the mountains, the transition from purple to orange was taking place, signaling the coming of the newborn sun. He looked at his watch. It was too early to get up. He shut his eyes again and prayed in the Spirit. His mind suddenly jumped to their trip to Roswell. He wondered what they would find. With all of his heart, he found it very hard to believe in men from outer space. There had to be a better explanation.

"Help me!"

Father turned his head and looked to where the cry had come from. He was standing in a hot desert. The voice was that of a small child and seemed to be originating just over a ridge in front of him. As he walked toward the ridge he heard the voice again.

"Help me!"

It was most certainly the cry of a small child. He walked to the top of the ridge and looked down. Below him in the ravine was a small girl about five years of age. She looked up at Father Macon and reached toward him with her arms.

"Help me," she cried. "The vampire is after me."

"What?" Father replied, walking to the small girl.

"The vampire wants my blood."

Father looked around then knelt down in front of the small child. "Sugar, there is no one here. You are okay."

"No," she screamed, "they won't stop till they get my blood."

Father reached for the child but she backed away.

"What is your name, Sugar?"

The child wiped her eyes then looked deeply into the eyes of Father Macon. "My name is Doris LePage."

A noise behind Father caused him to turn.

He opened his eyes as he heard Denise's bedroom door open. He looked at the ceiling then turned and looked again toward the kitchen. The sun was shining brightly through the large windows. He had fallen asleep again while praying.

"Good morning," he said.

"Oh, good morning, Rex. Did I wake you? I'm sorry."

Father sat up and looked at her. "You didn't wake me. I was having this weird dream about Doris LePage."

Denise wrinkled her nose. "Is that her name?"

Father laughed. "I don't know. But in the dream, that's what she told me it was."

Denise walked over to the couch. "What happened in the dream?"

Father quickly recounted the content of the dream. Denise frowned as he mentioned the part about the vampire. When he finished she laughed and shook her head.

"I didn't realize that priests had weird dreams like the rest of us."

Probably weirder," Father laughed. "I've learned that most of the time the weird ones are usually from the Holy Spirit."

Denise again frowned. "Whatever for?"

"To teach, guide or enlighten."

"You mean, God is trying to help us figure out what is going on in the desert of New Mexico?"

"Most certainly. That's the reason I'm here. He asked me to come."

"He asked you to come? Man! I thought God only talked to Moses."

Father laughed. "He talks to anyone who is filled with His Spirit."

"And dreams are the medium He uses?" Denise replied, nodding her head.

"One of the mediums He uses," Father smiled. "There are many."

"Amen," a voice confirmed from behind Denise.

She turned to find the Chief listening to their conversation. "You agree with what he is saying?"

"Absolutely," the Chief nodded. "My people have always believed that the Great Spirit communes with His creation. But, as much as I thought I knew, Father has taught me more."

"Well, then this thing should be wrapped up. We just let God tell us what is going on."

Father Macon laughed. "I wish it was that easy. Unfortunately for us, it doesn't work that way. We still have to do the legwork and the processing of information. God just pitches in where He sees fit."

"What if the Big Man doesn't pitch in?"

"Then we are on our own. But, like I said, He asked me to come out here. When He does that He will not leave us orphaned. If we remain open and obedient He will direct us."

Denise shrugged. "Should we go to Roswell? After all, that was my idea."

Father nodded. "I think so. We have no other leads and neither the Chief nor I have received anything to the contrary."

"Except the dream you just described."

"That's right. But that was not contrary. In fact, the dream really confirms what you shared last night about Dr. LePage. Before I went to sleep I was encouraged to pray for her. Then this morning I had the dream. If I'm right, she is important to solving this thing. How, I don't know. But, the dream knows. If we could interpret it, then the mind of the Spirit would be revealed."

"Would you mind sharing the dream again?" the old Chief asked.

"Not at all," Father replied. "The more we discuss it, the greater chance we have of interpreting it."

Father once again related the dream. Both the Chief and Denise listened intently, mulling over every word in their minds. The Chief had the same reaction as Denise had to the word vampire, but waited to question until after Father had finished.

"Why would a vampire be in the dream?"

Father laughed. "Chief, you know these things as well as I do. It's to transfer an idea."

"But why would a vampire want her blood?" Denise interrupted.

Father shook his head. "I don't know. But I really felt sorry for her. She was really scared."

"How old do you think she was?" the old Chief asked.

"I would guess about four or five."

"But why would Dr. LePage appear in the dream as a child?" Denise asked, her frustration revealed in her tone.

The Chief looked at Father. "You know, all the children that have been abducted have been about that age. A couple of them were a little younger, I think."

Father frowned, trying to make some sense out of the whole thing. "If Dr. LePage represents the children then who does the vampire represent?"

"Someone who wants their blood," Denise replied.

Father looked at her and squinted his eyes. "That's good. The blood represents life so someone wants their life."

Denise shook her head. "That doesn't make any sense. If that someone is the government, which we think it is, then how would they use the life of a child?"

"What do you think, Chief? I'm drawing a blank."

The Chief walked over to a chair and sat down. He looked up at Father. "What if the blood is not representative of life here? What if it means exactly what the dream said it meant?"

Father frowned. "You mean the government wants the children for their blood?"

The old Chief shrugged.

Denise looked at her watch. "Guys, we can continue this conversation in the car. If we are going to Roswell today, we need to be moving. Give me a few minutes in the bathroom then you guys can have it."

Father nodded. "Go ahead."

The Chief turned to Denise as she walked toward the bathroom. "Want me to rustle up some breakfast?"

"No, I've got an idea for finding our connection in Roswell. Let's eat there."

"Okay," the Chief smiled then turned back to Father as the bathroom door closed. "Wonder what she's got on her mind?"

"Search me. But remember she's the reporter."

Father got up and removed his shirt from the back of the couch and pulled it on. As he tucked the shirttail into his jeans, he turned back to the old Chief. "If it's blood they wanted, why would they take it from the kids? There are blood banks all over the state that are much more accessible and a lot less costly."

The old man's wrinkled face remained unchanged as he looked up at Father. "I don't know. They may not need blood at all. I was

93

just trying to help interpret the dream. You're right. It doesn't make much sense."

Father laughed as he pulled a comb from his jeans and dragged it through his hair. "You know there's not a lot about this whole thing that has made sense."

The Chief's response was interrupted by Denise's exit from the bathroom.

"Who's next?" she asked, looking at the old Chief then at Father Macon.

"I'll go," Father replied.

Denise smiled at Father as he walked past her and made his way to the bathroom. She walked over to the Chief.

"You guys get the dream figured out?"

The Chief shook his head. "No. We hit a cold trail."

"What if Dr. LePage's first name is Doris? No one has told us what her first name is."

The Chief smiled. "Then we know the dream was from the Great Spirit."

Denise laughed and shook her head. "You know, you guys are downright spooky."

The Chief threw his head back and laughed old loud. "What do you expect from a Indian medicine man and a Catholic priest?"

"What are you two up to?" Father asked, exiting the bathroom and walking over to the couch.

"I was just sharing with the Chief that you two would make a good team on a late night TV show."

"Why's that?" Father asked, looking at the Chief.

The Chief motioned with his hand toward Denise. "She says we're spooky."

"Oh," Father laughed. He bent down, reached into his bag beside the couch and pulled out his Bible. He thumbed through the pages as he stood up. *"Now we have received not the spirit of the world,"* he started to read. *"But the spirit which is of God that we might know the things that are freely given to us of God. Which things also we speak, not in the words which man's wisdom teaches but which the Holy Spirit teaches; comparing spiritual things with natural."* He looked up at Denise and smiled then continued reading. *"But the natural man receives not the things of the Spirit of God for they are foolishness to him."*

He closed the Bible, looked over at the Chief and winked.

"Okay, guys," Denise laughed. "I may be a natural girl and when it comes to this stuff, I may even be a fool. But when it comes to the spiritual mumbo jumbo stuff, I've always found that in the end there's some little guy behind the curtain working the levers."

The Chief laughed, slapped his leg and stood up. "But Dorothy, my dear, we're not in Kansas anymore. We're in New Mexico, the land of enchantment." He walked over to Denise and folded his arm against his side as if to escort her. "To Ros?"

Denise laughed and placed her arm in his. "To Ros," she repeated.

Father watched the two and joined in their laughter. "If you guys are waiting for me to sing, you're in big trouble."

They figured it would take a little less than three hours to get to Roswell. Denise was not too excited about taking her car so they decided to take the old Chief's truck. They knew it would be a rougher ride but the car was a rental registered in Denise's name. Her fear of the government became very obvious when she insisted that the old Chief drive.

Because of the length of the trip, Father put his clerics in a bag and placed them behind the seat. It was important to Denise that he take them. She said it would make their search a lot easier and finally convinced Father that he could change at a gas station restroom before they reached Roswell. He laughed at the idea but knew that it was important for her so he agreed.

They traveled east on Interstate Forty for a while then turned and headed south. The desert was beautiful but not uncomfortable in the early morning. By nine-fifteen they were only a few miles out of Roswell. Denise pointed to a small roadside sign.

"There's a filling station about a mile ahead. Father can change there."

"You're certain it's that important?" Father asked, also reading the sign.

"I've been a reporter for a lot of years. Many times it is hard to gain the trust of those you are interviewing. What we are looking for involves a very delicate subject to a lot of people, even in this town. That white collar is an immediate trust builder. People will tell you things in five minutes that they wouldn't tell the Chief or me in five years."

Father knew what she was saying was true. He had experienced it many times, total strangers coming up to him and sharing their life's story; unloading even deep secrets, all because of the white collar.

The old Chief pulled into the filling station and put gas into the truck while Father changed. The transformation was amazing. He stopped at the counter to buy a pack of gum and the clerk refused to accept any money.

"Oh, Father," he said, "there's no charge for that. Have a good day."

Father smiled and thanked him and walked outside toward the truck. Denise, who had been buying a pair of sunglasses, ran to catch up with Father.

"Well, what did I tell you?"

Father smiled and held the truck door open for her. "I just pray that I'm worthy of such honor."

"You've got my vote," she replied as she climbed into the truck. "You look very handsome."

Father looked at her and smiled. "Thank you."

The old Chief returned from paying for the gas and soon they were on the road again, each one of them wondering what Roswell, New Mexico would hold for them.

"Okay, Denise, what are we looking for?" the Chief asked as they all read the city limit sign.

"Let's look for a place to eat breakfast. A mom and pop place would be best."

They drove, looking for a small restaurant.

"How about that one?" Father asked, pointing to a small diner with a blinking flying saucer on top.

Denise laughed. "That's perfect, the *UFO Diner*. I hope the food's good."

The Chief pulled the truck into the parking area. Father opened the door, stepped out, and then waited for Denise to do the same.

"*UFO Diner*, food out of this world," Father read.

Denise looked at the sign Father was reading. "Sounds promising."

"I could eat a horse," the Chief added.

Father laughed. "I know what you mean. I'm kind of hungry myself."

"Well, let's check it out," Denise directed.

The diner certainly reflected the theme of the town. UFO paraphernalia was everywhere. Pictures of UFOs and wide-eyed aliens lined the wall. The waitress that seated the three was dressed in a silver space suit and her head was adorned with two antennae that bounced when she walked.

"My name is Beverly and I'll be your waitress," she announced as she placed a menu and a glass of water in front of each of the threesome.

"Boy, everyone sure goes in for this UFO business around here," Denise offered.

Beverly smiled as she took her pad and pencil from her pocket. "Yeah, it brings in the tourists and that provides jobs. It's also kind of exciting."

"Why's that?" Father asked.

"Well, if it's true, I think it's exciting that people from other planets are coming to earth and seeking our fellowship."

"So you think it is real and not fake?" Denise asked.

Beverly giggled. "I don't know if it is or not. But it does help to take the people's minds off of their everyday problems. For that reason, I hope it's not fake."

While they were talking, the Chief had decided what he wanted. As Beverly finished speaking, he pointed to the menu and informed her of his order. Father and Denise quickly followed. As Beverly walked away he looked at Father and laughed.

"Eat now, talk later."

Father laughed then continued to scan the restaurant looking at the decorations and memorabilia. The place was not very crowded. The breakfast crowd had ended an hour or so earlier. An old black and white picture on the wall to their right caught his attention. He got up from the small table and walked to where the picture was hanging. He was looking at it when he heard Beverly's voice.

"Father, your food is ready."

He turned and smiled at her, then turned back to the picture. "Beverly, is this the man who owned the ranch where the UFO supposedly crashed?"

She walked along side Father to where she could also see the picture. "Yes. That's Mac Brazel. He's the one who first found the pieces of wreckage."

Father nodded his head as he continued to look at the picture. Beverly turned and walked back to the table where Denise and the old Chief were already enjoying the food.

"Where's the best place to find out about all this?" he heard Denise ask.

He turned and walked back to the table, waiting for Beverly's answer.

She frowned as she poured more coffee in the Chief's cup. "We have the museum which is very good."

Father took his chair and placed a napkin in his lap. "Who is the area expert, the one who is thoroughly convinced that something crashed on Mr. Brazel's ranch?"

Beverly laughed. "That would be Hattie Haskel at the *Roswell Courier*. She's been with the paper since some time in the fifties and she probably has collected about as much information as the museum; maybe even more."

Father looked at Denise and nodded.

"Where can we find Hattie?" Denise asked.

Beverly turned and pointed toward the windows. "That's Highway 285 right there. It turns into Main Street farther on down. The *Courier* is about six blocks down on the right. You really can't miss it." She laughed and looked at Father. "You guys aren't connected with the government in any way, are you?"

Father shook his head. "No, why?"

"Hattie hates government men. She calls them G-men. If you were from the government the only thing you might get from Hattie was a good cussin."

Everyone laughed and Beverly left. Father bowed his head and prayed quietly. The Chief had about cleaned his plate but put his fork aside and bowed his head also. Denise, apparently uncomfortable, mimicked the old chief. They waited until Father looked up, then picked up their forks and continued eating.

"Sounds like Hattie is our person," Denise said, wiping her mouth with her napkin.

Father nodded then finished swallowing. "Sounds like she might be on our side, too."

Denise frowned for a second then laughed. "Oh, you mean anti-government."

"Yeah. That should help us."

"How much should we share about what we know?" the old Chief asked.

Father smiled. "I was just thinking about that. I guess we should wait and see. But, if it gets down to brass tacks, I would be willing. What do you think, Denise?"

"I agree. If she despises the government that much, we know she's not going to betray us."

Father was just finishing his last bite when Beverly returned.

"Can I get you guys anything else?"

Father smiled and shook his head. "No, thanks. I'm full. It was good."

Denise and the Chief joined Father in shaking their heads.

"Well then, you folks have a good day," she shared, placing the bill on the corner of the table.

Father picked up the piece of paper. "Beverly, thanks for your help. We appreciate you being so pleasant."

Beverly smiled. "Thank you, Father."

As she walked away, Father pulled out his billfold and placed some money with the tab on the table.

"Let me help with that," Denise offered, reaching into her pocket.

"No," Father objected. "This is on me."

Denise and the Chief thanked him then together they walked back out to the truck.

"Six blocks on the right," Denise said as she slid along the seat next to the Chief.

"Hattie Haskel," Father added as he slammed the door.

The Chief pulled the truck to the edge of the parking lot, looked both ways then eased out onto the highway. He drove slowly as they all three looked for the *Courier* building. Denise was the first to spot it.

"There it is," she pointed.

There was a small parking area to the side of the building, which had a few empty spaces. The Chief pulled into one and shut off the engine. He opened the door and climbed out then waited until he was joined by Father and Denise. Together, they walked to the front of the building.

"*The Roswell Courier*, Editor Mark Davis, Editor Emeritus Hattie Haskel," Father read out loud as all three of them stood staring at the front door.

The Chief opened the door and held it for them to enter. They walked to a reception desk where they were greeted by a young woman.

"May I help you?"

Denise reached into her pocket and withdrew one of her business cards, handing it to the young woman. "We would like to talk to Ms. Haskel."

The young woman studied the card for a moment then looked up at Denise. "Just a minute please." She picked up the phone, punched one of the buttons then waited. She read Denise's credentials into the phone, waited a few seconds then put down the receiver. "Hattie says to come on back. It's down the hall, second door on the left."

They all thanked the young woman then followed her directions. The hall consisted of glassed-in offices that contained different people in various stages of office work. A couple of the people waved as the three made their way along. When they got to the right door, again the Chief opened it for the group to enter.

They were all surprised by Hattie. But they could tell by the look on her face that Hattie was also surprised by them, especially Father Macon's collar.

Hattie stood as they entered the room and smiled. Father guessed her to be about seventy. She was a small, thin woman with bleached blond hair. She had large earrings that hung down about an inch and her lipstick was as red as fire. Her skin was wrinkled, but heavily powdered and her eyebrows had been drawn in. She looked like she had had a makeover and they had used a little too much of everything.

"Ms. Cameron," she said, extending her hand across the desk.

Her voice was low, almost manly. Denise shook her hand then introduced Father and the old Chief. After exchanging greetings, Hattie offered the threesome a chair then sat back down.

"What can I do for you?"

Denise looked at Father Macon then at the Chief. She could tell by their facial expressions that she had been appointed speaker. She turned and looked at Hattie.

"For the last few days we have been in Albuquerque investigating the cave in and the government's presence there."

A large smile came to Hattie's face. "Let me guess. You've been jerked around so much that you wouldn't know the truth if it fell on you?"

Denise smiled. "Close, but through sources of our own we happen to know what they really found in the cavern. But it's so strange that we wanted to know what actually happened here with the UFO crash. We thought there might be some connection."

The smile dropped from Hattie's face as she leaned closer toward Denise. "Was it a flying disk?"

Denise shook her head. "No, but something just as strange." She looked at Father who nodded his encouragement for her to continue.

For the next twenty minutes Denise summarized everything she knew about the cavern and its contents. Hattie sat mesmerized as Denise told her about Gabe Running Deer and what he had seen in the cavern. She shared about Gabe's death, the missing children, and the concocted press release about the two Indian mummies.

When Denise finished, Hattie leaned back in her chair. She chewed on her lower lip for a few seconds then looked up at Father Macon. "Are you a real Catholic priest?"

"Yes, ma'am," Father nodded.

Hattie half smiled then took a deep breath. She looked at Denise. "I'm going to be up-front with you so that you'll know from the start where I stand. I think our Federal Government is nothing but a bunch of liars. I think they are basically evil and full of deception. I wouldn't trust a G-Man as far as I could throw one and with my size that's not very far. They care nothing about the constitutional rights of the private citizen and as far as they are concerned the end always justifies the means. They wouldn't think twice about killing you or destroying your credibility if they thought you were a threat."

Denise shook her head. "But why? What is it they want?"

Hattie turned to Father. "What did the first man sell his soul for?"

Father Macon frowned. "Knowledge?"

Hattie smiled as she looked at Denise and nodded. "Knowledge. Man gave up everything God had given him for knowledge. It hasn't changed to this very day. In the right hands, knowledge is power and it is wealth. Do you really think for one minute that this country is run by the President or by Congress? Hell, no!" She looked at Father. "Excuse my French, Father."

Father smiled as she continued.

"This country is run by people with big money. The President and the Congress are merely their puppets. One wrong move from a government official and they're done. The big guys sic the news media on their victim with the task of destroying the person's credibility in the eyes of the public. The American people have been conditioned to believe anything they see and hear on TV so, in reality, it's a fairly simple task. Think back over the last twenty years at the number of people whose lives have been destroyed at the hands of the media."

"But," Father objected, "What knowledge can they glean from the canisters that would be that valuable?"

Hattie didn't answer but picked up the phone and punched one of its buttons. "Connie, this is Hattie," she said into the receiver. "I'm going back to my study. If anyone calls or comes looking for me, I'm out of the office. Okay, thanks."

Hattie hung up the receiver then stood up. "Come with me. I want to show you all why the government is so interested in what was in that cavern."

CHAPTER FIVE

The Tree of Knowledge of Good and Evil

The three followed the old woman through the building until they came to a door. It was well away from the main part of the business. Hattie removed a string that supported a key from around her neck. She placed the key in the lock and slowly opened the door. Father looked at Denise. Her eyes were wide with anticipation.

Hattie found the light switch and brought the dark room to life. It was a fairly large room with bookcases on one wall, stacks of boxes on another and shelves of small boxes on the third. A desk, a couch, and two chairs sat in the middle of the room.

"Have a seat," Hattie offered, as she turned and locked the door.

The Chief looked at Father and frowned as he watched the old woman locking the door. Father shrugged his shoulders then sat beside Denise on the couch. The Chief waited until Hattie had taken a seat behind the desk then eased into one of the chairs.

Hattie took her arm and waved it around her head. "You might say this is my secret room. It contains everything I have found on the Roswell incident. If the government knew what I had here, it wouldn't be here long."

"What did happen out there in the desert?" Denise asked.

"A lot more than you've been told, I assure you. When Mac Brazel found the debris scattered across his farm, he was not sure what he had found. But he knew that he had never seen anything like it before."

Hattie pushed her chair back and got up. The others watched as she found a small box and brought it back to her desk. She turned and looked at Father. "How much do you know about the UFO crash?"

Father shrugged his shoulders. "Not much. All I know is that some people say the crash involved a UFO and the government says it was a weather balloon."

Hattie smiled. "Okay that's good, because that's where I'm going to start. Any time research is done there needs to be a base for the experiment or what we will call a control." She took something out of the box then walked over and handed it to Father. It was a photograph of a young girl with a kite looking object. Denise leaned over and studied the black and white photo then looked up at Hattie for an explanation. Father handed the photograph back to Hattie who turned and handed it to the old Chief.

"This old photograph is of Jean Campell of Circleville, Ohio. On July the fifth, nineteen forty-seven, Sherman Campell, Jean's father discovered this UFO on his farm. As you can see it was a six-pointed star shaped kite that was fifty inches high and four feet wide. The whole thing was wrapped in foil. Nearly every newspaper in the country carried the story because UFO phenomenon was a hot topic in the summer of 1947. The local sheriff identified the UFO as a weather balloon with highly visible serial numbers etched across its exterior. Now get this. Jean Campell was allowed to keep the balloon for as long as she wanted without the slightest hint of governmental badgering."

I show you this because this is the way the government handled weather balloons that were found by civilians."

Father Macon looked at Hattie and smiled. He knew what she was trying to do and he realized that this old newspaper editor was a sharp lady. "What you're saying is that the government handled weather balloon sightings that way until Roswell."

Hattie smiled and nodded her head. "Exactly. The weather balloon that supposedly crashed at Roswell contained the same type of debris as that found in Circleville. How do I know?" Hattie walked back over to her desk and removed another photograph from the small box. She took it over and handed it to Father. "This is a picture of Brigadier General Roger Ramsel holding some of the so-called UFO. You can see that it is the same type of debris as the kite in the Campell photo."

Denise looked at Hattie and frowned. "So the way the government handled the Roswell crash site was entirely different than the Circleville incident?"

Hattie threw her head backed and laughed. "Oh sweetheart, there wasn't any comparison. The most extreme security measures were implemented around the Roswell crash site. There was an inner circle of guards and an outer circle of guards with sharp shooters stationed on every high ridge around the area."

Father looked at the old Chief. "Sounds the same as what is going on at Chaco Canyon right now."

Hattie nodded her head. "That's what I'm telling you. The government has procedures they follow for every type of incident. Roswell was no Circleville."

"But Chaco Canyon may be," Denise added.

"You can count on it. These G-men will stop at nothing to protect whatever it is that they have found."

"But why?" Father interjected.

"I told you. They want the knowledge that these discoveries bring and they'll destroy anyone and everyone who gets in their way."

"What kind of knowledge are you talking about? And who gets to use this knowledge?'

Hattie looked at Father and smiled. "That's the best part about Roswell but let's not get there so fast. I've got some other things I want to show you." She walked back over to the desk and removed a small jar and another photograph from the box. She walked back to Father and handed him the photo. "This is the crash where the debris was found. There is no debris left because the government took every piece they could find and they left no stone unturned. They scoured the entire site several times. Weather balloon, my foot."

Father looked up at Hattie. "This photograph shows a huge trench in the ground."

"That's right. The impact of the object tore a gash in the earth almost a hundred yards long. No weather balloon could do that." Hattie took the jar and unscrewed the lid. She dumped the contents into her hand. "This is what was found on the sides of that trench." She held her hand out toward Father.

The old Chief got up and walked over to the couch and stood behind Father and Denise. He looked at the material. "It looks like a mixture of sand and glass."

Hattie nodded. "That's exactly what it is. But, if you'll look closely you'll see that the sand has been melted into glass."

Father looked up at Hattie. "The object that made the trench was hot enough to melt the ground as it impacted. There's absolutely no way a weather balloon could do that."

"Bingo, Padre."

"But how about Mac Brazel? It was his ranch. Surely he got to watch while they cleaned up the debris."

Hattie chuckled. "Sweetheart, they kept Mac under armed guard for seven days until the G-men plucked his farm clean. They wouldn't let him use the phone and they put him through hell while he was under house arrest at Roswell Army Air Field. You told me they killed your friend because he knew too much. You under estimate these people. They'll kill in a heartbeat." Hattie once more walked back to the box on her desk and returned with another photograph. She handed it to Father. "This is George Wilcot. He was the county sheriff at the time. When Mac Brazel found the debris he reported it to Sheriff Wilcot who in turn reported it to the Army Air Force. But not before he did some investigating. He visited the crash site and saw the alien bodies. But, when the G-men showed up they made the site off limits even to Wilcot. And they told him if he ever leaked anything about the incident both he and his family would be killed. He knew they meant it. It had such an impact on his life that he never wanted to be sheriff again."

Father frowned. "Did he ever tell anything?"

Hattie shook her head. "He didn't but later his granddaughter did. She said that before his death, George shared that when he got to the site there was a large burned area and a lot of debris. It was in the evening and the light was bad but he said he saw four aliens. He described them as having large heads with dark eyes. All four were wearing shiny silver suits. He said, also, that they were much smaller than humans."

Denise looked up from studying the picture. "Did Mac Brazel ever say he saw the aliens?"

Hattie laughed. "Oh, no, no, no. You see there were actually two crash sites."

"Two?" Father exclaimed.

"That's right. The first impact was on the Brazel ranch. That's where most of the debris was found. The debris was scattered for three-fourths of a mile along a path that was several hundred feet wide. The object came to rest about five miles away near Corona, New Mexico on the Foster Range."

"And that's where the alien bodies were found?"

"That's right. The object came in on a southeast trajectory. It was during a violent thunderstorm. But it hit with enough force to dig the trench I showed you and melt the ground. At impact it was traveling so fast that it flew five more miles before coming to a stop. To give you some idea, the crash site is forty-five minutes from Roswell. The impact area where the debris was found is over two and one half hours away."

Father shook his head. "I don't get it. You mean that a story of this magnitude has been kept quiet all these years through fear and intimidation? That seems impossible."

Hattie's eyes narrowed as her expression changed to a deep frown. "Father, you underestimate these people. I have spent my life researching this thing and every time I get a good lead no one will talk."

"But that was over a half century ago," Denise objected. "What could they do to the people now?"

Hattie motioned with her head toward the old Chief. "The same thing they did to your friend in Chaco Canyon. But," Hattie smiled, "a few people are starting to come forward." She turned and walked to the other side of the room. She opened one of the small boxes, withdrew a manila folder, then walked back to Father Macon. "This is probably the most exciting. It is the story of a man named Gerald Landerson." Hattie opened the folder, revealing a wad of papers. "According to his story, his family had just moved to New Mexico from Indiana. They were staying at his uncle's house and decided to go out into the desert and do some rock collecting. One of his other uncles was a big rock hound. All together there were about six who struck out on the expedition. They were following an old dry creek bed when they came around a corner and found a silver disc stuck into the side of an embankment. Needless to say they were excited. As they approached the disc they found three bodies lying in the shade of the disc. Two of the bodies showed no signs of life but the third was alive, but barely. A fourth "being" was sitting next to the bodies and he was apparently unhurt. Landerson said the alien reacted fearfully to the approach of their group. One of Landerson's uncles tried to communicate with the creature in both English and Spanish but it was apparent that the alien did not understand."

112

"What did the creature look like?" Denise interrupted.

Hattie smiled. "That's interesting. His description is very similar to that of Wilcot's, humanoid but much smaller in stature. Big dark eyes recessed in a large, almost out of proportion head. All four of the creatures were wearing silver flight suits. Landerson did point out something that was very interesting. He said he actually touched the disc and it was like a freezer. Somehow it was providing relief for the creatures in a desert with a heat index of 114 degrees." Hattie thumbed through the papers then continued. "Mr. Landerson goes on to say that another group of people suddenly made an appearance. They were a team of archaeologists who had seen the fiery object fall to the earth the night before and had decided to check it out. They were out in the desert looking for Indian artifacts."

"How many were in that group?" Father asked.

"Landerson says there were six. Five of them were college students. The sixth was their instructor who spoke several foreign languages but was unfruitful in his attempt to communicate with the alien. Landerson was only a young boy at the time and he said he finally mustered enough courage to get close to the alien. When he did the being looked at him in a way that caused him to sense what the alien was actually thinking. He felt the fear of the creature and experienced a feeling of tumbling over and over. He said he believed he relived the crash. He could sense the terror and the loneliness that the alien was feeling. His experience was interrupted by a large group of government troops. They swarmed over the area very quickly and began pushing the civilians away from the craft and the creature. Landerson said that the alien went berserk when it saw the soldiers."

"I guess so," Denise sighed. "Poor little guy."

Hattie nodded her head in agreement. "There's one thing about Landerson's story that was very odd. He said that the soldiers were not impressed with the alien. They didn't gawk or seem the least bit surprised at the sight of the creature. It was as if they had seen this sort of thing before."

"You mean this wasn't the first time they had encountered an alien?" Father added.

"Yeah. They knew what it was and Landerson said that they also knew the value of the find. He said that entire battalion of soldiers soon had the site surrounded. It looked like a war zone."

"All for a weather balloon," the Chief laughed.

Hattie turned and looked at the old Chief. "You told that right."

"But why didn't Landerson come forward before now?" Denise asked.

"He said in his interview that the G-men threatened them. He said the army officers in charge told his uncle and his father that the government would take their kids away and they would never see them again if they said anything about the downed aircraft."

Denise shook her head in disgust.

"I'm telling you, sweetie, these people are vicious and evil. I believe they'd kill their own mother if it served their purpose. In fact, I believe they would have killed every civilian at the crash site if they knew they could have gotten away with it."

Father Macon jumped to his feet and shook his head in frustration. He turned and looked down at the little woman. "But why, Hattie? I still don't see what they've got to gain. What is worth the death of so many?"

A large smile came to the face of the old woman as she raised her hand, extending one bony finger in the air. "Ah ha. Now comes the most amazing part." She got up and walked again to the wall of boxes. She reached into one of the small boxes that lined the shelf and withdrew a tiny object. With closed fist she made her way back to the group. When she reached Father she opened her hand. In her palm was a small black object with three fine wires protruding from it.

"What is that?" Denise frowned.

Hattie looked at Father Macon, waiting to answer Denise's question.

Father looked at the object then at the old woman, slowly shaking his head.

"It's a transistor. This one thing has revolutionized this country's society. It has made this present computer age possible."

Denise took the tiny object from Hattie's hand and studied it more closely. "But what does this have to do with the spaceship and the aliens?"

Hattie laughed. "This is alien technology. Our scientists robbed this technology from the spaceship."

"Oh, come on Hattie," Father laughed. "I thought some scientists in California invented the transistor."

The old woman shook her head. "That's where you are wrong. From what I can find, there was a rash of UFO sightings during the Second World War. AT&T, or Bell Labs as they were known back then, was given the job of translating the 'radio' signals that emanated from the alien spacecraft. When the crash occurred here at Roswell they were given the task of decoding and dissecting the electronics of the spacecraft. Up to this time electronics used

115

vacuum tubes and rectifier diodes that allowed the transfer of power in only one direction. Who would have guessed that simple sand or silicon coated with a layer of arsenic and other chemicals would produce a semiconductor that led to the transistor? Before the Roswell crash there was no research in silicon. The scientists knew that a low voltage semiconductor was possible but no one had been able to produce the technology to fabricate such a device. No one, that is, until the scientists got ahold of the downed spacecraft.

"I know it sounds like science fiction but I've been able to trace the plight of the downed spacecraft. It was carried from here to Wright Air Force Base where it was partially dismantled. It was then shipped to the Bell Laboratories in Murray Hill, New Jersey. Once there, the alien switching device, or transistor, became a priority of the Lab and the Department of Defense. To prevent possible retaliation from the aliens the government built anti-aircraft batteries in the mountains that surrounded the Lab. These were not to protect against man's attacks. They were there to protect against an alien attack. These battery units even held mock drills especially during heightened UFO sightings."

Denise looked up at Father, checking his response to Hattie's story. "That's really incredible."

Father nodded. "It certainly is. So Hattie, you're saying that all the secrecy and all the threats are due to the technology that is obtained from these discoveries?"

"Absolutely! Can you imagine all the money that's been made from transistor and semiconductor technology? Not only that, I've found that even our laser research and solid state circuit research has been enhanced by the alien technology, not to mention

116

technology that we can't even began to understand; stuff that is hundreds of years ahead of our present technology. To the right people this is worth megabucks and they are not in the mood for sharing."

"You mean," the Chief interrupted, "that Gabe Running Deer was killed to protect technology?"

Hattie nodded. "I'm afraid so."

"But this is our government."

"Chief, you of all people ought to know that the government is run by people with big money. What they did to your people they do to anyone who stands in the way of their objective."

"And what is their objective?" Denise asked.

"Power and control, sweetie, power and control. Knowledge is power. It's been that way from the beginning and it's still that way. This country lives by the golden rule: Those with all the gold make the rules. They release enough knowledge to keep the people comfortable. That's all. The remainder is kept by a select group. And that group will kill anyone and everyone to protect what it knows. I didn't tell you before but the head of Bell Lab's circuit research was a man named Dr. Jack Norton. He was somewhat of a maverick and was credited with the discovery, in 1943, of a type of vacuum tube that made wide TV broadcasting possible. He was appointed in 1947 to general manager of the project to 'discover the transistor' and was very staunch in his research. Unfortunately Dr. Norton was mysteriously murdered in 1972."

"What do you mean, mysteriously?" Denise frowned.

"He was covered with gasoline and set ablaze."

Father looked at the old Chief. "He was like Gabe. He knew too much."

"Exactly," Hattie nodded. "But if you're right, the technology found in the cave in Chaco Canyon could make the transistor look like chump change. We're talking immortality here."

"She's right, Father," Denise added, excitedly. "I never thought about it before, but imagine what this could do to the world. If we could truly freeze people and bring them back to life, the implications are staggering. I could be put to sleep then wake up and play with my great grandchildren."

"And sweetie, people would pay through the nose for the opportunity."

Father Macon rubbed his chin. "Hattie, do you think the crash here at Roswell and the capsule in the cave are related?"

"You mean do I think that the aliens put the capsule there?"

Father nodded.

"I don't know but I would say yes. They're just too close geographically and the technology is just too similar and too far above our present capabilities. Where else would they come from?"

"I'm not sure but as a man of God I just can't understand how beings from another galaxy or planet would fit into the salvation plan of God Almighty."

Hattie smiled. "I see your point. But, I've never been much into the religious scene myself so I don't have any sacred cows to protect."

Father laughed. "Hattie, you'd make a great Christian. From what I've seen already I can tell your morals are better than many who profess a relationship with Christ."

"A woman doesn't need God to know that you get out of this old world what you put into it. Treat people right and they'll treat you right. Pretty simple, pretty straightforward. That's why I hate the G-men. They care for no one."

Father looked at Denise and grinned. "Hattie, we appreciate your time and your help but I still believe there's got to be another answer besides outer space. How about inner space?"

"You mean our past or our future?"

"Yeah. What if these people are time travelers or what if they are from a period in our past?"

Hattie laughed. "You sound like Bill Staples."

Denise looked at Father and then frowned at Hattie. "We met Bill Staples at the press conference in Albuquerque. He lives in Santa Fe."

Hattie nodded. "That's right. He writes for the paper there. He's a big Roswell man, too. Only he thinks like you, Father. He says the aliens are not aliens at all but time travelers. He says the government is well aware of their activities. According to Bill, the government calls them Time Skippers. I think he's wrong but it might do you good to talk to him."

Denise reached into her pocket and took out a card. "I've got his card. In fact he's staying at the same hotel in Albuquerque that I am. He's there investigating the Chaco Canyon incident also."

"That sounds like Bill."

Father winked at Denise. She knew it was his way of saying it was time to go. She nodded and smiled her response.

Father turned to the old woman. "Well, Hattie, we can't tell you how much you've added to our search. It has been both enlightening and educational."

"I'm glad I was able to help." She turned and looked at Denise. "Denise, I don't mind what you print but I ask that you not mention me or this room in anything you write. I'm sure you understand?"

Denise smiled and took Hattie's hand. "I understand."

Hattie nodded then led them to the door. The little woman's concern was demonstrated as they watched her unlock the door. She waited as the small group exited the room then she turned and re-locked the door. They thanked her again after she had escorted them to the front door. Each one said good-bye then silently walked to the truck.

The silence remained until the truck was well away from Roswell. Father looked at the sky out through the windshield. He just could not accept visitors from another planet.

Denise, too, was deep in thought. She wondered if Bill Staples was still in Albuquerque. She hoped so.

The Chief thought about what Hattie had said about Gabe being killed to protect technology. What a waste! Gabe was a good man. If that were true then the old woman was right. The white man had not changed. First it had been gold, then land, and now it was technology. The blood of the red man was still being spilled to assuage the greed of the white man. The anger started to rise in his heart when he remembered the children.

"We didn't ask Hattie about the children."

Father looked at him and frowned. "You're right. But, I don't think she would have been able to offer an opinion. Nothing like that happened during the spacecraft incident. No one has ever said anything about missing children in relation to the Roswell incident. For some reason I feel that this is special to whatever was found in the cave."

"I did mention the children when I told Hattie about the cave." Denise added. "The fact that she didn't mention anything afterwards means that you are probably right. Maybe Bill can offer some assistance."

"You may be right. I do think we should talk with him. What do you think, Chief?"

The Chief continued to watch the highway. Father could tell that his friend was disturbed. "I think it would be a good thing. When we were at the press conference, he approached us. If you remember, it was because of Denise's question about the missing children. He may be able to help us."

Father continued to look at the old Indian. "You okay, Chief?"

"Yeah. I was just thinking about Gabe and what Hattie said. I just cannot believe the lack of value that some people place on life. Gabe was a good man and a good son. Ben counted on him in his old age. Now he is gone - because of money?" The Chief angrily slapped the steering wheel.

Father Macon's heart hurt for the old chief. "Not money, Chief, greed. The Bible says that the love of money is the root of all evil. In this country it is a very big root."

"But when will we ever learn? It doesn't seem things have changed one bit since the time of my fathers."

Denise looked at Father, waiting for his answer. It was a good question.

Father Macon looked at Denise and then over at the old Chief. "It will change, my friend, when man realizes that he is a spiritual being and not a human being. Flesh lasts only for a season. The spirit is forever. Jesus said store things in heaven not on this earth.

When we learn that lesson then the greed and the lust for materialism will stop."

"Will that ever happen, Father? I kind of feel like the Chief. It doesn't look like it's getting any better. In fact, in my opinion, it's getting worse with each generation."

"God is patient with His children because He knows the power of the world on our minds. But even His patience is limited and if we do not turn on our own, He will provide the atmosphere for our minds to be renewed to the truth."

Denise frowned. "What do you mean, 'provide the atmosphere?' That sounds foreboding."

"God has a time-frame with mankind. This world - or dispensation, as God calls it - will not go on forever. God has a plan that has been in motion from the beginning of time and it will, one day, come to fulfillment. To gain as many souls as possible, God will allow certain things to transpire so as to 'shock' the minds of the people and help them to re-think ideas or mind-sets. Hattie was right. Knowledge is the key. But, knowledge that is not the truth is meaningless to God and His Kingdom. Man, however, hangs on to knowledge that makes his world comfortable or supports his lifestyle and mind-set. Truth, to that kind of mind, can be very threatening and easily rejected. But God knows that when the prevailing mindset is interrupted, it opens the mind to seek a new mindset. And sometimes the greater the impact the interruption has on the heart of the person, the more the mind is forced to seek. It is in the seeking that the mind can be introduced to the truth."

Denise smiled. "Is that what's happening to me now?"

Father frowned. "I don't understand."

"This Chaco Canyon thing. My mind is straining like everything, trying to understand what's going on here. My mind-set, as you call it, and my beliefs have most certainly been challenged. As a reporter, I like to think that what I write and report is the truth. But, if I understand you right, that may not be so."

Father nodded. "That's right. I have done the same thing. I have preached from my pulpit what I thought was the truth and then, years later learned that what I had taught was not the truth. It makes one understand that the truth is very precious and that absolutes should be studied very thoroughly before they are proclaimed as absolutes."

"Then what is the use of printing anything? How can a person know the truth when they have it?"

"Good question," Father laughed, looking over at the old Chief. "But, the truth has one unique characteristic that validates or confirms it every time. Know what that characteristic is, Chief?"

The old Indian nodded his gray-haired head as he continued to drive. "The truth always bears good fruit."

"Absolutely,' Father confirmed. "The truth always affects man in a positive way, causing the life of the man to be enhanced. It may not appear that way at first. But, with time, the effect is realized. That's why it is compared to bearing fruit. Fruit takes time and certain conditions before the tree or vine produces it."

The Chief turned and looked at Denise. "My forefathers had a saying. 'Keep the roots of the corn stalk clean and the ear will be big and full of grains.' They weren't just talking about corn."

"By clean you mean filled with truth?"

"Yes, exactly, but my forefathers also realized that the fruit produced did not cease with each generation. That which was brought forth in one generation would be passed on to the next. Thus, much more the need to make sure that the roots were filled with truth. Once contaminated, the re-cleansing of the roots was a very difficult thing to achieve." The old man took a deep breath. It revealed the depth of his frustration. "Once the roots of my people were strong and clean but the white man introduced ways that contaminated my people and now we are struggling to cleanse the roots." His mind once again turned to Gabe and his tragic death. He looked over at Father. "Sometimes it seems an impossible task."

Father knew he was referring to Gabe. "I know, my friend. But remember that with the Great Spirit all things are possible."

The Chief smiled. "In times like this it is that thought that renders me comfort. I know in my heart that someday God will give the red man back his pride and restore all that was stolen by the greed and injustice of the white man."

"Boy! Chief, that's what I call faith."

The Chief looked at Denise and smiled, then at Father Macon. It was a tall order but both men had witnessed the power of God and they knew that He was able. It was only a matter of time.

The truck drove back toward Albuquerque. The group's conversation had changed direction many times but only when they were at an intersection a few miles from the old chief's house did it turn toward Bill Staples.

"Do we want to go to my house or do we want to go and find Bill?" the Chief asked, pulling the truck to a stop.

Denise shrugged. "I don't think I could sleep a wink if we waited until tomorrow. I say we go now."

Father laughed. "Spoken like a true reporter." He looked at the Chief. "What do you think?"

"Okay with me. I just hope he's still at the hotel."

Denise's expression revealed that she had not thought of that. "Yeah, that would be bad if we drove all the way in and he wasn't there." She paused to think for a minute. "How about this? Let's drive until we find a phone and then stop and call." She reached into her pocket and withdrew the card. "I've got his room number."

"Sounds good to me," the Chief replied, turning the truck onto the road toward Albuquerque.

They only had to drive a few miles until they spotted a gas station. It was small and in need of repair but it had a phone booth attached to one of the rundown walls. The Chief signaled then pulled the truck into the station's parking area, stopping in front of the small glass and metal chamber with the word, 'PHONE' above it. Father opened his door, got out, then watched as Denise fumbled with her billfold as she made her way into the booth.

"She's a good woman," the Chief said as he watched her through the windshield. "She has a good heart."

Father, still holding the door, looked into the truck at the old man. "She is here for a much greater reason than reporting a story in Chaco Canyon."

The Chief smiled. "You have felt that too?"

Father nodded. "I believe that she has been called here by God just as much as you and I."

"I agree, but I don't have a clue why."

Father laughed. "Me neither. But, heck, I don't even know why I'm here."

"That's true. But, you and I know that with time that will be revealed." He pointed his head toward Denise. "She doesn't have that advantage. Even though she's a reporter, I don't think she's hanging in for a story."

Father looked over at the phone booth where Denise was now carrying on a conversation. He turned back to the Chief. "Why would she tell you she's here?"

The old Chief shook his head. "I don't think she knows either. You remember when we fought the Manitou a few years back? I didn't have a clue why I was there but I knew I was supposed to be. Later, I *knew* why I was there. So much of my life had been designed by the Great Spirit for that time and space." The Chief laughed. "You know, I'm an old man but it seemed like my life really started from that time on." The Chief again nodded his head in the direction of Denise. "I somehow believe it will be the same for her."

Father smiled. He knew exactly what the Chief meant. The Chief's life had started at that time because the old medicine man had made Jesus the Lord of his life, causing, even for him, a spiritual rebirth. Now, because of that rebirth, the life of the Chief was being directed in a very real and dynamic way. Father knew what the Chief was saying in his own way, that Denise needed that same rebirth. He looked at the Chief, "I have confidence that she is here for a reason. She has something that the Lord needs to use in this incident. It was the same with you when we faced the Manitou. And somewhere in the stream of that adventure you realized that something was missing. Even though you knew of the Great Spirit you didn't know Him personally. It was your humility that opened the door for the Lord to reveal this."

The Chief laughed. "I don't know if it was humility or God's grace, but I'm thankful it happened. And I pray that it happens to our young reporter."

"Amen," Father agreed.

The slamming of the phone booth door caused both of the men to look in Denise's direction. The smile on her face revealed that Bill Staples was still in Albuquerque.

"Are we in luck?" Father asked as he dropped his arm from the door, allowing Denise to pass and slide back into the truck seat.

"Gentlemen, we are indeed. He is still at the hotel and he said he would be glad to talk to us."

"All right," the Chief laughed, turning the key in the ignition.

They pulled back to the edge of the highway and waited as an Army jeep passed. The two men in the jeep slowed down and looked the trio over as they passed.

The Chief turned and looked at Father. "Boy! That was certainly a 'be all you can be' look."

Father laughed. "You can say that again." Father turned and watched as the jeep continued on down the highway.

Denise watched, too, then turned back to the Chief. "Bill said something's up."

Father turned and looked at her, his face in a frown. "What?"

"Bill said that something is going on. The military has been swarming all over Albuquerque for the last few hours."

Father turned and looked again down the road. The jeep had disappeared. "I wonder why."

"Bill didn't know, but he said it must be something pretty serious. The military had just finished searching the entire hotel."

"What? When someone searches for something that usually means they've lost something."

Denise nodded, her mind attempting to come up with an answer.

The Chief laughed. "Maybe one of their Indian mummies walked off on them."

Father's eyes narrowed. His mind, too, was searching for any idea that might fit this strange behavior by the men in uniform. He slapped the steering wheel and looked at the Chief. "Let's go talk to Bill."

CHAPTER SIX

The Defector

The Chief pulled the old truck out onto the highway. They were each filled with anticipation. They passed two more military vehicles before they reached the city limits of Albuquerque. Both times it seemed a stare-down contest by the passengers in each vehicle.

"Man!" Denise frowned as they drove through town.

It looked as if martial law had been declared in Albuquerque, New Mexico. Military vehicles and personnel were everywhere.

"I believe you're right, Chief," Father said softly. "One of the mummies did walk off."

They drove slowly, amazed by the number and activity of the military. The scene reminded them of an anthill.

The civilian traffic was light, and more than once the passengers of the old truck were scrutinized as it passed by. The faces of the Army men revealed that whatever was going on, it was serious.

They found the hotel and an unexpected parking place across the street. Men with fatigues, helmets, and M-16's were standing outside the entrance.

The Chief shut off the engine and stared at the men. "Think we ought to go in now?"

"I'm not sure we can get in," Denise added, watching two of the men salute then climb into a jeep and drive away.

"Well," Father finally offered after a few minutes of silence. "We've not done anything wrong and we need to get into the building, so I say we give it a shot."

Denise looked at him and smiled. "That's true. It's not like we are fugitives. I don't know why I'm so reluctant. Besides, it might give us a chance to find out what's going on."

Father looked at the old Chief and nodded his agreement. Both men opened their doors and Father waited until Denise had climbed out before slamming his. There was no traffic so they made their way across the street. Denise led the way with the old Chief and Father at her side. Two soldiers guarded the large sliding door of the hotel. Denise turned to one of the guards.

"Are we allowed to enter?"

The soldier nodded. "Yes ma'am, go right ahead."

The trio approached the door and paused as it automatically opened. Once inside the lobby Denise led them to the elevators. Another soldier stood at attention guarding their entrance. He merely nodded to the group as Denise pushed the lighted button on the wall. She started to speak to the young soldier when the elevator door opened revealing three other soldiers. Denise recognized the rank of one of the men as they smiled and walked past her.

"Major," she called.

The man turned and faced Denise. "Yes, ma'am?"

"What's all the activity about? We've been out of town and just returned. Is everything okay?"

The major smiled. "Everything is fine. There is nothing for you and your friends to be concerned about. Someone out at the archaeological site has stolen part of the discovery and we're just trying to get it back. We had information that the person or persons might have come here to this hotel."

"Did you find anything?"

The major again smiled as he shook his head. "I'm afraid not but we are still looking."

"But, you say it's safe?" Father ventured.

"Absolutely. Just go about your regular activities. It's completely safe."

Denise caught the elevator door as it started to close. "Sounds good. Thanks, Major."

The major tipped his hat then turned and disappeared around the corner.

Father and the old Chief walked into the empty elevator while Denise held the door. Father looked at her as she allowed it to close. "I wonder what's going on out there?"

Denise shook her head and pushed the button for Bill Staples' floor. "I really believe that they have lost something. How and what I don't know."

Father frowned. "How could someone steal anything out there with security as tight as it is? It would take a group from *Mission Impossible*."

The old Chief watched the lighted dial as the elevator climbed. "He's right, Denise. The guys that watch over this sort of thing are the best in the military."

"I know, but if something wasn't missing why would they be here in this hotel looking, and with this many troops?"

131

Father shook his head. He didn't have a clue. He prayed silently in the Spirit as the elevator came to a stop and the door opened. "Holy Spirit, help us," he prayed quietly.

Again the two men followed the young reporter until she stopped at the door to Bill's room. She knocked softly. They watched as the door opened, revealing the small man they remembered as Bill Staples. Father guessed him to be about fifty years of age. He was nearly bald.

"Well, you did make it," he greeted. "I was about to give you up. Come in."

The three made their way into the room as Bill held the door. He had to look up to smile at the old Chief. He waited for them to enter, looked both ways down the hallway, then closed the door.

"Bill, this is Chief Walking Cloud and Father Rex Macon," Denise introduced.

Bill shook hands with the two men then offered for all of them to find a seat. The room had a large king-sized bed that allowed room for only one armchair, a desk and chair. Both Father and Denise took a seat on the edge of the bed. The old Chief pulled the desk chair out and sat down. Bill continued to stand.

"So, you guys got to meet Hattie?"

Denise laughed. "Yeah, she was a neat lady."

"She certainly is. That is, unless you are a government man."

They all laughed.

"She sure knows a lot about the Roswell incident," Father added.

"She does indeed, and I think she knows what she's talking about."

"She said that you had a different theory about the origin of the UFO."

Bill looked at Father as he took a seat in the armchair. "That's correct. I, too, have spent a lot of time researching the Roswell incident, and I'm just not convinced. I was born in a small town south of Roswell called Greenfield. I lived there as a youngster and I remember the incident very well. It was the main topic of discussion for years and it sparked in me the desire to learn more about 'outer space.' Since then I've spent a lot of hours trying to prove the existence of beings from another planet or another solar system." He shook his head revealing his frustration. "It's just not there." He looked at Denise. "Think about this. In the case of the aliens, what would be the reason for staying so covert? As long as it has been, they have had adequate time to learn everything there is to know about us. They know we are no threat. In the case of the human race, our society has been so plagued with extraterrestrial novels, movies and books that the fear by the general public, I believe, has been removed. If they were going to hurt us, that would have already happened. They certainly have the one-up on our technology. I know we have these cases of UFO abduction but nothing has ever been proven there either. To me it just doesn't make any sense."

"You do believe that something extraordinary crashed at Roswell?" Denise asked.

"Most definitely. But, I believe that it had its origin in this world."

Father was glad to hear this. He looked at Denise and smiled, then turned back to Bill. "Hattie said that you thought that they were time travelers."

The small man nodded his head. "That's right. That's where Hattie and I differ. I'm sure she told you."

"She did, but do you have anything to back up your theory?"

Bill smiled. "No, not really. But I think I have as much as those who purport the extraterrestrial theory. Let me ask you a question. What if you had the ability to time travel and nuclear weapons were threatening the time *you* lived in?"

Father shrugged his shoulders. "I would probably go back in time and try to do something about the proliferation or construction of nuclear weapons."

"Bingo," Bill laughed. "That's what I would do too. And, I think that's what they did. Mankind was pretty much new at nuclear technology when we dropped the bombs on Hiroshima and Nagasaki. We were amazed at the destructive ability of splitting the atom. UFO sightings were common over the skies of Europe, during World War II. They were especially prevalent over Germany where the V-2 rocket delivery system was being perfected. After the war, we placed that same rocket technology in the hands of German-born scientist Werner Van Bran. His expertise was guided missile systems. That, plus our nuclear research, took place only a few miles down the road from here at White Sands, New Mexico. If a race from the future wanted to warn us or change the future of nuclear technology, this would be ground zero."

"So you think they were trying to make contact with us and somehow lost control of their aircraft?" Father asked.

"I don't know about contact. That's possible. But I'm sure they wanted to try and keep an eye on us. The crash is also interesting. From what I have found out over the years, the propulsion system for these flying discs somehow works using magnetic fields. The earth is surrounded by electrically charged particles forming magnetic fields that extend many miles out into space. We know from our technology that electricity can create or alter magnetic fields. Records show that there was a severe thunder and lightning storm around that part of New Mexico the night the disc crashed. Now this may be too simple but if the UFO were from outer space they would know about the dangerous effects of electrical storms and know to steer clear. But, if that disc were coming from the future through a time portal, then they would not know about the storm and would be well into it before they could do anything.

"To me that would also explain the covert atmosphere around these flying discs. Their mission would be merely to observe and not interfere."

"Unless it threatened the planet and man's existence?" Denise added.

"That's correct." Bill nodded.

"But according to the accounts of the crash, the beings didn't look a thing like us. They had large heads, small bodies and large eyes. We would be hard pressed to call them human."

"You're right, Denise, but you just said that they would not interfere with our activities unless we were a threat to the future. We don't know how far in the future these beings have come from, but they are here for a reason. Now consider this. We know that the human race over the years has adapted to its surroundings causing quite a diverse change in skin color as well as other bodily features. Let's jump this evolution process thousands of years into the future and add a nuclear exchange that almost destroys the planet. Where would the safest and most likely refuge be for a race of people at this time?"

Denise studied the question.

"Underground," the old Chief added before Denise could answer.

"Exactly, Chief. And what would a being look like that had adapted to small confined spaces and dimly lit surroundings?"

Denise laughed. "That's pretty amazing. They would be small in stature to facilitate ease of movement and they would have large eyes for gathering smaller amounts of light."

"That's correct, and that doesn't take into consideration possible mutation from radiation or lack of exposure to the light of the sun. If those factors are added in, there's no telling what a human from the future might look like. Heck, he could have four ears and three hands."

Father rubbed his chin, trying to analyze all that Bill had shared. "Bill, you've certainly done your homework. Hattie said that the government is well aware of these time travelers. She said they call them time skippers."

"That true. Over the years this sort of thing has been hard to keep secret. But, I must say that this government has done a darn good job. I have some sources, however, and they say that these beings have met secretly with our government several times. President Truman was supposedly the first." Bill laughed and brushed back the small patch of hair that he had above his right ear. "Many critics of Truman say that the greatest mistake of his presidency was not allowing General MacArthur to invade China during the Korean War. But what if the beings told Truman that it was the wrong move? What if this was the needed change in history that prevented a future nuclear disaster?"

"So, if I understand your theory, these 'beings' have been coming and going for a long time. The Roswell crash was an incident where the machinery they were using malfunctioned and prevented them from returning to their "time.""

"That's right, Father," Bill nodded. "History is full of UFO sightings and Roswell is not the first recorded crash."

Denise frowned. "You mean there is another?"

Bill looked at Father. "Have you ever heard of the Dropa Stones?"

Father shook his head. Bill looked at Denise and then at the Chief. Both shook their heads silently.

"In 1938 a Chinese archaeologist by the name of Chi Pu Tei found a number of caves in the Baian-ara-Ula mountains. It was on the border that divides China and Tibet. The walls of the cave were like glass as if the tunnels had been artificially carved by extreme heat. In the caves they found several burial sites. They were very old. The skeletal remains were strange in appearance and measured about four feet in length. The bones were small, very frail and spindly. But the skulls were large and out of proportion to the rest of their bodies. The eye sockets were also much larger than normal. At first they thought the remains were some sort of unknown mountain gorilla. But, when they began to look around they decided they were human. There were pictographs on the walls of the caves showing in great detail the sun, moon, the stars and the earth." Bill smiled, "But the greatest discovery was buried on the floor of the cave. They found discs carved out of stone. The discs were about nine inches in diameter with a three-quarter inch hole in the center. Etched on the face of the discs was a line that spiraled out from the center to the rim. They checked the age of the discs and concluded they were between 10, 000 and 12,000 years old."

"You mean they found more than one?" Father asked.

"Oh my, yes," Bill laughed. "They found 716 in all and each one had the groove from the center to the rim. But this is the exciting part. The groove was not a groove at all. On close observation the groove was found to be a thin line of carved hieroglyphics so small that they needed magnification in order to be detected. It was a language carved in these stones by some intelligent group of people. The stones were catalogued and stored away until 1962 when Dr. Tsum Um Nui carefully transcribed the tiny microscopic writing to paper. He then undertook the task of deciphering the hieroglyphics. What he found was astounding. In fact the Chinese establishment would not let him publish the translation nor even speak of it. Finally, however, after two years and much persistence they let him publish his findings. The title of his work was, *The Grooved Script Concerning Spaceships Which, As Recorded on the Discs, Landed 12,000 Years Ago.*"

Denise laughed. "That's what the writings on the discs said?"

Bill nodded. "Yes. The discs tell of a space probe from a distant planet that crash-landed in the area of the Balan-Kara-Ula mountains. They called themselves the Dropa and they took refuge in the caves. Just like the beings at Roswell, they were unable to repair their spacecraft so they were marooned on Earth."

"But in that case," the old Chief objected, "the space probe was from a distant planet."

"That's true, Chief. I've thought about that, too. But, the person deciphering the writings would consider any place away from Earth another world. Another place in time would seem to be a distant planet."

"But," Denise added. "What would be their purpose going back so long ago? There was nothing to fear back that far."

A huge grin came across Bill's face. "That's where you're wrong, my dear." He got up and walked to the desk where his briefcase was resting. He opened it, removed a handful of papers, returned and sat down. He held up the papers. "I just happen to have these with me. Don't ask me why, I just put them in at the last minute."

Father looked at the Chief and grinned. Bill thumbed through the papers then handed one to Denise.

"Tell me what these look like?"

"Oh my, gosh," Denise exclaimed, pointing to the pictures. "These two look just like airplanes and that one looks exactly like a modern day helicopter." She handed the paper to Father Macon.

"This last one looks like some type of hover-craft with a large antenna."

"Yeah," Bill agreed, "or maybe a flying disc."

Father turned and handed the paper to the old Chief.

Bill pointed to the paper. "Those are Egyptian hieroglyphics found in the temple of Abydos. Are they a product of a vivid imagination? I don't think so. In ancient India these things were called Vimana. They were aircraft of some sort. The ancient Sanskrit writings are full of this stuff. So much, in fact, that it can't be overlooked. Listen to this. In the Sanskrit Samarangana Sutradhara, it states, 'Strong and durable must the body of the

Vimana be made, like a great flying bird of light material. Inside one must put the mercury engine with its iron heating apparatus underneath. By means of the power latent in the mercury which sets the driving whirlwind in motion, a man sitting inside may travel a great distance in the sky. The movement of the Vimana is such that it can vertically ascend, vertically descend, move slanting forwards and backwards.' Vimanas were described as double-decked, circular aircraft with a dome and portholes along the sides."

"Sounds like our flying saucers," the Chief interjected.

"Absolutely," Bill agreed. "But it gets better. Apparently there were two dominant civilizations on this planet at the time. One was in what is now India. It was called Rama. The other was somewhere in the middle of the Atlantic Ocean. It was called Atlantis."

Denise started to speak but Bill anticipated her question.

"That's right, the same Atlantis we hear so much about."

"But I thought that was all myth," she frowned.

"Don't be so sure. In these ancient texts they were known as the Asvins and apparently there was a great war between Atlantis and Rama in which both used these Vimana. The ancient Mahabharata describes the awesome devastation of the war. One weapon that was discharged from the Vimana was a projectile that had all the power of the Universe. It produced an incandescent column of smoke and flame as bright as a thousand suns and rose miles into the air. The text describes how the people's hair and nails fell out, the birds turned white, and food and water were not fit to eat and drink. To escape the effects of the blast the soldiers threw themselves into the rivers to wash themselves."

The Chief grunted and shook his head. "Sounds like Hiroshima."

Bill smiled. "Exactly, like a nuclear blast. Archaeologists in the last century were excavating an ancient Indian city called Mohenjodaro. They found skeletons holding hands as if the destruction had happened in a second and the remains were the most radioactive ever found. In fact they were along the same line as those found at Hiroshima. The walls and brick of the city were literally fused together."

"And that was how long ago?" Denise asked.

"Somewhere in the range of twelve to fifteen thousand years."

Denise smiled. "About the same time as the Dropa. Do you think they were traveling back in time in an attempt to prevent the war or change the course of history?"

Bill shrugged his shoulders. "I don't know. But according to the documents Atlantis was not the utopian place it has been cracked up to be by modern writers. Apparently they had the technology and the temperament to go along with it. I picture them as the evil empire in the movie, *Star Wars*. They were literally a black cloud of influence."

Father Macon had been listening intently to Bill when he felt the little man's words move his spirit. "A black cloud of influence," he repeated.

Denise turned and looked at him. She could tell by the way he repeated Bill's words that something was going on. She looked at the Chief and frowned.

"Bill, where in the Atlantic do you think Atlantis was located?" Father asked excitedly.

Bill shook his head. "I don't know. Some say it was a continent in the middle of the Atlantic that completely sunk after a huge cataclysm. A few say the Azores are the tip of Atlantis. Still, others say it was located off the east coast of Florida close to what is now the Bahamas."

Father looked at the old Chief and nodded.

"What's going on?" Denise demanded.

"It's the dream."

"What dream?" Denise continued to frown.

"The day before I came out here I had a dream in which I saw a black cloud come out of the Atlantic Ocean and cover the earth. I heard a voice say, 'And darkness was on the face of the deep.'"

Father shared the rest of the dream as the others sat spellbound. Denise was the first to respond. "The cloud was blown away by the wind but the cloud returned over New Mexico?'

Father nodded. "That's right. And if I'm right Atlantis was somehow involved as the source of the darkness the first time and it is again this time around."

"Are you saying the canisters are from Atlantis?" the Chief asked.

"What canisters?" Bill interrupted before Father could answer. He waited, looking from the old Chief to Father, for an explanation.

Father inhaled deeply realizing that the Chief had let the cat out of the bag. But, Bill had shared honestly with them and Father believed that he was a part of God's answer to this strange occurrence so they agreed to share what they knew. Together they revealed what was in the cave. Bill sat quietly, his eyes expressing his excitement. Father related most of the information with both the Chief and Denise adding things that they thought were important. When they had finished Bill sat back in his chair.

"Man! No wonder the military is all over this place. No telling how long those canisters have been there."

"Well, if you're right about your time line, it could have been 10 to 15 thousand years," Father answered.

"And you think they're from Atlantis?"

Father smiled. "When you mentioned the black cloud, the Holy Spirit quickened my spirit and I immediately remembered the dream I had. I believe that Atlantis was where the first cloud originated. Why or how I don't know. But whatever happened there, God viewed it as something dark and dangerous, thus the symbol of the black cloud. So when did the wind blow the black cloud away and cleanse the earth? I believe that was the Holy Spirit in Genesis, Chapter One, verse two. *'And the Lord said let there be light.'* The Light of God destroyed the darkness. But the cloud began to reform and it was really terrible in my dream. It was powerful and stifling. The fact that the cloud is reforming has God concerned."

"Man, that's heavy!" Bill exclaimed. "I didn't realized God involved Himself with the things of this earth to that magnitude."

Father smiled. "The Lord is always concerned about the welfare of His children."

Denise had been thinking about the dream. "When you first called out for help, your voice was that of the Chief's."

Father nodded his head in agreement.

"That was the Chief's call for help. Is the sound of the many waters or the sound of the children's voices the cry for help from the children who are disappearing?"

143

"I don't know, but it could be. The dream is certainly making more sense now."

"Do you get many dreams like that?" Bill asked, intrigued by Father's gift.

"Yes I do. It one of the ways that the Lord guides me. Sometimes they seem impossible to understand. But with time and patience they almost always unfold into giant steps of enlightenment."

"That's really amazing. Do you have to be a priest to get that type of revelation?"

Father laughed. "Everyone who makes Jesus the Lord of their life has the same opportunity. The prophet Joel said that in these days young men would dream dreams and old men would see visions."

"Does that include women, too?" Denise asked.

Father nodded. "Women, too."

Denise giggled. "I was just thinking that if I had that gift I could help you with the dream you had this morning."

"What was it about?" Bill asked, still fascinated about Father's gifting.

Father looked at Denise. "It was about Dr. LePage." He laughed, almost too embarrassed to share any further. "She was about four or five years old and she was being chased by a vampire."

Bill's countenance immediately changed. He frowned then rubbed his chin.

Father noticed the change. "What's the matter?"

"I had an interview with Dr. LePage this morning and she was as nervous as a long-tailed cat in room full of rocking chairs." Bill looked at Father. "I remember wondering, 'What is chasing this woman?'"

The room was quiet for at least a minute. Each person looked at the other, wondering if this, too, was something important.

Denise broke the silence. "Did she talk about the cave?"

Bill shook his head. "I've interviewed a lot of people in my years with the newspaper. No matter what I asked she seemed to always come back to the subject of herself."

"I don't understand."

"She seemed to be trying to convince herself of something. She shared how she loved her country and how she was a good doctor who wanted the best for mankind."

"Did she mention the mummies?"

"No, not one time."

"Did you ask her about the missing children?"

Bill paused then nodded. "Yes, I did. And thinking back that caused her even more apprehension. I remembered how Dr. Laird had reacted to your question at the press conference and so I thought I would just see how she would handle the same question."

"How did she handle it?"

"Not very well. She started asking me questions about loving my country and sacrificing myself for the betterment of all people. She asked me if I had a child could I give it up for the good of others."

Denise frowned and looked at Father Macon. "She asked me the same thing." She looked back at Bill. "Right after the press conference Dr. Laird and Dr. LePage came to my hotel room under the guise of hiring me for a public relations position. I know what

145

you mean about nervous. And she asked me the same type of questions, really weird stuff."

"Is her first name Doris?" Father asked.

"No, it's Angela," Bill answered. "Why?"

Father shrugged. "In the dream the little girl told me she was Doris LePage."

"No it's Angela. I'm sure of that. But you know the funniest thing about all this is that while we were talking this morning I felt like I was hearing her confession and here you are a Catholic priest. I wish you had been there. The last thing I told her was that all of us have to listen to our heart and try to be true to its direction."

Father smiled. "That's good advice for all of us, Bill."

"Amen," the Chief added with a chuckle. "And the wind asked the freshly fallen snow, 'Which animal in the forest is your favorite?' And the snow answered, 'The purity that you see on the mountain-top or on the meadow is a reflection of my dedication to the truth. Whether it is a blowing leaf leaving a small wisp of an impression on my head or a raging herd of buffalo scaring my back for miles, I record each detail as it is. The minute I choose a favorite I lose the ability to be snow."

Denise laughed, not understanding the proverb. "Which translated means?"

"Anytime we become something other than what we were created to be, we cease being ourselves. No matter how good the intent."

"Is that what Dr. LePage is dealing with?"

The Chief nodded. "When we are not ourselves our heart is the first to let us know. Sometimes it is unrelenting in its conversation."

Denise looked at the Chief and thought about her own conversation with Dr. LePage. The Chief was right. Something very intense was going on inside the woman.

Father looked at his watch. "It's getting late. We need to be heading home."

Bill was about to comment when the phone suddenly interrupted him. Bill looked at Father Macon and frowned. "I wonder who that could be this time of the night?"

He walked over to the desk and picked up the receiver. The others watched silently as he put the phone to his ear.

"Bill Staples here."

His eyes grew wide as he listened to whoever was on the other end. "Hold on just a minute." He covered the mouthpiece with his hand and looked at Father Macon. "It's Angela LePage. She says she needs my help. She said the entire military is after her because she has freed the experiment."

Father Macon looked at Denise, searching for an answer in her face. He looked back at Bill. "Tell her you'll help her. Find out where she is."

Bill nodded, removed his hand and then repeated Father's question into the receiver. He turned again to Father.

"She's at the old Canton Silver Mine."

Father looked at the Chief. "Do you know where that is?"

The Chief nodded. "It's about twenty miles north of here. Fairly close to Ben and Gabe's place."

"Tell her to stay put. Keep out of sight and we'll try to be there as soon as possible."

Bill again repeated Father's instructions into the phone. Satisfied that she understood, Bill said good-bye then hung up.

The small group stood looking at Bill, his face revealing the questions that were on everyone's mind. The Chief was the first to speak.

"Now we know what's got the military in such an uproar."

"What did she mean, 'I've freed the experiment'?" Father frowned.

Bill shook his head, realizing the question was directed at him. "I don't have a clue. Whatever the experiment is, however, its freedom cost Angela LePage a lot. Her voice was filled with fear and desperation." He looked down at his watch then up at the old Chief. "How long will it take to get to the mine?"

The Chief scratched the back of his head, his wrinkled brow exposing his concentration. "Normally not long. I would say thirty minutes tops, but with the military as thick as fur on an otter, I can't say."

Bill's eyes widened. He had not really considered the military. Suddenly he realized that what they knew made them a dangerous target. He looked at Father. "Doesn't the Bible say something about counting the cost before beginning an endeavor?"

Father nodded. He knew what Bill was thinking.

Bill looked at the others. "The minute we make contact with Angela is the minute we become part of the defection. We will be fugitives and wanted by the government, just like her. I think each one of us needs to consider that before we walk out that door."

Denise took a deep audible breath. She looked at Father then at Bill. "There are things going on here that make me question the intelligence and the morality of my government. I hope they are not true, but I have to find out. It may be the reporter in me, but there is no way I could walk away from this thing and ever live with myself. Every time I looked in a mirror I would hold some disdain for the face looking back at me. It's worth the risk to me."

Bill smiled then looked at Father Macon.

"I'm here because the Lord asked me to come. There have been many times when this thing seemed stonewalled and then suddenly a door opened. My job will not be done until I find out why this is so important to the realm of the Spirit."

The old Chief nodded his head as Father finished. "I agree completely, but I must also find out what is so important that it would once again require the lives of my people. I think I owe Ben Running Deer that much."

Bill smiled. "Then it is settled." He looked at his watch. "It's late and four people walking out of here at this time of night might draw some suspicion." He looked at Father. "What do you think?"

"I agree. Denise knows the way to the Chief's house. You take your car and let her show you the way. The Chief and I will meet you there then head to the mine from that point. Is that okay Chief?"

The Chief nodded. "I think that would be great. That way if we are followed, we will know it and they couldn't say much if we were just going home."

"That's good," Bill agreed. "You guys go ahead and leave. Denise and I will wait ten minutes then head your way."

149

The Visitor

The small group said their good-byes then Father and the Chief quietly made their way out of the hotel. The military were everywhere and each small group of soldiers stationed at various places eyed the two men as they passed. Both were glad to get to the truck. Nothing was said as the old Chief backed the truck out and headed out of town. A roadblock had been set up at the city limits but the soldiers quickly motioned the old truck and the two men through. Father looked back as the truck distanced them from the roadblock.

"How do you think they will explain this to the public?"

The Chief kept his eyes on the road. "These people are masters of deception and lying. They will find a way."

Father turned back around and looked at the old man. "Deception and lying, certainly not characteristics of the Spirit we serve."

"Jesus said that Satan was a liar from the beginning. Satan is also a master of deception. Who would you say these people are serving?" He looked over at Father, waiting an answer.

"I know things like this make our government look bad, but not everyone in the government is bad. The government is made of individual people and for many of these individuals there are limits. When these limits are met, good people rebel. That's what happened, I think, with Dr. LePage. She went along with the deception up to a point. Beyond that point, her heart would not let her alone. The truth became more of a force than the lying and deception. One person filled with the Light can destroy the lying and deception perpetuated by thousands. That's the gift of the One we serve. A single candle can light the darkest of rooms."

"And for us that single candle is Angela LePage."

"Exactly," Father nodded. "That's the beauty of the Lord. She is the answer to our prayer. Years ago the Holy Spirit may have put her in this position just for this time. When she joined this military adventure she would never have accepted that she would be its betrayer. But something deep in her heart that only the Lord knew about became the instrument that He used to set her limit."

The Chief smiled and looked at the priest. "That is amazing; the power of a broken heart."

"Isn't it something?" Father laughed. "Dr. LePage has something hidden in her heart that caused her great pain and distress. To the Lord that is a broken heart. But, whatever this military experiment is, it has triggered that place in her heart that is broken."

"And she can't stand the pain."

"And she can't stand the pain," Father repeated. "The pain has become the instrument of deliverance for others. Isn't it strange how many times that's the way it is. The redeemed alcoholic becomes a way out for other alcoholics. The redeemed prisoner becomes a way to freedom for other prisoners."

"And a redeemed Indian medicine man becomes a way of life for his native people." The Chief looked over at Father. "Like I said, pretty amazing."

Father nodded and smiled. "It certainly is."

The old truck seemed to know its way home. It became a safe haven as they looked back toward the way they had come. Only thick darkness covered the landscape. The Chief eased the truck into its parking spot but did not turn off the engine. The two men looked beyond the darkness, trying to discern the first signs of a car's headlight. They waited.

151

CHAPTER SEVEN

Enoch

The Chief continued to stare out into the dark night. He slowly brought his watch up to his eyes. He squinted to see the numbers in the dim light provided by the dash lights. "It's been forty minutes."

"It seems like two hours," Father added, breaking his silent prayer time.

They continued to watch until the Chief suddenly turned and switched off the engine. He opened the door and stepped out into the darkness. Father could hear him praying in the Spirit. He paced along the side of the truck for a few minutes until he stopped and ducked his head inside the cab. "Think we need to go back and check on them?"

"They'll be here. There's no reason for them to draw any suspicion."

The Chief smiled. "I've already been down that road and you're wrong. They're reporters. But they're not from the same paper. Now answer me this. Why would two reporters who represent two different newspapers be together, heading out of town at this time of night?"

"Good question."

"Something else, if you were Angela LePage and you were trying to blow a whistle on this whole thing, who would you seek out above all others?"

"I would find a good reporter," Father replied, realizing that maybe there was room for suspicion, and a reason for concern. He was about to agree to go back and look for them when he saw two lights break the distant darkness. "Looks like we can sit tight." He smiled and motioned toward the lights with his head.

The old Chief pulled his head out of the cab and turned toward the lights. "Praise God," he breathed.

The men watched the two lights become larger as they drew closer to them. Both of their hearts were beating rapidly when the blinker light came on and the car pulled into the yard.

"You had us worried," the old Chief sighed as Denise stepped out of the car.

"Did you guys get stopped at the roadblock?" She asked, shutting the door.

"Just a slowdown and wave through," Father answered, coming around the front of the truck.

"We were stopped and searched."

Father looked at the chief and frowned. He watched as Bill got out of the car and made his way to where the three were standing. "What did they do?"

Denise took a deep breath. Father could tell she was shook up.

"They asked us to get out and then they checked every inch of the car. They asked us for identification and wanted to know our destination."

"What did you tell them?"

Bill pointed to the old Chief. "We said we were going to visit the Chief."

Father looked at the Chief. "What do you think?"

The Chief's answer was delayed as he stared back down the road. "Looks like they didn't believe you."

The others turned and watched as two more sets of headlights

153

became visible on the distant road.

"Let's get inside," the Chief encouraged.

The three men quickly followed Denise into the house.

"Father, turn on those lights over there," the Chief instructed. "Let's make it as easy as possible for them to see that we are here."

"Good idea," Father answered, flipping on the switches that lit up the kitchen and small hallway.

The Chief pulled out one of the chairs around the breakfast table. "Bill, you and Denise sit down with me. Father, you go into the back bedroom, leave the light off and watch from the window. Let's see what our friends end up doing."

Father nodded then made his way back to the Chief's bedroom. He stood to one side of the window and watched silently as the lights on the highway grew stronger. Father caught himself barely breathing as he watched the two vehicles slow as they approached the turn off to the house. It was two military jeeps. Father couldn't tell how many men were in the vehicles but he could definitely tell that they were scoping out the place. Both jeeps came to a stop and one of the drivers shined a flashlight onto Bill's car then onto the Chief's truck. Father could tell by the focal point of the light that they were checking out the license plates. After about four minutes they turned out the light and headed on down the road. He watched until he could no longer see any trace of their lights then walked back to the kitchen.

All three sets of eyes greeted him as he entered the room, walked over to the table and sat down.

"They stopped and checked out the license plates then drove on down the road."

Denise's eyes grew wide as she looked at the Chief. "There's no way they could know anything."

"That's right," the Chief agreed. "But put yourself in their

154

shoes. This must be something very valuable and they're not taking any chances. Father and I were talking before you arrived. Whatever this is, they don't want the press to get ahold of it. For you two to be out this time of night, you have to admit, looks suspicious even if you're not paranoid."

"So what do we do? If they're watching us, we'll lead them right to Dr. LePage."

The Chief smiled. "We have an advantage. I've been here long enough to know this area very well. If they are watching and waiting for us to move then it has to be from a distance great enough to hide the lights of their own vehicle. But out here the smallest light travels very far, and so if we can see them, they can see us. They think that if we move we will have to use our lights thus giving up any chance of unobserved activity."

Denise looked at her watch. "But, it's been nearly two hours since Dr. LePage called and she's soon going to start thinking that Bill's not coming. She might try to run and then we will lose any chance of re-contact."

"I totally agree."

"So, what do we do?"

The Chief got up and pointed out the large kitchen window into the darkness. There is a road behind my house that leads to the main road that leads to the old mine. It's not much of a road. In fact, it's just a cow path. But, it will take us to where we can get to the mine undetected."

"There's only one problem, Chief," Bill frowned. "If the men in those jeeps have been assigned to keep tabs on us and they come back and see your truck is missing, they're going to know that we sneaked off. That in turn will prove that we know something and that all of us are involved. We then become high profile suspects right along with Dr. LePage."

The Chief nodded sadly. "I've thought of that, Bill, but we're not left with many options. Denise is right. If we don't get to Dr. LePage soon she may panic and take flight. Her sacrifice would be for nothing."

Denise stood up. "I say let's move." She looked around at the others.

Father stood also. "We don't have any other options. Let's do it."

Bill looked at the Chief and smiled. "I hope it's worth it."

The Chief nodded and stood with the others. "Only one way to find out."

Bill slapped the table then stood up. "Chief, you're the man. Lead the way."

"We'll take my truck, but Father you'll have to drive. We can't use any of the lights so I'll walk in front of the truck and be your eyes. I know the road and when we get over the mountain we'll be out of sight and able to use the lights again."

Father nodded then started toward the door. The others followed. Denise reached over and turned off the lights.

"No, Denise," the old Chief scolded. "Leave the lights on. We want them to think that we're still here."

Denise smiled her understanding and flipped the switch back on. Together they left the house and quietly made their way to the truck. Father got behind the wheel. Denise slid over next to him, allowing Bill to climb aboard and shut the door. Father started the engine and backed the truck away from the house. At the Chief's sign they began the journey.

There was only a partial moon but coupled with starlight it allowed Father to see the Chief very well for about twenty-five feet.

"They'll be able to follow us in the morning," Bill said softly as he too watched the old Chief. "The desert dirt around here is as powdery as flour, and they will have no trouble determining where we went."

Father looked over at Bill. "Hopefully by then it will be too late."

"He's a remarkable man, isn't he?" Denise shared, watching the old Indian, trying to change the negative atmosphere. "Not very many men his age could walk at that pace and keep it up for as long as he has."

"He's a very remarkable man," Father agreed. "Not only is his body still in good physical condition but his mind is as sharp as most men's half his age."

"How did you guys meet?"

Father looked at Denise and smiled. "That my dear, is a very long story."

"Maybe sometime you can share it with me?"

"You're on."

They drove for a long time. All eyes were on the Chief. They all agreed they could see better than before. Denise wondered if it was getting lighter, but they all decided that their eyes were getting adjusted to the darkness.

"We're starting up the mountain," Father revealed.

As he was speaking the Chief turned and walked back to the truck. He bent over and looked into the cab. "We are getting ready to go over the mountain. The road is narrow but not that dangerous if you will stay right behind me. As soon as we get on the other side we can use the lights."

Father nodded as the Chief turned and began walking in front of the truck. He motioned with his hand for them to follow.

They climbed for a good while. Father couldn't see much but what he could see made him glad that they couldn't see. He was sure the tires of the truck were not more than a foot or two away from the edge of what he could make out was a huge drop-off. He prayed in the Spirit to ward off the fear and was glad when the nose of the truck started down, revealing that they would soon be able to use the lights. Father wondered how much farther as they continued their descent. After about twenty minutes he stopped the truck as the Chief once again approached the window.

"You can turn on the lights now. I'll hop in the back and give you directions on how to get to the mine."

Father nodded as the old man climbed into the back of the truck. He knelt behind the cab and stuck his head around to Father's window. "Okay, let's go."

Father switched on the lights, bringing the desert floor and the old road to life. The Chief was right. It wasn't much of a road. Carefully he followed what he thought was the path and soon they were back on level ground. The road improved the farther they traveled and soon they were able to develop some speed. The Chief gave Father directions that eventually led to the main road to the mine. It wasn't much of a road either, but it was gravel and definitely more traveled.

Father stuck his head out the window. "Denise wants to know how much farther?"

"Tell her about two more miles. We should be there in a few more minutes."

Each one of them was filled with anticipation as those last two miles were covered. Rusted mining equipment lined the road revealing that they were getting close.

"I wonder how long this mine has been abandoned?" Denise asked, not taking her eyes off the road.

Father held his reply until he guided the truck across a small washed out ravine in the road. "I would say by the shape of all this old equipment that it has been inactive for a long time.

"We're here," the Chief announced as the headlights of the truck revealed what appeared to be the main entrance to the mine. It was a large hole in the side of the mountain surrounded by huge pieces of abandoned mining equipment. Father brought the truck to a stop and shut off the engine. He left the lights on as he and the others got out of the vehicle. They walked to the front of the truck, looking to each side for a sign of Dr. LePage.

Bill put his hands to the sides of his mouth. "Dr. LePage," he yelled. He looked at Father when there was no reply. "Think we are too late?"

"I hope not. Try again."

Bill nodded. "Dr. LePage," he called louder.

Once again there was only silence.

"Where would she go?" Denise asked desperately.

"I'm here," a voice called out from the mine entrance.

The group watched as Dr. LePage appeared in the dark mine opening and made her way toward them. "Can you turn off the truck lights please?"

Father walked back to the truck and extinguished the lights. He watched as the young doctor made her way over to Bill.

"Thank you for coming, Mr. Staples," she said, extending her hand.

Bill took her hand and greeted the woman with a smile. He could feel her hand trembling. He held onto it. She received the compassion and fell against Bill's chest sobbing. The others gathered around her. Denise placed her hand on the woman's back.

"I am so scared," she sobbed.

Bill guided her over to a piece of mining equipment that resembled a bench. "Sit down here and tell us what's going on. You are among friends. You know Denise. This is Chief Walking

Cloud and Father Rex Macon. He is a Catholic priest. We are all here to help you."

Angela sat down, then looked up at each of the group. She smiled as her eyes met Denise's. "Thank you for coming."

Denise smiled and nodded.

Father reached into his back pocket, removed a handkerchief and handed it to the woman. She took it from him and wiped her eyes.

"Thank you. You don't know how much relief you are to me."

"We're here to help," Bill offered. "But how can we help?"

Angela took a deep breath and looked up at the starry sky. "It seems so much like a dream. I keep hoping I'll wake up and it will all be over."

"What will be over, Dr. LePage?" Denise asked. "What's going on around here?"

Angela shook her head, "Oh, where to start?"

"How about the beginning," Father encouraged.

The woman smiled and nodded. "Yes, the beginning. I was working in Washington for a branch of FEMA when our department received an urgent message. The forest fires here in New Mexico had uncovered something very unusual. It was top secret. In less than three hours we were on our way to Chaco Canyon where the local National Guard unit had set up a perimeter around the secret find. When we entered the canyon what we found was extraordinary."

"Let me guess," the old Chief interrupted. "What you found were two time capsules containing a man and the bones of a dead thing."

Angela's eyes widened in surprise. "How did you know?"

"My friend Gabe Running Deer was one of the men who found the capsules and reported them to the authorities."

160

"Oh, no," she cried, tears running down both cheeks. "I am so sorry." She looked up at the old Chief. "They killed him to keep him quiet."

The Chief looked at Father in disgust.

"We know," Father inserted. "We found where they had cut his brake line."

Angela nodded. "That's the way they work. They always make it look like an accident."

"But why does it have to be so hush-hush?" Denise asked.

"Because they are never sure how the public will handle the discovery. Especially a discovery like this."

"Go on," Father encouraged.

"We took the capsules back to the nearby military base and made up the story about the Indian mummies. Along with the capsules was a container that was full of thin metal plates. They were like sheets of paper only metal, and on each metal sheet was some sort of writing. The language and deciphering teams were called in, and after only a couple of days the entire cache of writings were deciphered. They said the language was very similar to a blend of ancient Cuneiform and Hebrew. The plates described how to bring the man and beast out of hibernation. It was a most interesting process. It far exceeds anything we have today. But..." she began to cry again. "The desire to bring the man back to life far exceeded any moral or legal conduct that is conducive of a modern, civilized society. One of the ingredients needed to revive the man was the blood of infants. It seems that there is an enzyme in blood that has the potential to bring immortality to the flesh, but the enzyme disappears around the age of five."

Again the Chief interrupted. "So you kidnapped the Indian children and sacrificed them for your project?"

"Yes," she cried, and once again tears streamed down her

cheeks. "I am so, so sorry. The blood *had* to be fresh so the babies were transfused immediately. It hurt me so much to see the life drain from their little helpless bodies."

"Now I know why you asked me those questions that day in the hotel," Denise sighed.

Angela nodded. "Those questions weren't for you, Denise. They were for me. I was trying to convince myself that I was doing the right thing. All for God and country you know?"

"But why so many children?" the old Chief asked.

"Because we found that the enzyme only had a short time of duration. It kind of builds on itself. At first we had to transfuse the man every couple of days and then once a week. We were up to two weeks when I realized that I couldn't take it any longer. Enoch objected, too."

"Who's Enoch?" Denise frowned.

"Enoch is the man we revived from the capsule."

Father looked at the Chief. "What do you mean he objected?"

"After we revived him, he quickly gained the ability to speak our language. His mind is far above anything in our world today. When he found out we were sacrificing children to keep him alive he tried to escape. He began to talk to me and tell me about his civilization and how he had come to be in New Mexico. He begged me not to kill any more babies. His pleas finally made me realize that it was not worth the cost. I couldn't kill another infant so tonight between shift changes, I helped him escape."

"You mean he's here?" Denise exclaimed.

Angela pointed. "He's in the cave. I told him to stay put until I came back."

All four of them looked toward the mine entrance and then at each other.

"He's dying though."

"Because of the blood?" Father asked.

"Yes, but there's something else. He's from another time, a time when the earth was pure and clean. The air has changed so much since his time that he has trouble breathing. Even if we had the blood, he would have to stay in a special chamber the rest of his life to just survive. He says he could handle that but he cannot handle the death of another child for his sake."

Father shrugged his shoulders. "So what does he want?"

Angela smiled. "He wants to go somewhere away from all the science and simply be allowed to die."

The group stood silent. Everyone realized the significance of this discovery to all of mankind, but they knew that Angela was right. The Chief looked up at the night sky.

"It will be light in about three hours. Whatever we are going to do we need to get moving in that direction."

"But I don't know what to do, Chief," Angela objected. "All I know is that we need to get Enoch to some place where he can enjoy his last days on earth in peace."

A huge smile came to the face of the Chief. "I've got an idea." He turned to Father. "Ben Running Deer's place is just over that hill. If we can talk Susie into it she can lead us to the hidden burial cave of the Anasazi."

"Is it far?" Angela asked.

"Probably four days by foot."

Angela shook her head. "Enoch would never make it. Like I said he has trouble breathing, and his last transfusion was only a couple days ago. At best he's only got a week or ten days."

The Chief took a deep breath searching for a solution. "Can he ride a horse?"

"Yes, I think so. Like I said he's very intelligent. His learning curve is way off the page."

"Good. Bill, you and Denise wait here with Angela. Father and I will be back in an hour or so."

Denise reluctantly gave a nod of acceptance then watched as Father and the Chief walked back to the truck. They shielded their eyes as the truck lights came to life.

"What's on your mind, Chief?" Father asked as the old man turned the truck around and headed out of the mine entrance.

"Ben has a few horses and Susie knows the way to the burial cave." He turned to Father and laughed. "You ever been on a horse, Padre?"

"I'm no John Wayne, but I've ridden a couple of times."

"That's good. I just hope everyone else has, too. The way to the burial cave is fairly demanding but once we make the first canyon it will be hard for the military to find us."

"Do you know the way?"

"I've been there only one time with Susie. I don't think I could find it. We need her to show us."

The old truck bounced on the gravel road as the Chief fought the wheel. He was driving faster than he needed to on the rough roads but time was not on their side. They had to be under way before sunrise. A chopper in the air could see for miles in this desert and they would be sitting ducks. They needed the cover of darkness until they reached the canyon.

The dogs around Ben's place ran out into the headlights as the Chief pulled the truck to a stop. He shut off the engine just as the door to the house flung open. Susie stood in the doorway, a rifle pointing in the direction of the truck.

"Hold on, Susie," the Chief called. "It's me."

"That you, George?"

"Yes. It's me and Father Macon. We need your help."

Susie lowered the gun as the two men approached. "What are

you guys doing out here this time of night?"

The Chief motioned to the door. "Let's go in and I'll explain."

For thirty minutes the Chief and Father Macon tried to give a shortened version of what had happened. Susie listened intently without interrupting. Her eyes widened as they shared of Enoch and how the scientists had sacrificed the babies to keep him alive. Her anger was dampened when she heard that Enoch was dying because he refused to be a part of their infanticide. Father nodded as the Chief shared how they needed her help to find the sacred burial grounds of the Anasazi.

"Without your help, Susie" the Chief pleaded, "the military will find Dr. LePage and Enoch for sure."

"I will help," she smiled. "But we only have six horses. The rest we have turned out to pasture. It would take a couple of days just to find them. "

The Chief frowned. They needed seven horses for everyone in the group to go. Six horses meant that someone would have to stay behind. That was not good.

"Do you have enough supplies to last us for a week to ten days?"

Susie smiled. "You have Gabe to thank for that. He has enough gear and food stored out back to get us through a couple months if need be. I always thought it was paranoia but he knew the white man better than I did. He said the government would starve the people if it was needed to fulfill their agenda. He was prepared if it happened."

The Chief smiled. "It seems that he knew their heart well."

"So well that it killed him," she returned.

The Chief nodded his head. He knew her pain.

"Come on," she motioned as she got up. "I'll show you where the supplies are stored and then you two can load the truck while I

165

saddle up the horses."

Father and the Chief followed Susie outside and around to an outbuilding behind the hogan. They watched as she opened the door and pulled a string attached to a light in the center of the ceiling. The light flooded the room revealing shelves loaded with canned goods and camping supplies.

"Praise the Lord," Father exclaimed. "This is amazing. It's as if Gabe knew what we were going to need."

Susie looked at Father and frowned. "It's a shame he's not the one leading you to the sacred burial grounds."

The Chief took Susie's hand. "Maybe he is."

Susie smiled. She knew what the old medicine man meant and she had no problem in accepting it. "You guys hurry and finish up here. I'll get the horses."

The Chief nodded as he and Father began to load themselves with supplies.

It was another thirty minutes before they had the truck loaded. They knew they were running out of time but it was all they could do. The Chief was tying the last of the supplies down to the truck bed when they heard the sound of the horses. Out of the blackness Susie appeared riding on one horse and holding reigns to five others. She looked down at Father and smiled.

"They're at the old mine," the old Chief yelled. "We'll go ahead and you come as fast as you can."

"Sounds good," Susie yelled back. "I'll leave a note for daddy then head that way."

The Chief nodded then motioned for Father to climb aboard. Father waved to Susie then got into the truck cab. He watched as the Chief turned the key and quickly put the truck in gear. He, too, knew that time was growing short. They had to be on their way to the canyon in less than two hours. He prayed quietly for God's help.

"Why only six horses?" Father asked, after they had driven a few miles.

The Chief shook his head in the glow of the dash light. "My heart is saddened that one of us will have to choose to stay behind. The decision rests with the Lord. That is the reason for the six horses."

The Chief was right. Everything had been provided when it had been needed. The six horses meant that someone was not supposed to go with the group. The answer was on both of the men's minds as they pulled the truck up to the entrance of the mine.

Denise came out of the opening to meet them. Father could tell as he slammed the truck door that Denise was excited. He could see it in her face, even in the light of the truck lamps.

She waited until they met at the front of the truck. "He is amazing."

"Who?" Father frowned.

"Enoch. Wait till you meet him."

She grabbed Father's hand and led him into the mine. Small torches lined the walls along their path.

"That's convenient," Father commented, looking up at the torches.

"Yeah, Enoch made them. He is something else."

Denise led Father and the Chief back to an opening a short distance into the mine. It, too, was lit by the same type of torches. As they approached, Father saw Enoch. He stared as they continued to approach the man.

"Father Rex Macon, this is Enoch."

Father extended his hand toward the man as he studied his features. Enoch was about six feet six inches tall with a thin to medium build. He looked like a normal man except that his head was slightly bigger from his eyebrows to the crown of his head. He was dressed in a silver uniform, making him look like the Hollywood pictures of Frankenstein. His eyes were dark but in the light of the torches they gave off a purple hue.

"Hello, Father Rex Macon," Enoch smiled, as he grasped Father's hand.

The smile changed as he held onto Father's hand. They stood looking at each other until Denise introduced the Chief. Enoch smiled at Father, released his hand and turned to the Chief.

"Enoch, this is Chief Walking Cloud."

The two shook hands and once again Enoch seemed bound to the old Chief. They stared at each other until Denise loudly cleared her throat.

"Gentlemen, I understand that time is of the essence. We must get going."

The two men released their hands and smiled at each other as they turned to face Denise.

"Father, could you instruct us in what we are to do?"

Father nodded. "Susie Running Deer will be here any time now. She is bringing the horses that we will need to get to the sacred burial grounds. The supplies are in the back of the truck that we will need while we are there. We must get them loaded quickly and be on our way. We must be to the first canyon by daybreak. There is, however, one problem." He looked at Denise and sighed. He started to continue but was suddenly interrupted by Susie's entrance into the mine. The young Indian made her way toward them but stopped when she saw Enoch. She stared at the man. "Anasazi," she said softly.

"What?" Denise asked.

Susie didn't answer but continued to stare at the stranger.

Father finally broke the silence. "Everybody, this is Susie Running Deer, our guide. Susie, this is Bill, Denise, Angela, and this is Enoch."

Susie greeted each person but still seemed mesmerized by Enoch.

"Father, what is the problem?" Denise asked.

"What?" Father frowned, then remembered. "The problem is that we only have six horses. One of us will have to stay behind."

Silence filled the small room of the mine. They had been brought together. It seemed a shame for one to be left behind.

"Except for Enoch," Father suggested, "I think it would be best if we all drew straws. The shortest straw stays behind."

"There's no need to do that."

Father turned around to face Bill.

"I can't go," Bill said, shaking his head. "I'm a diabetic and my medication is back at the hotel. I take two shots of insulin each day."

Father could see the disappointment in Bill's eyes. "Bill, are you sure?"

"I'm sure. I wouldn't make it past the first day without the medicine. I've been thinking about it, though. This is probably for the best. I can drive the Chief's truck back to his house and if I can get it there right about dawn then maybe they'll never know we left."

Father looked at the Chief. "I think he's right, Chief."

The Chief nodded. "I think it's an excellent idea. It also gets the truck further away from us. If Bill's not discovered before he gets back to the house, there is no way they can track us. It buys us extra time."

"Then it's settled," Bill grinned, fighting back the tears.

"Let's move everybody," Father shouted, then slapped Bill

lightly on the back.

The group departed the mine and began to load the supplies from the truck onto their horses. Susie had brought feed sacks that served as ideal storage bags for the supplies and camping gear. What had seemed impossible had become a reality. Every bit of the supplies from the truck had been loaded onto the six horses.

Father walked over to Enoch. "Ever ridden a horse before?"

"A Sackwa, yes; a horse, no. But they are similar."

Father smiled then walked over to Bill. He was leaning against the front of the truck.

"I do envy you, Father," he said as he continued watching the others prepare their horses. "An opportunity comes along like this only once in a lifetime." He motioned with his head toward Enoch. "That man has things to share that I would like to hear. I know he has answers to many, many questions."

"When I get back I will share what I have learned."

Bill looked at Father and smiled. "Fair enough."

Father reached into his pocket and pulled out a small note. He handed it to Bill. "This is a phone number and the name of my secretary. Could I get you to call her on Saturday and tell her that I may be a few days? Tell her not to worry."

Bill took the note and placed it into his shirt pocket.

"Father, it's time," the Chief called.

Father extended his hand. "Take care, Bill."

Bill shook Father's hand with tears again filling his eyes. "You, too."

Father turned and walked to his horse. Susie was holding the reigns.

"You know how to work one of these things, Father?"

"With a beautiful teacher like you how can I fail?"

He grabbed the saddle horn, put his foot in the stirrup then swung his other leg over the horse. Susie handed him the reigns.

"I'm impressed," she smiled.

"Thank you, ma'am" Father smiled, then pretended to tip his hat.

Susie giggled then walked to her horse. She spent little energy in climbing aboard. "Everyone ready?"

She waited until each member of the small group gave some sign of readiness.

"Let's ride," she shouted.

Bill watched as they each waved then turned their horses in behind Susie's. In no time at all they were lost in the darkness. Bill waited until he could hear them no longer then turned and climbed into the truck cab. His imagination was overly active as he headed the old truck back toward the Chief's house. It cruelly taunted him about all the things he would miss.

The small band rode until the sun began to appear over the horizon. They were still a couple of miles from the first canyon. It was a very vulnerable time. They all listened for any sounds of aircraft. Fortunately, none ever came. Father thanked the Lord for his protection. As Susie announced the entrance to the canyon, they all let out a loud cheer. For now they were safe.

CHAPTER EIGHT

The Revelation

Susie raised her hand into the air, signaling the others to stop. She stepped down and walked back to Father. They had reached the bottom of the canyon. A small river coursed between the high walls of rock and the light of the bright sun glistened on the water's surface. It was a beautiful sight.

Susie looked up at Father, shielding her eyes from the sunlight. "It's getting pretty hot, and I think by the looks of everyone that it would be best to stop. No one got any sleep last night and we've all had a rough morning. I would suggest that we rest then head out again this afternoon when it gets cooler."

"I think that sounds great, Susie. I for one could use a rest. My legs already feel like Jell-O." He looked back over his shoulder at Enoch. The slumped-over posture of the large man's body revealed its fatigue. "It's important that we look after Enoch. It might be best if we take our time."

"I understand." She pointed up the canyon. "There is a large overhang just about a quarter mile up the river. It will provide shade and concealment."

"Sounds wonderful."

Susie walked back to her horse, mounted, then again motioned with her hand for the little band to follow. The horses followed

172

single file along the edge of the river. The scenery would have been exhilarating if everyone had not been so tired. When Susie finally yelled at Father and pointed to the large overhang he praised the Lord. The last quarter mile had seemed like ten.

The overhang was large enough for the party to ride under. Each one dismounted and stretched their legs. Audible sounds of relief sounded among the small group. Susie rounded up the horses and led them down to the river to drink. Father clapped his hands to get the group's attention.

"Susie has decided that it would be best if we traveled during the cool of the day. None of us slept last night so let's all take a few hours and get some rest. Find a place where you can spread out your bedroll and we'll rest until this afternoon."

It was cool under the overhang. Sand covered the bottom, which provided a softer support for the bedrolls. The old Chief approached Father as he watched the others walk down to the river to remove their bedrolls from the horses.

"I may be overly cautious, but do you think we need a sentry?"

Father shook his head. "I don't think so, Chief. I think we're fairly safe here. We all need the rest. It'll be okay."

The Chief smiled and nodded. Father could see the fatigue in the old man's eyes. The rest was important for them all.

Susie finished watering the horses and tied them away from the group but still under the overhang. She removed her bedroll and walked over to where Father was spreading his out in the sand. The others were already resting in various spots along the floor of the overhang. There was little movement.

"Didn't anybody have to be rocked to sleep, looks like."

Father looked around at the others then nodded. "Yeah, last night was very taxing on us all. Nothing like extreme stress to wear the body out quickly."

"That's for sure." Susie pointed to a spot a few feet from Father's bedroll. "Mind if I join you?"

"Not at all. Need some help?"

"No. I've done this many times."

Father laid back on his bedroll. He turned and watched Susie finish her preparation. "Thanks for helping us out, Susie."

She turned and smiled. "It seemed like the right thing to do." She looked over to Enoch's bedroll. There was no movement. "When I saw him in the mine last night, I *knew* it was the right thing to do."

Father frowned. "What do you mean?"

Susie brushed her long black hair out of her face then looked deep into Father's eyes. "I'll show you when we get to the burial cave." Susie smiled, then rolled back onto her bedroll. "Have a nice rest, Father."

"You, too," he said as he turned and lay back against the soft material of the bedroll. He stared at the rock ceiling above him, trying to remember back to the previous evening when Susie had walked into the mine and met Enoch. He remembered that she had been captivated by the man's appearance, but then, he had been too. What was she talking about? His memories of last night caused him to recount his handshake with Enoch. Something had happened to Enoch during that handshake. The strange man had felt something. And it had happened again when Enoch shook hands with the old Chief. It was like he didn't want to let go of them. Father rubbed his eyes. He was just too tired to think about it. He thanked the Lord for being with them, and for His guidance and protection. He started to pray in the Spirit but he didn't get far.

Father's eyes opened to the sight of orange rock above him. It took a few seconds for him to remember where he was. The smell of bacon frying was too inviting to turn down. He sat up and looked around the site. The others were sitting around a fire where Susie and the Chief were cooking. Denise and Angela sat talking with Enoch. He carefully picked himself up and walked toward the group.

"Well, look who's up," the Chief greeted. "Sleep well, my friend?"

"Like a rock," Father laughed. "How long have I been out?"

The Chief looked at his watch. "About 6 hours."

"Wow, I must have been completely wiped out."

"We all were," Denise added. "It was a wild night."

Father looked at Enoch. "How are you doing?"

"I am doing all right."

Father smiled. "That's good. But, I've been wondering. What's a Sackwa?"

Enoch laughed. "A Sackwa is an animal that we rode for pleasure much like you do these horses. It looked something like your horse but a little larger. Its feet were much larger and more round than the horses and it had two humps on its back."

"Sounds like a camel," Denise laughed.

Enoch frowned as he looked at Denise. "Camel is a new word for me."

"A camel," Denise explained, "is the animal that we have now that fits the Sackwa you described."

"I see," Enoch nodded.

"Where do you come from, Enoch?" Father asked.

The Chief and Susie stopped what they were doing and

gathered around close to the stranger. They were interested, too, in what he had to say.

"I come from a great land that was situated in the center of a vast ocean. The island was called Atlantis."

Denise and Susie's gasps caused Enoch to frown. He looked at Denise. "Why the surprise?"

"Because we have heard of Atlantis but most people thought it was only a myth."

"Oh, it is, or at least it was, very real. I can assure you."

Father walked over to a large boulder and sat down across from Enoch. "Our stories say that it was destroyed in one day by a huge earthquake."

Enoch looked at Father. "I am not sure about the one day but Elwa destroyed Atlantis."

"Who is Elwa?"

"Elwa is the creator of all things. Angela says you call Him God."

Father looked at Angela and smiled then turned back to Enoch. "Why did Elwa destroy Atlantis?"

"Because the people of Atlantis persisted in their disobedience to all that was pure and right. We knew it was coming. Elwa had warned us many times but most refused to heed the warning."

"And you came here to escape the destruction."

Enoch smiled. "You are a wise man, Father. You see Atlantis was a gift from Elwa but the people abused the gift for too long. Before the warnings even began, I knew that it could not last. We were a technology and science minded people. Science controlled and motivated everything on Atlantis. Very few paid any attention to Elwa and his decrees. Our temples became empty and those dedicated to Elwa's service diminished to just a handful. One night I had a *fordova*, or what you call a dream. In that fordova Elwa asked me to leave, to go to a land that He would show me for very soon Atlantis would be no more. What you call air travel was very common in Atlantis. The capsules that your scientists found me in were called *Coufre*. They were designed to prolong life for hundreds or even thousands of years. It was the general belief that people would grow in abilities and capabilities with time. We never imagined that knowledge would go backwards. As a precaution, however, the knowledge needed to revive me and Atalore was enclosed and inscribed on metal plates. The metal was designed to withstand any form of corrosion or decay."

"Atalore was the beast in the other capsule?"

"That's correct. Atalore was a genetic creation called the Monstobi. They were our protectors and our workers. They were designed to be physical giants in stamina and stature but they were infants in their ability to think. Atalore was my personal bodyguard."

"Gabe described it as a man with a bull's head," the Chief added.

"That's right. The scientists of Atlantis were very well versed in what you now call genetic manipulation and mapping. The ones called to serve Elwa opposed the entire thing furiously but public opinion and public sentiment became the rule of Atlantis. The Monstobi were created to be simple of mind because with their tremendous strength they could easily overpower and overtake the average man. They thought like children but were fierce fighters and very hard workers. They were bought and sold like cattle."

"Were they only male?" Father asked.

"At first all were male, but with time there came abuses. The Monstobi were human from the neck down and capable of sexual bonding with human females. At first it was unlawful and any female caught bonding with a Monstobi was immediately incarcerated and surgically sterilized. Those impregnated with the Monstobi were treated the same and the offspring were destroyed. Later, however, it became sport in the ranks of the wealthy. It was forbidden entertainment and it grew rampant. So rampant in fact that it was impossible to stop. Huge crowds gathered to watch and encourage the strange activity. Naturally the number of those impregnated increased which left the officials with a tremendous dilemma. Many of the women, knowing the rules, hid in the zones away from the main city and had their offspring. The minds of these offspring, however, were not so childlike but their bodies still maintained their tremendous strength. The zones around the cities became unsafe for human traffic. Faced with a tremendous problem, the officials developed a type of weapon that could chemically sterilize the Monstobi through the medium of drinking water. Within a hundred years the Monstobi Rebellion was brought under control and the Monstobi once again became the slave of the man. I never agreed with the creation or abuse of the Monstobi. I didn't want Atalore to come with me but the others insisted that I might need the protection."

"Did Elwa destroy Atlantis because of the Monstobi?"

Enoch shook his head. "Man's creation of the Monstobi was terrible but it was only part of the reason Elwa brought destruction to Atlantis. When we began killing the infants, that's when the downfall started. The people on Atlantis lived to be very old by your standards, some reaching the age of six and seven hundred years. But that was not enough. Immortality became the desire of the people and the men of science came together to give it to them. By accident they found that young babies and children carried an enzyme in the blood that, when filtered and combined with several other agents, could actually stop and even reverse the aging process. The only problems were that the blood had to be fresh and in enough quantity to produce a sufficient quantity of the enzyme. So..."

"...so the babies were sacrificed," Father added.

"Yes, I'm afraid so," Enoch continued. "The knowledge of the enzyme spread like a cancer and the demand became so great that millions of babies were sacrificed. It became common practice for women to give birth just so they could kill the baby and obtain the enzyme."

"How could anyone do such a thing?" Susie asked. "Where was the compassion?"

Enoch looked at Susie. "There was none and that was the reason Elwa had to destroy Atlantis. As the babies were sacrificed in huge numbers, the compassion disappeared. It became one person against another. Entertainment turned into barbaric practices, the more destructive and bizarre, the bigger the crowds."

"Didn't anyone try to speak out and put a stop to it?" Denise asked.

"Yes, some tried, but they were quickly destroyed. The madness continued, I guess, right up to the end."

"That's why when he found out that we were killing the infants to keep him alive," Dr. LePage offered, "he tried to stop us and then tried to escape."

"Because you knew that we were heading down the same path to destruction," Father added.

"Yes. In fact I could see the same coldness in the eyes of your scientists and their same disregard for human life. Each time I watched them drain the blood from those tiny bodies I tried to warn them of the consequences but they paid my pleas no mind."

"We convinced ourselves that the end justified the means," Dr. LePage explained. "The huge advance in science was worth the death of a few children. But Enoch is right about the loss of compassion. The lives of those children meant nothing to the men on the team. They would have killed five hundred if that's what the project demanded and never batted an eye. One of the doctors on the team made the comment that if we could replicate the process then it would put an end to abortion. The babies would be too valuable to abort. They would be delivered and sold to firms who harvested the enzyme."

Father shook his head. "Nothing like logical insanity. The abortionists deny that the baby has life, but it contains so much life that now they wait to kill it *after* it's born to rob its life."

"How long have your people been aborting their young?" Enoch asked, looking around at the group for an answer.

"For almost a quarter of a century," Angela replied, tears welling in her eyes.

"That is not good," Enoch frowned, shaking his head. "You must warn them. Tell them to stop."

Everyone looked at Father, expecting him to answer. Father took a deep breath. "We have told them to stop, but they refuse to listen."

"Then their fate will be like that of my people. Elwa is patient, but when He moves, the end will come swiftly. It is so simple: Elwa is life; to refuse life is to refuse the Creator. Rejection of the Creator brings the opposite of life."

"Death," the Chief added.

"Exactly, and death has many forms. When death is accepted it becomes an attitude, which leads to a way. Logical insanity you called it. Once a way, it becomes a force, which feeds upon itself. Like a whirlwind it sucks in every bit of death from everyone and everything and pushes it down to a vortex, which becomes the huge finger of destruction. The more the whirlwind is fed the greater the power of the finger becomes."

"But not everyone accepts this attitude of death," the Chief objected.

"That is true, Chief. I saw it in my day. But the whirlwind has the uncanny ability to deceive and blind. Those caught in its dance will swear on all that they possess that it is the truth. While, to those on the outside, the lie is very obvious." He looked up at Angela and smiled. "Ask Dr. LePage how drunk her scientific friends were on the 'wine' of discovery."

Tears again formed in Angela's eyes. "Very drunk. And I went right along with them."

Denise reached over and took Angela's hand. "But you put a stop to it."

Angela began to sob. "But it was too late." She jumped up and ran away from the group. Denise looked at Father and frowned then got up and walked over to where Angela stood weeping. Denise put an arm around her, which turned into an embrace. The others watched as the two women stood holding each other.

"Her pain is strong," the Chief said sadly.

"Yes," Enoch added, "but it is the pain that allows her to overcome her blindness."

Susie looked at the women then back at Enoch. "I do not understand."

"There have been those that Angela admired and trusted that have taught her the way of death. It is obvious that she received the way and became part of its force. But, there is something deep within her heart that has rebelled against death's way. Whatever it is causes her great pain when she confronts it. Each confrontation, however, leads to a greater awareness that she has been lied to by those she trusted the most."

Father continued to watch the two women. He knew what Enoch was saying. "And as that awareness grew she refused to be a part of death's destruction. Once the blinders were removed she was forced to make a choice that went totally against the system."

Enoch smiled at Father's wisdom. "That is correct. There are always a few who see past death's deception."

"But she said she was too late," Susie questioned. "What did she mean by that?"

Both Enoch and Father shook their heads. The answer to that question lay deep in Dr. Angela LePage's heart.

They watched the women walk back toward them. Denise laughed as she reached the others. "Man, I'm starved. What do you guys have cooking over there, Chief?"

The others understood it was her way of saying that it was time to end the conversation.

"It's almost ready," the Chief replied. "I got so wrapped up in what Enoch was saying that I forgot my kitchen duties."

The others laughed, even Angela. Once again the pain had passed.

Susie looked down toward the river then back at Father. "It's cool enough for us to travel now, too. We've got four or five hours before sunset."

Father nodded. "Okay, let's eat and get back on the trail."

The trail was not really a trail at all but part of the riverbed. When the river flooded there was no trail, only the river bordered by tall walls on either side. Father would have been contented to just sit and listen to Enoch but he knew they had a mission to fulfill. He had not noticed Enoch having any difficulty breathing until the large man exerted himself. Then it became very obvious. It saddened him that the man was dying.

The small band finished their meal, cleaned up the area and packed their horses without much conversation. Susie packed quickly then helped the others until everyone was ready to ride. With a wave of the hand she started their methodical journey up the canyon. They passed many overhangs like the one where they had rested. It was obvious that over time the water had been a powerful force against the red rock walls. The air temperature was warm but the air coming off of the cold river made the ride pleasant. Susie was wise to travel only during the cooler parts of the day. Father wondered how far they would have to ride. As far down as they were in the canyon, he knew that the sun would set early for them.

Susie knew it too, and she was aware that the little band she was leading was not used to being on a horse all day. Time was valuable; she knew that. Enoch was slowly dying, but the safety and well-being of the others was just as important. She decided to ride for an hour then rest for fifteen minutes. Everyone, including Enoch, was strong enough to handle that cycle.

The Chief was like a duck in water. This was his ultimate environment. He enjoyed every rock, every small wild flower and every sparkle that reflected off of the river's surface. He was home and it was good that he was here. He was helping Enoch with his journey. The "Way of the Owl" as his people called it; the journey through darkness to the light of the new day. In his younger days he had walked the journey with many of the older men in his tribe. As they neared their death, they would choose two of the younger men in the tribe to "walk the way" with them. Most of the time it was a two or three day journey to the burial ground and during the trip the older man would give an account of his life and relate vital teachings to the younger men. In this way wisdom and the knowledge of the ancients were transferred to the succeeding generations. The young men would then attend to the dying man, honoring him with their servitude until the last glow of the funeral pyre. Age was something held in high esteem by his people and it was a thing of great honor to be chosen to make the journey with the "old one." It had been many years since he had made one of the trips but he had thought about them many times as he, too, had grown older. Now here he was again. The cry of a red-tailed hawk flying high above the canyon broke his concentration. A frown came to his wrinkled face. It was not a good sign. The red-tailed hawk was a mystical sentry for the Indian, sent by the Great Spirit to warn his brother, the red man, of eminent danger. His dark eyes scanned the high cliffs, his ears searched the sounds in the wind.

Susie had also heard the hawk. She raised her hand signaling the group to halt. Father watched as she, too, searched the sky and high cliffs. After a couple minutes she turned in her saddle and yelled at the others. "Rest time, let's take about fifteen."

She didn't have to tell them twice. Everyone was ready for the break. Denise laughed as she stepped down from her saddle. "Man, my legs feel like rubber."

Angela was quick to agree. Father watched as Susie rode back to the Chief. He could see the concern on her face. He kicked his horse lightly, guiding it toward the two.

"Everything okay?" he asked, as he brought his horse alongside Susie's.

She didn't answer but looked at the Chief who again looked up along the rim of the canyon.

"They're looking for us."

Father frowned and looked at Susie. She nodded her head in agreement.

"How do you know?"

"Listen," the Chief instructed.

Father sat quietly, listening hard for whatever he was supposed to hear. After a few moments he shook his head. "I don't hear anything."

Suddenly the cry of hawk again broke the stillness. It's cry much farther off than before.

The Chief smiled. "Our brother the hawk is warning us that trouble is ahead."

"Do you think that Bill told them where we were going?"

"He couldn't have. He didn't know where we were going. This desert is vast and there is no way he would have told them which direction we were headed unless he was tortured."

"Or threatened," Father added.

The old Indian's eyes narrowed. Father was right. Angela had shared how cold and insensitive the military and her fellow scientists were. Bill was tough but, if the military thought he knew something, they would apply whatever pressure was needed. He looked at Susie.

"Is there another outcropping or cave nearby?"

Susie nodded then pointed toward the way they were headed. "There's a big one about a hundred and fifty yards farther up in front of us."

"Good. Why don't we spend the night there?" He again looked up to the rim of the canyon. "It'll be dark soon and we need some time to set up camp." He looked at Father. "That okay with you?"

"Hey," Father laughed, "this is your and Susie's forte. Whatever you say."

The Chief smiled. "Let's get everyone back on their horse."

Father pulled on the reins and turned his horse toward Denise and the others who were stretching their legs on the bank of the river. He looked down at Enoch who had taken a seat on a large boulder.

"I hate to put a quick end to the rest period but we've decided to set up camp early a little ways up river."

"Any problem?" Angela asked.

Father motioned with his head toward Susie and the old Chief who were still talking. "Chief seems to think that we might need to be cautious."

Denise laughed. "There's no way anyone could find us out here." She looked at Enoch then back at Father, and frowned. "Is there?"

Father shrugged. "I don't know what their capabilities are. I think it would be tough but they probably have technology that we know nothing about." Father could see the effect his answer was having on Dr. LePage. Her eyes grew wide with fear. "But, I trust Susie and the Chief. They know what they're doing out here. So let's get mounted and we'll be making camp in a few minutes." Father watched as they all climbed back in the saddle, then he led them over to where Susie and the Chief were waiting. Without saying anything Susie again took the lead. The others fell in line, single file, behind her. The Chief waited to the last, his eyes still scanning the sky above the canyon.

The overhang was at least as big as the first one where they had previously stayed. It was really a strange sight. It looked as if a huge slice had been carved out of the bottom of the canyon wall. Mechanically it seemed impossible for the huge rock wall to stand with so much of its base missing, but the overhangs were plentiful along the river and none showed any signs of caving in. For the group it made an excellent shelter. Susie again took care of the horses while the Chief started a fire. The others staked out various places along the floor of the overhang, unrolling and arranging their bedrolls.

Father threw his bedroll onto a sandy area then walked over to where Enoch was sitting quietly, his eyes closed.

"You okay?"

Enoch smiled without opening his eyes. "I am fine. I am sorry for putting all of you in so much danger."

"Each one of us is here because we want to be. Sooner or later we all have to make a stand for something."

Enoch opened his eyes and looked at Father. "You are wise for your age. Dr. LePage tells me that you are a priest of your God."

Father nodded. "That is true but I believe that my God is the same as your Elwa. We have a book called the Bible that is the historical record of God's relationship with man. One of the first names for God in that book is Elohim."

"Who wrote this book?"

"We believe that is was written by men inspired by the Spirit of God."

"Does it mention Atlantis?"

Father shook his head.

"But you say it is a historical record? How far back in the past does it go?"

Father smiled. "We believe it goes back to the introduction of man on this planet."

Enoch frowned, producing many wrinkles across his large forehead. "And you think this book is reliable?"

Father started to answer but was interrupted by Denise and Dr. LePage.

"Mind if we join you?" Denise asked.

"Not at all," Father answered, "I was just sharing with Enoch about the Bible. He was wondering if it mentioned Atlantis."

Denise laughed. "I can answer that and I'm not much of a Bible scholar. Atlantis has always been a myth fabricated from the writings of Plato."

"But," Angela held out her hand toward Enoch. "As we can see, it was no myth. How could something so large be missed by the historians?"

Father ran his hand through his hair, thinking about the question. He could tell that it was mainly directed toward him. "My guess is that since Atlantis was completely destroyed there were few survivors and no written records to pass on." He looked at Enoch and smiled. "Until now."

"There had to be other survivors. I was not the only one to whom Elwa revealed the fate of Atlantis. I am sure of that. Why there is no record of their fate, I do not know."

"How did you come to leave Atlantis?" Denise asked.

"As I shared before, the evil in Atlantis grew to a point that the land became unfit for decent living. The disrespect for life, the depravity, the barbarism was beyond anything anyone could imagine. These were highly intelligent people and yet they seemed to lose all sense of reason. It was like they were drunk on human blood. It was so bad that I lost all my faith in mankind. I saw no way for it to get any better. So, I asked Elwa to take me out of it." He looked at Father Macon. "I meant I wanted to die. It was that bad. That became my *tatwa* or prayer as you call it. Soon after that, I began to receive visions of the island sinking under a great flood. I had no idea what they meant but they became so real and so vivid that after a while I understood what was about to happen. A few of the others who secretly served Elwa also began receiving the visions. Then one night an Anaki appeared to me in a dream and told me that Elwa wanted me to flee Atlantis for it would soon be destroyed."

"What is an Anaki? Father interrupted.

"I think you call them angels."

A huge smile came to Father's face. "I'll be."

"What?" Denise frowned.

"It just hit me. It says in the Bible that Enoch was not, for God took him. I think we now know where God took him."

"You mean you think that this Enoch was that Enoch?" Denise questioned.

Father looked at Denise and nodded. "It sure seems to fit. In the Bible Enoch was taken by God before the great Flood came to destroy an earth that was totally wicked. Where God took him to has never been determined."

Denise laughed. "All I remember about the Flood is Noah and his ark."

"Noah?" Enoch asked. "Do you mean Noah of the river?"

Denise looked at Father, wanting him to answer.

"Who was Noah of the river, Enoch?"

Enoch paused as if trying to remember. "Noah was an open servant of Elwa, a very rare thing. He lived outside the city on the banks of the great river. I was told that at one time he was highly respected for his wisdom. I never met him, but everyone called him insane. That is the reason, I guess, that he got away with his open support of Elwa. When he and his sons started building this huge vessel, he told everyone that Elwa was going to flood the entire world in retribution for the people's wickedness."

"That's the same Noah in the Bible," Denise said excitedly.

Father nodded, waiting for Enoch to continue.

"Of course, no one listened, just more insanity. He became the recipient of much ridicule. Many went out from the city to see the spectacle. He was still building on the vessel when I left Atlantis."

Father looked at Denise then at Angela. He knew they were all thinking the same thing. Angela finally broke the silence.

"He is the same one."

"But why now?" Denise added. "The coufre, as you called it, has been hidden in that cave since the dawn of time." She turned to Father Macon. "Why now?"

Father shook his head. "I wish I knew. God definitely has his hand in this, but still too many puzzle pieces missing." He looked at Enoch. "Did Elwa tell you anything about your journey or your mission?"

Enoch frowned, his huge forehead again filling with wrinkles. "He said to tell no one except those who I was sure were His followers. He said there would be those who would try and stop me, and that I would be rewarded for my obedience."

"Did any of your people try to stop you?"

"Not that I am aware. But you must realize that while I was in the coufre I knew nothing of what was going on around me. I knew nothing of Atalore's death until I asked Dr. LePage."

"So you knew nothing of what this area looked like when you landed?"

Enoch shook his head. "Nothing."

"Listen," the Chief interrupted, raising his hand in the air.

The entire group froze, straining to hear beyond the lapping of the river against the rocks. Susie was the next to hear it. She frowned and looked at the old Chief. Suddenly each face in the group revealed that, they too, were hearing it.

"What is that?" Enoch asked softly.

No one answered as the sound grew nearer and louder. Father could see the panic in Dr. LePage's eyes. He smiled then took her hand. He prayed silently against the fear as the small group stood like stone. The smile returned to his face as the sound grew more faint. He looked at Dr. LePage and nodded "all clear" with his head. He could see the relief return her body to calm. He squeezed her hand then let go.

The Chief was the first to break the silence. "Our brother the hawk was right."

Susie nodded. "They are looking for us. That's for sure."

"What was that," Enoch asked. "Some type of flying machine?"

"It was a helicopter," Father explained. "They are a form of aircraft used by the military. Susie is right. They are looking for you."

Enoch shook his head. "They do not want me. They want the knowledge I have. They are drunk on the possibility of immortality. I have seen that drunkenness before on the faces of hundreds of the scientists on Atlantis. It swept like a dark cloud over the entire country."

Father looked up into the face of Denise. They were thinking the same thing. Before they could say anything the old chief clapped his hands together. "That's it!"

Father laughed and nodded his head. "You're right."

"What?" Susie frowned.

"The dream," Denise announced.

Dr. LePage looked at Denise, waiting for an explanation, then at Father. "What dream?"

The group listened intently as Father recounted the dream that had brought him to New Mexico. By the time he finished everyone knew the dream's interpretation. "God destroyed Atlantis because they were drunk on the blood of their children. That drunkenness is the dark cloud and...

"Now it's trying to raise its ugly head once again in this country," Denise interrupted.

"Exactly," Father agreed. "The same black cloud is forming over New Mexico."

The old chief sighed deeply. "The first voice you heard was mine asking you to come out here. The next voice was the sound of children's cries. It was the sound of a great waterfall."

The small group stood quietly, trying to deal with the magnitude of the revelation.

"It is my fault," Enoch said softly. "I have brought this on your young ones."

Father Macon felt his spirit quicken. "That's not true, Enoch. This was already set in motion before you arrived. He looked at Dr. LePage. "That's true isn't it, Angela?"

Dr. LePage looked startled. She looked at each face in the small circle as they waited for her to answer. Tears formed in her eyes then fell down across her cheeks. "You're right. We've been working on this technology for a long time. The main work has been done not far from here. Just down the road at Los Alamos."

No one said anything. They could see the struggle going on in Dr. LePage. She wiped her eyes then continued. "It began by accident. Some noticed that the effects of radiation fallout were more tolerated by infants. We traced the reason to the blood. We knew there was something there. Enoch's sudden appearance only confirmed that we were on the right track and very close to the discovery."

Denise felt a knot form in the pit of her stomach. "How many babies have you sacrificed in the process?"

Dr. LePage took a deep breath, tears forming again in her eyes. "Too many," she stammered, then burst into tears.

Father walked over to her and put his arms around her. She melted into his chest as she continued to sob.

"Angela, what you have done has taken a lot of courage. Not one of us in this group condemns you. You are a scientist and we understand any scientist's dedication to his or her work. We also understand that work can sometimes make great demands on us. I praise God you finally listened to your heart."

"Hear, hear," Denise added.

The Chief nodded and smiled. "Amen."

Angela sniffled, wiping her eyes. "Thank you. You don't know how much I appreciate every one of you."

The Chief started to speak but suddenly stopped. He put his finger to his mouth to invoke silence. One by one the group acknowledged the sound. It was the helicopter returning. Everyone remained still until, once again, the sound faded in the distance. The Chief looked at Father. "They know something. That one was closer than the last. They're probably running a crisscross search pattern over the area looking for us."

Denise frowned. "Darn it. That means they got to Bill."

"Don't blame Bill," Angela said, still wiping her eyes. "You don't know these people. They are determined and they will let nothing stand in their way. I can assure you that they would threaten or even torture Bill if they thought he knew anything." She looked up at Susie. "You brother is proof of that. Every one of those men who first saw what was in the cavern are all dead."

"It was the same in my day," Enoch added. "It saddens me to think that man has not changed in all these years of time. The thirst for power and immortality drives men to become savages. Nothing stops men like that except Elwa. If it continues, I am afraid that your people will come to the same end as mine."

Father looked at the old chief. It was all starting to fall in place now. "Enoch is here as a witness."

Denise looked at Father then the old Chief, waiting for an explanation. "A witness for what?"

"When Father had the dream," the Chief explained, "it was the Lord revealing to him the magnitude of the problem. Long ago, during the time of Enoch, mankind had become so depraved that God destroyed the earth with water to remove the evil. The number of babies slaughtered for the blood enzyme must have been outrageous."

Enoch nodded his head. "It was terrible. We became a society

193

of madmen. I saw babies sold at auction to the highest bidder just so the blood of that infant could be sacrificed for the enzyme."

"When men become so depraved that innocent life means nothing," the Chief continued, "the God of life is motivated to act. The extent of the depravity and evil was symbolized in Father's dream by the black cloud. When Atlantis sank beneath the waves, the black cloud vanished. But, it reappeared, in the dream, over the state of New Mexico. To God, the same evil and depravity was beginning again."

"In Los Alamos," Denise inserted.

"Exactly," the old chief nodded. "What the scientists were doing there was unleashing the same madness that had inflicted Enoch's people." He pointed to Enoch. "He is here as a witness to that madness and as a warning from God that if we continue in this research, this country is doomed."

A silence covered the small group as each one thought of what they had become a part of. They knew the old Indian was right. They were all part of a divine appointment. The thought seemed to empower Denise.

"Let me get this right." She looked at the Chief. "You're saying that God knew this was going to happen at Los Alamos so he took Enoch thousands of years ago, put him in a time capsule, and dropped him off just a few miles from Los Alamos just so that he would be found exactly at this time?"

The Chief smiled. "That's exactly right. But, not just so that he would be found, but so that he would be a witness against the depravity."

"That is so unbelievable."

"But they didn't listen!" Angela exclaimed. "They're out there right now looking for Enoch because they think he will help them finish the research."

The Chief shrugged his shoulders. "It doesn't matter. He has accomplished his mission."

Angela shook her head. "What do you mean? Nobody out there gives a rip about the babies or about Enoch. All they want is the knowledge. If no one listens to his message then how can his mission be finished?"

"Because *we* have heard his message."

Angela looked at Father, her face showing her concern. "I don't understand. What can we do?"

"It's not what we can do. It's what God can do through us. He's already used you in a tremendous way. He spoke to your heart and you responded. We have all done the same. God doesn't need a lot of people, just a few who are committed." Father made a small circle with his hands. "He has that here in this small group."

"But even with our commitment, we are no match for what's out there. They'll kill every one of us in a heartbeat if they deem it necessary."

"To the rational mind that seems possible and even probable, but the rational mind always leaves out one important factor."

"What's that?"

"God. You see, Angela, we are all here, not by accident but by design. Look around you. Everything and everybody that has been needed has been supplied. I have no idea how this is going to end, but I wouldn't miss it for the world."

The Chief laughed. "Me neither."

Their conversation was suddenly interrupted by a deep cough from Enoch. Susie grabbed him by the arm and slowly helped him over to a large rock. She could see he was getting weaker. She waited until the coughing subsided then found one of the canteens and poured him a cup of water. She looked at the Chief as she handed Enoch the cup.

Father intercepted the look. He turned to the old medicine man. "Will he make it?"

"I don't know. He's getting weaker by the hour. According to Susie we still have a day and a half of travel. And that's if we don't have to dodge the feds. They know we're out here somewhere and they'll keep looking until they find us. I just hope we get to the sacred burial site first." The Chief looked out toward the river. "It's getting dark and if I'm right they'll still continue to search for us using infrared or heat scanning. We should be safe under this much rock, but everyone needs to be very careful. They know it's hot out here and they're smart enough to figure that we most likely will move during the cooler parts of the day. They are also aware that Enoch, without the blood, will become a big burden for us. We just need to use extreme caution and let the Lord protect us."

Father smiled. "He will."

"He always has and I'm sure this will be no different." The Chief looked over at Enoch. He was still leaning up against the big boulder. Susie was over at the far end of the overhang, tending to the horses. "I'm going to get some food together for us. Why don't you check on Enoch?"

"I was thinking the same thing." Father turned and walked over to Enoch and sat down across from him. "How's it going?"

Enoch looked up and smiled. "It's a strange feeling knowing that in a few days I will cease to exist. Especially for someone who has lived as long as I have."

Father laughed. "You certainly win the top prize as far as I'm concerned."

Enoch started to laugh but it turned into more coughing. Father could tell that the huge man was having trouble breathing. Enoch finally brought the coughing under control then took another drink of water. As he sat the cup down, he cleared his throat.

"Father, I was wondering. What does your Bible say happened after the great flood?"

"It says that Elwa started all over again with Noah's descendants."

"Can you tell me more about that? I would really like to know."

"Sure, I'd love to."

CHAPTER NINE

The Sacred Burial Ground

Enoch sat listening intently to every word Father shared. It was a Biblical history lesson. Father started with Noah and recounted the journey of man from that time to the time of Abraham and how God or Elwa had made a covenant with him. Enoch only listened until Father's story recounted the exodus of God's people from Egypt.

"There was a time when I was a small child that my father recounted the mighty deeds of Elwa. Many times in my life I have felt His invisible presence but I have never seen such deeds as you and my father described."

Father nodded. "I would have believed that. The Bible says that you were translated through faith. Faith is a very powerful thing to God. It means we trust Him and act accordingly even though we don't see Him. Faith is no longer faith when we can see the things we're believing for."

Their conversation was suddenly interrupted by the calling of the Chief. "Hey, Father. You guys come on. Chow's ready."

Father turned toward the Chief and raised his arm, signaling that he had heard. He turned back to Enoch. "You feel like getting something to eat?"

"Yes, I do. In fact, listening to your story has actually made me feel better."

Father smiled. "I assure you the story gets much better. Elwa

198

actually becomes a man and walks on this earth."

"Why?"

A huge smile came to Father's face. "Because He loves us so much."

"Is He still here?"

Father paused for a moment. He stood up and pointed to his heart. "Yes, right here."

Again Enoch's huge brow looked like a crinkled piece of parchment. "I don't understand."

"Let's go eat and I'll tell you the greatest story ever told."

Enoch stood and brushed the sand off of his clothing. "If what you say is true then Modasavah was correct."

"Who is Modasavah?"

"He is what I believe you call a seer. He was also a very close follower of Elwa. He helped me prepare for my journey. He said that one day Elwa would come to earth as a man and take back what Anakicrey had stolen."

"And Anakicrey is?"

"Anakicrey means dark angel. He was the angel assigned by Elwa to protect and guide man. But Anakicrey became jealous of man. That jealousy spread to many of the other Anaki, and together, they formulated a plot. They worked with man until they gained man's complete confidence. Anakicrey then used that confidence to steal all that Elwa had given to man."

"The Bible says that man came to the point where he trusted Anakicrey more than Elwa."

Enoch's eyes grew wide. "The Bible says that?"

Father nodded. "It says that man handed over everything to the dark angel and Anakicrey became the ruler of this earth."

"Oh, that is very true. Everyone on Atlantis knew that Anakicrey was the true ruler of the island. Only what you call the "high government officers" ever got to see him but the decrees with his name on them were everywhere around the city."

"It's getting cold, you guys," they heard the old Chief yell.

Father didn't even turn. He just raised his arm again to inform his friend that he understood. What Enoch was sharing was much more fulfilling than food. "So you're saying that an angel was in charge of Atlantis?"

"Most certainly. But not just Atlantis, Anakicrey was ruler of the entire earth."

"So that is why your flight from Atlantis was so covert?"

Enoch frowned. "Explain covert."

Father motioned with his hands. "You know, done in secret; done without anybody knowing it."

"Everything on Atlantis concerning Elwa was done in secret. Noah by the river was the only open proponent of Elwa that I knew of, but everyone considered him insane. To anyone else it would have been a death sentence. A decree had been issued many years before I was born that the name of Elwa could not be spoken."

"Let me guess. This decree came from Anakicrey."

"Of course."

"So, how many followers of Elwa were there?"

"At the time I left Atlantis I was aware of only five. There were more followers before the babies started being killed. Once that became such an atrocity many came out of their silence and became vocal in their protests. They were arrested and were never heard from again. I was very young when that happened. The five I knew were very dedicated but kept silent in their belief."

Father smiled, remembering the story of Noah. "Everyone except Noah of the river?"

"That's right, but he was different. Everyone considered him so insane that no one paid him any attention. I don't think Anakicrey

200

considered him much of a threat. In fact, Noah and his family became what your people call a novelty. He lived by a river but he was building a boat that was so large that the nearest water that would float such a craft was 300 stegels away.

"Stegels?"

"A stegel is a unit of measuring distance. It's a little larger than your mile."

"Guys, I hate to butt in but I must be missing one heck of a conversation."

Father turned and smiled at the Chief. "You're right. What Enoch has been sharing is very fascinating."

The Chief motioned with his hand. "Well, let's go eat then we can all hear." He laughed. "Nothing like a good meal of beans and cornbread followed by conversation and fellowship around a campfire."

They all laughed and walked over to where the others were already eating. The Chief served Enoch and Father then dished himself a plate of the hot beans. He walked over to a rock next to Susie and sat down. He took a bite of the cornbread. "Well, it's not Cracker Barrel, but it'll keep us alive."

"It's actually very good," Denise offered. "Out here all the rules change. I'm just glad we've got something to eat."

The Chief nodded as he continued to chew a spoonful of beans. He turned and looked at Susie. "We have Gabe's foresight to thank for that."

Susie barely moved her head to acknowledge the Chief's words. Her face clearly revealed the struggle that was going on in her heart. She looked up at Enoch. She understood that this man represented a wonderful opportunity for mankind. But nothing he had to offer was worth the life of her brother.

Enoch seemed to sense her pain. "I am sorry, Susie. If I could have, I would have stopped them."

Susie's face inked out a slight grin. "I know. Enoch, I don't blame you at all. In fact, I admire you for standing your ground against killing any more babies, even to the point of dying for that stand. My people used to be that way. Too many of my people have adapted to the ways of the white man."

"But that can change," the old Chief inserted. "I see a time when the Great Spirit will give the red man back his dignity, and we will be like a huge fire in the darkest of night." He took Susie's arm. "Before that can happen we must learn to forgive. As hard and as painful as it is, vengeance belongs to the Great Spirit, not to us. The white man has allowed evil to control his mind for so long that he has become a slave and doesn't even know it. The red race is a simple people and that simplicity is the key. A simple story around a campfire with family is more important to us than having two hundred channels on a television. Integrity is more important to us than robbing the planet of all it has to offer." He looked at Enoch. "In the time of the flood when the earth was mad with evil, God found a man you call Noah by the river. Why? Because he had not gone the way of madness like the world. He had held on to his integrity, and one day God honored it. It is the same with the red man. If we will hang onto our integrity, one day the Great One will honor us." He turned and looked at Susie. "We must not, however, give into hatred and unforgiveness. Like a thief it will rob us of our destiny. God has given the white man revelation of Himself, but the white man's arrogance and greed has kept him from fully understanding what a treasure he really has been given. He proves that in the way he lives. One day in the midst of this madness, God will again look for a Noah. I believe with all my heart that it will be the red man. We were once a proud and noble people, but many of us have now become poor and dejected, a people with no honor and no home. One day the Great Spirit will use the humble to confound the wise and like a phoenix, we will rise from the ashes of despair." The Chief sat his plate on the ground next to him and took Susie's arm. "And Susie there's something that I must tell you."

Susie looked at the old man with respect and attention.

"Gabe and I have talked very much about the Great Spirit and about the God-man Jesus Christ."

Susie frowned and shook her head.

"I know you don't want to hear this because you associate Jesus with the white man and his religion. But Gabe finally saw what you refuse to see and became a blood brother to Jesus. I know you didn't know that because he told me not to tell you. But, Gabe is a part of everything that is happening to us now because he was sensitive to the Voice of the Spirit. All these supplies that you think he had stored for some great world shortage problem, they were for us. I talked with Gabe when he started storing this stuff. He didn't have a clue why or what for, and I didn't either, but he was obedient to the Voice. I believe that if he had never made covenant with Jesus Christ, *we* would not be here now. We would not have had the supplies needed for the journey. Thousands of years ago God sent Enoch here to *this* time and space to warn mankind. God will honor him for his obedience. God will do the same for Gabe. The Great Spirit is beginning to honor the integrity of the red man. I know that if you will let go of your unforgiveness, the Great Spirit will honor you also."

"What he is saying is very true," Father added. "This world does not belong to the white man or to the red man or to the black man. God does not look at a man's skin; He looks at the man's heart. Jesus said the pure in heart would see God. What the Chief is saying is right on. Gabe, in essence, gave his life for us. If it hadn't been for him, we would know nothing about what was going on with Enoch, and the government might have made good on their plans. We know now this would have eventually destroyed mankind just like it did Atlantis. Gabe was in that cavern because God put Gabe in that cavern. It cost him his life but how many others will live because of his sacrifice?"

Susie smiled and put her other hand on top of the Chief's. "My anger has made me blind. I knew something had happened to Gabe since he started spending so much time with you. He was at peace. The anger that he had carried for so long was replaced with a joy for life. It showed, and I guess I was jealous of that. I wanted him to stay angry like me."

Enoch had been listening to every word. He waited until he thought Susie was finished then turned to Father. "You said that Elwa had become man. Is this Jesus Christ, which the Chief spoke of, that man?"

"Yes," Father answered. "Everything I shared with you before about Noah, Abraham, and Moses was God moving on man to prepare for a time when God would become man. They were first called Israel, but later became known as the Jews."

The small group sat around the campfire, listening as Father shared with Enoch about Jesus' birth, life, passion, death and resurrection.

The old Chief stopped him long enough to rustle up a couple more sticks of driftwood for the fire. Sparks rose up into the air as the fresh wood hit the hot coals. "I sure am glad the Lord had this wood stored up for us under here."

"Amen to that," Father laughed, then continued with his story. He shared about Pentecost and how the Holy Spirit was given to anyone who would make covenant with God through the shed Blood of His Son, Jesus. He was about to tell about St. Paul's

The Visitor

conversion on the road to Damascus when Enoch interrupted him.

"What about me?"

Father frowned. "I don't understand."

"What if I make a covenant with Elwa? Will He give me His Holy Spirit?"

Father laughed at the magnitude of what was happening. Here was a man from the beginning of time, hearing the Gospel and wanting to receive Jesus as Lord. "Enoch, you make me feel like a powerful preacher. I wish everyone would receive my words as readily as you have."

Enoch shook his head. "Not just your words. They have only been an explanation. The first time we met in the mine, when I shook your hand," he turned to the Chief "and yours, too, I felt something go through me. It reminded me of Elwa. I now know what that was." Enoch pointed with his hand. "A while ago when we were over there, you said Elwa was in your chest. I now understand. When a covenant is made with Elwa, His Spirit comes into that person. You and the Chief have done that, and I can feel it when I touch both of you."

"But you didn't feel it in any of us?" Denise asked.

Enoch again shook his head. "Of all the people I have been exposed to, these two men here are the only ones. There was such a peace when I shook hands with them that I didn't want to let go."

The Chief laughed. "I remember that now. I remember thinking, 'What's going on here?'"

"Yeah, I remember it, too," Father agreed. "I had some weird thoughts go through my mind, but they were all related to old science fiction movies I had seen."

"You mean like he was trying to read our thoughts or steal our soul?" Chief laughed.

"Exactly," Father laughed.

205

Enoch joined the small group in laughter. "I'm sorry for that, but it was just such a warm and peaceful presence that I didn't want to release it. It reminded me of another time. I guess I felt like I was home."

Father smiled. "That Presence we have in us you can have in you."

Enoch nodded. "I would like that."

"Then simply pray this prayer with me. 'Lord Jesus.'"

"Lord Jesus," Enoch repeated.

"I thank you for dying for me. Because of my sinful nature I have missed the mark of perfection and I repent of that nature. Come into to me and be my Lord and Savior."

Father paused after each line, allowing Enoch the time to repeat the prayer. He could hear the others around him also repeating the prayer, even Susie. The Chief looked at him and winked. He nodded his head in approval as Father finished.

"Oh my," Angela yelped.

Father turned and looked at her. Tears were streaming down her face.

"I felt something right here," she said softly through the tears, pointing to her stomach. She continued to cry, covering her stomach with her hands. "I prayed along with you, also and it's like a...a...wonderful freedom."

"That's the love of the Father, Angela." Father explained. "You now have a covenant with the Him. His Spirit is now inside of you."

"I, too, can feel what she is describing," Enoch added excitedly. "It's like the empty feeling I had inside of me is now filled."

"But, I prayed it too," Susie objected. "And I didn't feel anything."

"Me either," Denise frowned.

Father laughed. "Ladies, that's okay. Some people feel something and some don't, but everyone who asks receives. If you prayed the prayer from the heart, you received." Father quickly looked back at Angela. "The Lord just told me that you've been carrying some very heavy baggage since a young age."

Angela again began to sob as she nodded her head. The others waited as she slowly gained enough composure to speak.

"When I was seventeen, I became pregnant. I knew I was too young and immature to raise a child so I had an abortion. My parents were very angry and unsupportive. My boyfriend and his sister helped me through the ordeal. The choice to abort that baby was one of the most terrible mistakes I have ever made. Not a day goes by that I don't think of that child." She looked at Enoch. "Every time we sacrificed one of the babies for the experiment I thought of my own baby. I guess that is why I could not stand it any longer." She looked back at Father. "You are right. At times it has almost been unbearable. It has been like a two ton weight on my shoulders."

The Chief slapped his knee. "My dear, you have been an instrument in the Lord's hand and now He has rewarded you for your obedience."

"Chief's right," Father added. "This whole thing could not have happened without you. It always amazes me how the Lord works things out. Your position on that government team was planned from the very beginning by God. He knew that one day the capsule would be found in the cavern, and He knew He had to protect its contents. So, He placed a young lady on the team whose heart was broken and needed mending. Your broken heart caused you to be sensitive to His promptings. You helping Enoch gain his freedom has resulted in you gaining your own. The sensation you felt was the Holy Spirit healing that area of your heart. The shame and guilt brought on by the abortion you had has now been removed."

"How long ago was that, Angela?" Denise asked.

"That was almost fifteen years ago. I just wish I knew whether it was a boy or girl."

"You have the Holy Spirit in you now," Father instructed. "Ask Him what sex it is. He'll tell you, and when He does give the child a name."

"Why's that?" Angela frowned.

"Because that soul is alive and one day you'll see it again. When you do it would be nice to call him or her by name."

Angela smiled. "Yes, I see what you mean."

The Chief got up and looked out beyond the light of the campfire. He carefully walked toward the opening of the outcropping. The others watched as he stood for a while looking out into the darkness. He then turned and walked back to the group. A huge smile covered his face.

"What's going on, Chief?" Father asked as the chief rejoined the group.

"Have you noticed that we have not heard the helicopters?"

Denise frowned. "But it's dark."

"That doesn't matter to the military. They fly just as well at night. They do, however, have trouble flying in storms."

Denise looked out toward the river, trying to see into the darkness. "What storm?"

"There's one coming."

"How do you know?"

The old chief smiled. "I can smell it. Can't you?"

Denise tilted her head back and put her nose up in the air. She took a deep breath then waited. "I don't smell anything but smoke."

The group laughed. They, too, had been trying to smell some

sign of the storm. None had succeeded.

Susie squinted her eyes and looked at the old Chief. She knew that he knew what he was talking about. "Odd time for a storm; they're extremely rare this time of year."

The Chief nodded. "I was thinking the same thing. It'll be here before morning. If it lasts very long it could make our journey more difficult."

"I'll say," Susie agreed, "it doesn't take much to turn this little river into a big one. If you haven't noticed we are actually traveling in the river bed. When the river gets up the nearest trail is a hundred feet straight up."

"Above the rim of the canyon, you mean?" Denise asked.

Susie nodded sternly.

Father stood up. "We must not worry. The Lord will get us safely to our destination. If there is a storm it is for a reason. I suggest we all hit the sack so we'll be rested and ready to go at sunrise. Good-night, everyone."

The others stood up, wished each other good-night, then carefully made their way to their bedrolls.

Father had positioned his sleeping bag just inside the circle of light provided by the campfire. He was in the process of spreading out the bed roll when he heard a cough behind him.

"Excuse me, Father. Could I talk to you for a few minutes?"

Father turned to see Denise standing over him. He smiled and patted the sleeping bag next to him. "Have a seat."

Denise accepted the invitation and quickly sat down. Father looked at her and waited for her to speak.

"I was wondering." She looked around at the others who were in various stages of preparing their own bedrolls. "Everyone here has a reason or purpose for being here." She looked Father in the eyes. "What is mine?"

Father reached up and scratched the side of his head as he thought about her question. "Denise, I don't know. You prayed with us tonight, didn't you?"

"Yes, I did, but was that why I'm here?"

"Someday that prayer will be the most important thing you will have ever done. If the Lord had to get you here to save you, then to me, that is enough reason. But, I think there's more."

Denise waited for him to continue. "And...," she finally said, gesturing with her hands for him to share his thoughts.

Father shook his head. "Denise, really, I don't know. You must be patient, for in time you will know. I now understand why Angela is here. Before tonight I didn't. God has a purpose for each of us, and sooner or later you will have your answer."

Denise smiled then stood up. Father stood with her.

"If you figure out anything you will tell me, won't you?"

Father laughed. "Always the reporter! Yes, I will tell you."

"Thanks."

"You're welcome."

Denise smiled then turned and walked back to her bed roll. Father watched until she seemed settled in then he looked around at the others. All were in their sleeping bags except for Enoch. He was sitting on his bed roll with his head facing up toward the rock ceiling. Father squinted his eyes in the dim light but still could not see well enough to determine if Enoch was all right. After about five minutes he finally decided that Enoch was okay so he knelt down and finished preparing his sleeping bag. He crawled on top of it and propped his head up with his hands. He stared at the dark ceiling above him, quietly praying for each of people in the group. Off in the distance he suddenly heard a clap of thunder. A smile came to his face as he thought of the old Chief's unique spirituality. Nature was important to him, but it was not a pantheistic god. Making Jesus the Lord of his life had not destroyed his relationship with God's creation, it had enhanced it. The Chief was proof that the red man could make Jesus Lord and not have to give up all the "old ways." The Great Spirit and the Holy Spirit were one and the same. The old Chief knew that, and he had helped Gabe to understand it also.

The fire had died down and now there was only darkness. Another clap of thunder sounded, but much closer than the first. He hoped the weather would not cause them delay. Enoch was losing strength by the hour and time was a valuable commodity. He shut his eyes and prayed for the Lord's protection and guidance.

"Father."

Father opened his eyes.

"Father," he heard again as he felt someone shake his shoulder.

The light was dim but he could still make out the outline of the Chief. "What is it?"

"It's Enoch. I think you ought to see this."

Father sat up and looked to where the Chief was pointing. Over to their right near the entrance to the outcropping was Enoch. He was standing, talking to a figure that appeared to glow.

"Who is that?" Father whispered.

The Chief continued to watch the two figures. "I don't know, but it's definitely not of this world."

Father looked around to see if any of the others were awake. The dawning light was getting brighter and it revealed that all the others were still sound asleep. Father turned back toward Enoch just in time to see the lighted figure disappear. They watched as Enoch turned and walked toward the river.

Father stood up and looked at the Chief. "Let's go talk to him."

The old Chief nodded and led the way out of the overhang. Enoch was kneeling down, washing his face in the river. He turned to look at them as they approached. His face glowed in the dim light of the dawn. He no longer looked sick and fragile. He looked twenty years younger. He smiled as he stood to greet the two men. Father was the first to speak.

"You are no longer dying."

Enoch smiled and nodded his head. "That is correct. The Spirit of Elwa has become my life. Thanks to you I am now *in* Christ Jesus."

Father looked at the Chief. "Then our journey is in vain."

Enoch grabbed Father's arm. Father staggered then caught himself.

"Whoa," he laughed. "The power of God is all over you."

Enoch quickly let go. "I'm sorry. You're right. What you call resurrection power is flowing through me. It is overwhelming to the human body."

"I'll say," Father laughed. "It felt like I had grabbed a hot electrical wire."

"I'll be more careful." He looked up at the dark sky. "Elwa is providing cover for us."

Father and the Chief looked up above the canyon rim. The clouds were dark, and they could see rain falling above the rim, but it was not raining on them.

"It's raining up there but not down here," the Chief said, still gazing at the area above the canyon.

Father looked at Enoch. "But, I don't understand. If you're not dying why do we need to continue our journey to the burial grounds?"

"Because it is the will of the Spirit," Enoch replied. "You were right. I have accomplished my mission, and now it is time for me to leave. I cannot stay. This is your world and your time. I am only a visitor with a message for the people of your time. I have delivered that message, and now I must go."

Father understood. "You are going to be taken again, but this time, to your reward."

Enoch smiled. "That is correct. I am out of place here. Elwa loves the people of this world so much that He sent me here as a warning. My world was destroyed long ago because of my people's depravity. The same thing will happen to your world if the hearts of your people do not change."

The Chief shook his head sadly. "Do you think we have a chance?"

"Yes, I do. You two, along with the others, have been called here because of your faithfulness and your clean hearts. Together you must convince the scientists to give up on their destruction of innocent life in order to recover the blood enzymes. It *must* stop. If they continue it will mean death for everyone."

"But Enoch," Father objected. "If you stayed we would be much more convincing in our message."

"I agree, but this is not my world. This is yours. It has been given to you to oversee. I asked Elwa to let me stay, but He said that man must learn to see with their hearts and not their eyes."

Father nodded. "With God it always boils down to faith. When we see it through our five senses it's not faith at all."

The three men were suddenly interrupted by the women who approached very carefully. They all seemed mesmerized by the glow of Enoch's face. Denise started to reach up and touch his skin but Father grabbed her hand. She frowned, then slowly looked at Father.

"What's wrong with his face? It's glowing."

"He is no longer dying. He has been reunited with God and the life of the Father is flowing out of him. It would not be wise to touch him. The anointing is so strong on him that touching him would overwhelm your flesh and probably cause you to faint."

"Look!" Susie exclaimed. "It's raining above the rim of the canyon but it's not raining down here." She looked at Father. "How is that possible?"

The others looked up to survey the strange happening. It was a weird sight. They could see it raining hard on the edge of the canyon rim, but not one drop made its way down to where they were.

"There are many looking for us," Enoch explained. "Elwa has clouded their vision in order to protect our journey. We must hurry, however. Now that it's light, we need to be moving on."

"But, why?" Angela objected. "If you're no longer sick, then why must we go on?"

"Because my time here with you is finished. I can no longer stay."

Angela did not understand. She looked at Father, her face filled with questions.

"Angela," Father shared, "God's mercy sent Enoch here to warn us of the impending doom of mankind if we continue with the research your team was working on. It has to stop. Enoch is a witness to the destruction that it will cause if it is allowed to continue. He has been obedient in delivering the message. Now he will be removed from the earth."

"But he can't go. They'll never believe us. I know those people and without him, we are wasting our time."

Father could see the concern in Angela's eyes. He was concerned, too. But, they had to put their trust in God and believe.

"We have to try," the Chief said, almost reading Father's thoughts. "We have to remember we are not in this alone."

Father looked at Susie. "Now that Enoch's health is not a concern, how long until the burial grounds?"

Susie thought for a second. "Ah, about eight hours. If we can stay in the saddle that long, we could be there by nightfall. But, that's a long hard ride." She looked toward the rim again. "If it continues raining like it is up there, this river bed could swell pretty rapidly and cut us off."

Enoch shook his head. "We won't have to worry about that. We will be safe all the way to the burial grounds."

"Then let's get going," the Chief directed. "We can eat on the trail. Susie, you get the horses, and we'll get our bed rolls together."

Susie turned and started toward the horses while the others walked back under the overhang. Each one quickly prepared their bedroll and within a few minutes they were all in the saddle.

It really was an amazing sight above them. It looked as if a protective bubble was over the entire canyon. With the amount of rain that was coming down above the rim there should have been water pouring down the canyon walls and crevices into the river. There was none.

Father wondered about the being of light that he and the Chief had seen talking to Enoch. He wondered who the being was. He kicked his horse and brought it up next to Enoch's.

"I was wondering. Who was the being you were conversing with early this morning?"

Enoch nodded, acknowledging the question. "That was Uriel, the Anaki that had warned me of Atlantis's destruction. He shared with me many things. He said that Anakicrey had been defeated but that his influence in the earth was still very strong. But he no longer had the rulership as he did during the time of Atlantis. You

215

have much more power to change the hearts of men than you realize. You and the Chief must encourage the others. The Lord Jesus has given you what you need."

Father smiled. He realized that this was the first time he had heard Enoch refer to Jesus as Lord. It made him realize, too, that Enoch knew what awaited them at the sacred burial grounds. He thought a long time about asking him, but decided to just wait and see. Looking up at the dark sky, he knew God was in control.

They traveled at a fairly good clip for almost two hours. No one objected when Susie stopped and suggested they take a rest. Father's legs felt like rubber. He walked around, exercising his muscles, stopping every few minutes to rub the backs of his legs.

"Kind of makes you appreciate what our early forefathers had to contend with," the Chief said as he approached Father.

Father laughed, bending over again to rub his tight muscles. "I was thinking the same thing. That is what you call grace in action. God knew I would never make it back then. That's why He let me be born at this time."

"Maybe you're just out of shape."

Father stood up, flexing his back. "There's no maybe about it."

The Chief pointed up at the dark sky. It was still raining above the rim but not as severely as before. "I've never seen anything like this out here. These storms never last this long, three to four hours at most."

Father surveyed the dark canopy above them. "God is giving us time to get Enoch to the sacred grounds. Without this the military would surely have found us and prevented us from reaching our destination. If I am right this will stay with us until we get to where we are going."

"Where are we going?"

Father looked at the Chief. "That's a good question. I asked Enoch about the lighted being we saw this morning. It was the angel Uriel. Enoch said he was the same angel that had warned him of Atlantis' fate. I am guessing that Enoch is somehow Uriel's responsibility." He looked to where Enoch was talking with Denise and Angela. "I am also guessing when we get to the burial grounds he will be translated."

"You mean taken into the realm of the Spirit?"

Father smiled. "Yes, exactly."

"But why wait and maybe be intercepted by the military? He could have just as easily been taken last night while we slept."

"I've asked myself the same question. Enoch is adamant about getting to the sacred burial grounds. I've wanted to ask him, but decided to just wait and be patient."

"I guess we have no choice."

Father bent over again stretching the muscles in his back. "You're right there."

As he straightened back up, they were joined by Denise.

"Chief, we were wondering if we might stop fairly soon and cook something? Everyone seems to be pretty hungry."

"Good idea," Father agreed, rubbing his stomach. "I could eat something myself."

The Chief shrugged his shoulders. "Sounds good to me. Tell Susie to find us a place."

Denise smiled. "She says there's a great spot just about a half mile ahead. She says we will soon be entering the area of the caves."

"Good," the old Chief answered, motioning with his hands. "Tell her to lead on."

They watched as she carried the message to the others then

217

climbed back on their horses. They waited until Susie gave the signal, then the tiny band formed a single line and started again along the edge of the river.

They rode for much longer than Father thought they should have to cover half a mile. Susie was right, however. He began to notice large cave-like openings in the face of the canyon. Some parts of the canyon wall had so many holes that it reminded him of red Swiss cheese. He wondered if this was part of the sacred burial grounds.

The sky had lightened somewhat but was still very overcast. Father Macon kept watching, waiting for Susie to signal that they had arrived at the right cave. He could tell from the actions of the others that they were anxious as well. Finally, after another thirty minutes he saw Susie throw up her hand. The group stopped and waited as Susie looked around. It was apparent that she was not quite sure of her location. She motioned for the others to stay put then kicked her horse into a gallop. She rode ahead for another fifty to sixty yards, then stopped and signaled for the group to come to her.

"I'm sorry," she apologized, when everyone had made their way to her. "It's been a few years since I've been here and this terrain has changed quite a bit in that time." She pointed to a large opening in the wall of the canyon. "There's the cave. We can stop here for a while to rest and rustle up something to eat."

Denise didn't need any more encouragement. She turned her horse and headed for the cave opening. The others quickly followed. As Father rode by Susie she grabbed his horse's reins and pulled him to a stop.

"I'm sorry it took so long getting here, but the good news is we are not very far from the sacred burial grounds. Another hour or so and we'll be there."

Father pointed to the many caves in the wall of the canyon. "Is this all part of the burial grounds?"

"No, not at all. My ancestors were very strict when it came to selecting burial sites. There were many things that had to be considered in that selection. Where we are going is no ordinary burial site. Very few of my people even know how to get there. You may be the first white man to ever have visited it."

Father nodded respectfully. His college degree was in Archaeology, and he understood completely what Susie was trying to tell him. He had worked on hundreds of burial sites and he appreciated each one's mystique and sanctity.

He looked at the sky. "Do you think we will make it to the sacred grounds before dark?"

"It's not my call, but I would not want to spend the night in the sacred cave. The spirits of the dead roam there and it would not be wise. I would suggest we stay here tonight, and then enter the sacred cave tomorrow morning."

"That sounds good to me. But, we'll have to see what Enoch wants to do. This is his call."

Susie smiled. "I understand."

By the time they joined the others, the old Chief already had a fire going. The driftwood was not as plentiful as before, but there was enough to get the food prepared. As they all sat around the fire eating, Susie shared what she had disclosed to Father about the location of the sacred grounds. As she finished, Father looked across the fire at Enoch.

"Enoch, this is your decision. We are all here for you and I believe that you are being divinely led. Do you want to go to the burial grounds today or wait until in the morning?"

"We are to stay here. This will be our last night together. Tomorrow we will depart for a time. Do not be afraid. Each one of you will be protected."

Father glanced at the Chief. He could tell that Enoch's words had stirred questions in the Chief's heart as well. They studied each other's face, wondering if it was appropriate to ask for more detail. The change in the old Chief's posture signaled that it would be more courteous to wait until later. Denise, however, was not ready to be as polite.

"What do you mean, we will be protected? From whom?"

"Elwa has used the weather to protect us from your military machines. Today, they could not fly. Tomorrow, they will find us."

Angela recoiled in fear and began to sob.

"Angela," Enoch commanded sternly, "do not fear. Put your trust in your Lord. He will protect you and see you safely home." He looked around the fire at each face. "Remember your mission. Your world is in a valley of decision. Do not allow *your* people to make the same mistake that *my* people did. Elwa is forgiving and long suffering but it will not last forever. The fact that I am here is a testimony to Elwa's great love for you and your people. Do whatever it takes to open their eyes. If they do not listen the punishment will be swift and thorough, I assure you."

The group sat quietly thinking about Enoch's words. Angela wiped her eyes with her fingers but Father could tell that she was still very worried. Denise put her arm around Angela then again looked at Enoch.

"Will they take you away from us?"

Enoch shook his head. "No."

"But you said this would be our last night together."

"Each of you has been a good friend to me, and I am very grateful. Sadly this will be our last night together. What happens to me is not important. I have only been a visitor here. My destiny has always been and is even now in the hands of Elwa. I am finally reaching the end of my path. Each of your paths, however, has now joined for a great purpose. Hear me. There lies the importance."

Denise had performed her share of interviews and she knew when one was finished. She knew Enoch was not going to share any more of what tomorrow held for the tiny group. They would just have to wait and see for themselves. Angela had stopped crying but Denise continued to offer her comfort. She could feel Angela's body quivering from the fear. It would be a long night, she thought, for Dr. LePage.

The overcast skies had caused darkness to overtake the cave much earlier than usual. Susie had taken care of the horses and the Chief had kept the fire going by searching the area for firewood. The floor of the cave was not nearly as smooth or flat as the overhang's had been, but everyone managed to find a spot for their bedroll within the circle of light provided by the fire. After unfolding his bedroll Father walked out of the cave and sat down on the edge of the river.

"Enoch was right. The clouds are breaking up."

Father turned to see the Chief looking up at the dimly lit sky. He, too, scanned the sky but it appeared to him as only shades of gray and black. There were no visible stars or moon. He made no comment.

The old Chief grunted as he sat down beside Father on the rocky ground. He picked up a rock and threw it out into the river.

"You think the task at hand is overwhelming?"

Father continued to stare out into the darkness where the rock had splashed. "It is not impossible but I think it will be very difficult."

The Chief picked up another rock. "I shouldn't have to tell you that with God all things are possible."

As the Chief flung the rock, Father turned and smiled. "It never hurts to remind me, especially when we're dealing with what seems to be an impossible mission."

"From what Enoch shared just now, it sounds as if you were right about him being translated. If the military finds us, I'm sure they will take his body and the world will never hear anything about this."

"If he's translated, there won't be a body. Except for the coufre and the metal plates there will be no evidence that he was even here."

"You mean God will kind of rapture him out of here?"

"If I'm right, yes."

"So it will be only our word against the government's."

Father nodded then picked up a rock and sailed it out into the darkness. He knew the Chief now understood the magnitude of their mission. They both sat quietly, occasionally throwing more rocks into the river.

The Chief finally put his hand on Father's shoulder. "Rex, we have to try."

"I know. But, it sure would have been a whole lot simpler if someone with a lot more political clout had been with us on this trip and heard the reason for Enoch being here."

The Chief laughed. "Come on, Rex. You've never seen God do it that way. He always uses the lowly to confound the wise. He will not fail us. He will give us what we need. But you know as well as I do that it will always boil down to faith. You never know. God may use this to not only stop Dr. LePage's team from developing the enzyme from the babies' blood; He may use it to stop abortion all together."

As the Chief finished speaking, the clouds parted allowing a momentary streak of moonlight to shoot through. Father turned and looked at the Chief.

"Was that an amen?"

The Chief laughed. "I believe it was."

They both sat in silence and watched as the clouds began to break up, allowing more of the moon to bathe them in its brightness. The river quickly picked up its glow and rays of light danced across the water's surface. As more of the stars made their appearance, both men knew that the storm was over. They had lost their blanket of protection. Tomorrow they would be open and exposed all the way to the sacred grounds. They would be truly in God's hands. Enoch had promised that God would see them all safely home. In their hearts, both Father and the Chief knew that was true. They were at peace.

Father picked up another stone and tossed it out into the river. This time he could also see the splash. He stood up and looked down at the Chief. "Tomorrow should be exciting."

The Chief stood up and brushed off his pants. He smiled and nodded his head. "I was thinking the same thing."

They walked back to the cave. Inside they found everyone already wrapped up in their sleeping bags except Denise. She was sitting on a rock by the fire, staring down into its glowing embers. She turned and looked at the two men as they approached. Father could see the concern in her eyes even in the dim light of the fire.

"Shouldn't young girls your age have a curfew?"

She smiled. "I couldn't sleep. My mind's going ninety to nothing with what-ifs."

Father and the Chief sat down on a large rock across the fire from her. They looked at her, waiting for her to continue. She pointed to Angela's sleeping bag.

"I feel so sorry for her. She is mentally exhausted. She knows that if the military finds us they will kill her. She's hoping Enoch is wrong."

"Enoch's not wrong. The storm has passed and the moon is shining like a noon-day sun. Tomorrow should be high skies. They will find us but they won't hurt us. Remember Enoch said we would all make it home safely. Besides, God needs us."

A large frown covered Denise's face. He could tell she did not understand.

"We've got a mission to accomplish when we get back and God's counting on you."

The frown on her face changed to a smile which quickly changed to a chuckle. "When I graduated from college with my degree in journalism, my Aunt May was so excited. She said she was going to ask the Lord to give me a 'headliner.'

"A headliner?" Father repeated.

"Yes. A headliner is a once in a life time story. Something that is so big that it makes the headlines in every newspaper. A story, she said, that would impact the world and make it a better place for humanity."

The Chief cleared his throat. "Sounds like your Aunt May knew the Lord?"

"Yes, she did. Every time the church door was open, she was there. She loved to sing. I went with her many times. Every time we went she encouraged me to give my heart to the Lord." Denise shook her head as if regretting her stubbornness. She looked at Father. "It just never felt right."

"I know," Father encouraged. "That's okay. She'll be glad to hear that you have now."

Denise took a deep breath. Tears rolled down her cheeks. She took the collar of her shirt and wiped them. She sniffled, then wiped her eyes. "I wish I could. She died two years ago."

"I'm sorry. It sounds like she thought a lot of you."

"Oh, she did. She was my biggest fan. She was always concerned that I was going to end up on an assignment in a third-world country and be kidnapped by some left-wing militia group. Now I may end up in an American military prison that nobody ever heard of for kidnapping a man who came from the island of Atlantis. Now if that doesn't sound like a fairy tale..."

Father laughed as he stood up. "Denise, you'll be all right, but we are all going to be too tired to function if we don't get some sleep." He pointed at the fire. "We're losing our light fast so let's all find our bedrolls."

"Good idea," the Chief yawned.

The three said their goodnights then found their sleeping bags. Father was right. The fire died quickly, leaving the cave engulfed in darkness. He prayed silently for all of them and especially for Angela and Denise. He wondered what the next day would bring. He would like to have talked for days with Enoch but it was not meant to be. The visitor from Atlantis was an amazing man. He loved God and God loved him. He had been an obedient messenger. Now if they could just get the people to believe his message.

CHAPTER TEN

The Reunion

Father was awake when the rays of the morning sun began to enter the cave. His night had not been restful. He had prayed each time he woke up until he dozed back off to sleep. What seemed so strange was that he felt the Lord encouraging him to pray for the military. Not the entire military, just the ones looking for his tiny group. He thought it was an odd request but he had been obedient. It was this obedience that had kept him awake to watch the morning light completely fill the cave.

The old Chief was the first one to stir. Father watched as he climbed out of his bedroll and made his way toward the cave entrance. The old Chief had commissioned himself "keeper of the fire" and Father knew he was headed outside to find more driftwood to use as fuel. No one else moved so Father put his hands behind his head and continued to pray.

Thirty minutes passed and Father began to become concerned about the Chief. Carefully he unzipped his sleeping bag and was in the task of crawling out when he heard the Chief returning. He sat watching as the Chief entered the cave with an armful of driftwood.

"Looks like your hunt was successful."

The old Chief dumped the wood into a pile beside the bed of ashes from the previous night's fire. He looked at Father and smiled. "This morning I was remembering my childhood. As a

226

small boy I would carry the wood in for my mother. Sometimes I would have to go a long ways to find some, but I never returned home empty handed. I thought I might break my record this morning."

Father stood up and stretched his back. "I was beginning to get a little worried. How far did you have to go?"

"I had to go a fair ways farther up the canyon. The river here comes almost up to the canyon wall which leaves very little opportunity for debris to get caught and lodge. Luckily, I found a spot where a huge limb had become caught when the river was at a higher level. The Lord is good."

"Amen to that," Father laughed.

"Amen to what?" Denise asked, rubbing her eyes as she approached.

"The Lord is good," Father repeated.

She shook her head as she finished as huge yawn. "My Aunt May would have been right at home with you guys. I believe that was her favorite saying."

"Smart woman," the Chief said as he knelt and began to place the wood for the fire. Father and Denise watched as he assembled the wood in just the right order then pulled a pack of matches from his jeans.

Denise looked at Father and winked. "I thought Indians always started fires by rubbing two sticks together."

The Chief looked up at her and grinned. "We do. Watch this." He took out a single match and struck it against one of the larger pieces of driftwood causing the flame to burst forth. "One stick against another; works every time."

Denise laughed. "You know we've lost something really valuable when the American Indian substitutes age-old tradition for the white man's technology."

"Especially when that substitution becomes epidemic," Susie added as she joined the group.

Denise could feel the coarseness of her comment but she forced a smile.

Susie looked down then back up, her scowl changed to a smile. "Sorry, I didn't mean to wake up on the wrong side of the bed. Struck a cord there, I guess."

"Good morning, Enoch," Father greeted cheerfully, causing the others to turn and watch as the tall visitor made his way to them.

Enoch didn't say anything as he joined them. He smiled and nodded to each one then turned and watched as Angela came from behind him to complete the tiny band. He greeted her with a huge smile as she stood next to him. She frowned as he stared at her.

"What?"

"This will be one of the happiest days of your life."

She continued to frown as she looked deep into his eyes. "Why? What's going to happen?"

Enoch looked across at Father. "Does not your Bible say that those who come to God must believe that He is and that He is the Rewarder of those that diligently seek Him?"

Father smiled. "Yes, it does. That's Hebrews 11:6, but who told you?"

"The Holy Spirit has been teaching me 'The Written Truth' as He calls it. I find it very fascinating." He turned back to Angela. "You were willing to risk your life to save me and the children. Your love for those children has caused God to grant you a great reward. He was moved by your love. Know that nothing this day will harm you."

Angela continued to wait, hoping there would be more of an explanation. Suddenly she squealed as a burst of excitement shot through her. "I know, I know."

Enoch silenced her by placing his finger up to his mouth. She was like a firecracker ready to explode. She began to jump up and down, laughing excitedly. The others looked at Enoch to explain. He only shook his head. They knew that what he had given her was just for her, but whatever it was had chased all fear and worry out of the heart of Dr. Angela LePage. They continued to watch as the laughter turned to tears, prompting her to run out of the cave. Father looked to Enoch for permission to go help. Again he shook his head.

"Leave her alone. She needs this time for herself. She has made a huge sacrifice that is very pleasing to God. In fact, all of you have. All will go well today. Do not be afraid."

Denise started to speak but again Enoch silenced her with a finger to his lips. "No more questions. Let's eat breakfast and be on our way. This is the day that the Lord has made."

Father smiled. He was amazed at Enoch's knowledge of the Word. He was quoting scripture and he didn't even have a Bible. What a blessing to hear the Voice of the Holy Spirit that plainly.

The Chief soon had the coffee ready. A breakfast of hot coffee and raisin bread wasn't much of a meal, but it would at least keep them going.

After eating his fill, Father received an okay from Enoch to take Angela some of the food. He had the Chief fill a cup, then cut off a large slice of the bread. He squinted as he walked out of the cave into the bright sunlight. It took a few seconds for his eyes to adjust, and he was able to spot Angela a few yards down the river bank. He walked up to her. She was sitting on a large rock, staring out toward the river. She turned and looked at him as he approached. He smiled as he offered her the cup and bread.

"You, okay?"

She reached out and took his offerings. "Wonderful." She started to take a bite of the bread but stopped and looked at Father. "You know, God is not anything like the world has Him pictured. I have never felt such love."

As she said the word, love, a flood of revelation poured into Father. A huge smile came to his face. "God is going to let you see your son today."

Angela's eyes grew wide with excitement. "He told you?"

Father nodded.

"I know. He told me, too. And He said it was a boy. Wow!" She looked again out across the river then quickly back at Father. "What will I say?"

"My advice is just let it happen. Don't worry."

She took a bite of the bread then again stared out into space. "Yeah, I'll just let it happen."

Father could see she was deep in thought so he turned and started back to the cave. He took a few steps then stopped and looked back toward Angela. "We'll be ready to go in a few minutes."

She didn't respond. He smiled as he watched her chew the mouthful of bread but continue undaunted in her stare. This was definitely a day that the Lord had made.

By the time Father made it back to the cave, Susie and the Chief had gotten the horses ready and the gear packed. They had even taken care of Angela's bedroll. The Chief was extinguishing the fire as Father approached.

"Everything okay?" he asked, stomping the last pile of embers.

"Everything's fine, but Angela won't need her horse for the rest of the journey."

The Chief looked at him and frowned. "Why? What's wrong?"

"She's so high she's going to float all the way."

The Chief laughed as he kicked dust from the cave floor over the dead coals. "As Aunt May would say, the Lord is good."

Susie, along with Denise and the Chief, led the horses out of the cave. Angela was kneeling by the river, washing out her coffee cup. She stood and handed the cup to the Chief who stored it in the gear bag on his horse. The air was thick with anticipation as each one of them mounted and began following Susie up the river's edge. Enoch and Father knew Angela's "reward" but the rest of the group were left to only imagine. The Chief thought about it but quickly decided he would find out when it was the right time. Susie's mind was occupied with trying to remember landmarks and trail markings. She had been to the sacred burial grounds several times but it had been a long time since her last visit and the trail was definitely unfamiliar and cold.

Denise couldn't get her imagination on anything other than Angela's reward. Her mind went through hundreds of scenarios, each one causing her to become more frustrated. She was most impressed with the radical change that had occurred in Angela. Last night Angela had been a basket case, full of fear and trepidation. This morning she was bubbling over with excitement. It was something Enoch had conveyed to her, but what? Did Father Macon know? Would he tell her if she asked him? She was about to gather enough courage to ask him when she saw Susie hold up her hand. She stopped with the others and waited. She watched as Susie looked around feverously then yelled, "Get up against the canyon wall. Get out of sight."

She was wondering what was going on when she heard it. Off in the distance she could hear the sound of a helicopter. The others heard it too and quickly brought their horses over against the wall of the canyon.

"Stay as still as you can," the Chief called.

There was no overhang and they were out in the wide open. If they stayed still they might blend in with the surrounding terrain. As the chopper came closer each one of them became as rigid as the rock wall beside them. Suddenly it passed over the canyon almost right above them. For a moment the sound of the rotors was harsh and invading, and then it was gone. Everyone stayed frozen until the sound was completely inaudible.

Denise was the first to speak. "Do you think they saw us?"

No one answered immediately. The Chief pulled his horse out away from the canyon and looked at the sky, listening more intently.

Shaking his head he looked at Father Macon. "I don't see how they could keep from seeing us. We stand out like a sore thumb down here." He looked at Susie. "How much longer to the sacred grounds?"

"We have maybe an hour, an hour and a half at the most."

"I say we pick up the tempo."

"There is no need to worry," Enoch interjected. "We will be okay. Go ahead, Susie. Lead on."

Susie looked at the Chief who nodded his agreement. With a motion of her arm she again led the single line of horses and riders toward their destination.

Each one of them wanted to believe Enoch but that did not keep their ears from being trained toward the sky. Father knew that as close as the chopper was above them there was no way a military eye would miss seeing the group. Still, the chopper did not return. God had blinded them before with clouds and rain, maybe now he had blinded them with the sun. Surely they would have circled or returned for a closer look if they had seen something. In his heart, however, he knew Enoch was correct and they would be discovered. He thought about Angela and the impact it would have on her to see the son that she had never seen. He laughed to himself as he thought of God's goodness and mercy. Before she was even a Christian, she had gotten the Creator's attention because of her tremendous love. She was willing to give her life to save the lives of those tiny babies and in the process she became the instrument of freedom for Enoch. No wonder God wanted to reward her by healing her deepest hurt. The irony of it all; the baby that she had not wanted would now become the greatest reward that God had to offer. She would get to witness that life rejected did not mean life denied. What she thought was a blob of flesh would now meet her face to face and she would know that God is a God of the living.

Father was so excited he wanted to shout. He asked God, if possible, to let him witness the reunion of Angela and her son. "In fact," he prayed softly, "let all of us witness it."

The sun had risen to where it was almost peeking over the lip of the canyon. It reminded Father how long they had been in the saddle. He kept looking for Susie to give them a break but she continued to press onward. He was about to suggest they stop for a rest when she raised her hand. Everyone stopped and she pointed to the canyon face just ahead of them. About midway up the wall was the painting of a huge thunderbird, its wings spread as if guarding this part of the river.

"We are close," she shouted. All of these caves from this point forward are burial sites but the one we are seeking is just up ahead."

As they continued on, the markings on the canyon walls were

like graffiti. Father studied each one carefully. Suddenly he pulled heavily on the reins. "Whoa." He sat looking at the panel before him. He turned toward the old Chief. "Hey, Chief, Enoch come here."

The entire group rode to where Father was. Susie came back to join them. On the wall in front of them were painted three figures, two dressed in white robes and one in black with horns coming out the sides of his head. It looked just like the Holy Ghost panel in Chaco Canyon. Under the figures was a line of what looked like letters. They were very odd shaped.

"Atlancho," Enoch read.

Father looked at him and frowned. "What?"

"It says, Atlancho. It means men from Atlantis."

Father looked at Susie. "Your father called them Olantcho. Remember the story he told us?"

Susie nodded excitedly. "The tale was true. I knew it was. I have heard the story since I was a child."

Father looked at Enoch. "But who put it there? Did the people who brought you stay long enough to paint that?"

Enoch thought for a moment then shook his head. "I don't know." He turned and looked at Susie.

"Come," she said, "there is much to see."

The archaeologist in Father began to rise. If the markings were authentic it meant they were pre-diluvian. The strange letters under the drawings reminded him of Egyptian hieroglyphics. He continued to study them until the rest of the group had passed him. He finally turned his horse in line behind the old Chief, watching for similar markings on the walls of the canyon.

Susie continued for about another two hundred yards then once again held up her hand. She waited until the others caught up with her then stepped down from her horse. She pointed to a small opening in the side of the canyon. "We will have to leave our horses here, the opening is too small."

Father looked to where she was pointing. "It was a huge flat wall with an opening about the size of a fifty-gallon barrel. Above the opening were more markings that resembled the ones they had just seen. Father stepped down from his horse and led it over to the opening, his eyes fixed on the strange lettering. The others soon joined him. He looked at Enoch as he pointed to the markings above the opening. "What does it say?"

"It says," he paused, "we are here."

Father waited for him to continue. "Is that all there is?" he asked when he realized that Enoch had finished the translation.

Enoch nodded. "That's all it says."

Denise moved in between Father and Enoch, looking first to the message then to Enoch. "What does it mean?"

Before Enoch could answer, Susie reached for the reins of Father's horse. "Let me get the horses settled and then you shall see."

Each one of the group handed Susie the reins to their horse then watched as she led all of the horses back down the river to a small overhang. When she had them secured, she walked back to the group.

"Inside we will find torches." She looked at the Chief and grinned. "You still have your fire sticks?"

The Chief patted his jeans pocket. "Right here."

"Good." She looked around at the group. "We will pass through an entrance tunnel then break out into a large room. Everyone stay close, and remember, my ancestors are buried here."

As soon as she finished speaking she ducked into the entrance. Father was next followed by the others. The way was narrow. They each had to bend over and move along by shuffling their feet. After about forty feet Father stood up and looked around. There was enough ambient light for Susie to find the torches that had been stored for such an occasion. She waited until the old Chief entered the room then held up the torch for him to ignite. As it came to life she handed it to Father then held another torch against it. As the second one burst into flame the room became very well illuminated. The entire group stood looking around.

The walls were covered with burial chambers that had been hewn out of the rock wall. Old bones, wooden pieces, clay pots, feathers, and various artifacts were everywhere.

"Wow!" Father exclaimed, "this is awesome."

"Come," Susie encouraged, "this way." She had lit another torch and handed it to Enoch. He waited for Denise and Angela, then fell in behind. The Chief went next with Father taking up the rear. All walked in reverent silence except for Father. He was so amazed by what he saw that he couldn't keep quiet.

"Chief, this is unbelievable. I've seen a lot of burial grounds but none that could hold a candle to this one."

The Chief nodded. It was something to behold. Every wall was covered with the burial places. Some of the pottery was finely crafted and ornate. Many of the skeletons were still covered with bits of leather or cloth.

Father thought how many museums would have given anything to have the artifacts from just one of the burial places, and they were as far along the wall as the torch would permit him to see.

The large tunnel that they had been following seemed to go on forever. Father calculated that they had walked for at least a hundred yards back into the earth. He was surprised when Susie's torch revealed that they had come to the end. As he caught up with her, he found them staring at a large wall with only two burial chambers. Between the burial places the wall was covered with writings.

"Atlancho," she said as she pointed to one of the skeletons. Father moved his torch closer to the skeleton. The skull was unlike any he had ever seen. The cranium was the same size and shape as Enoch's. He walked over to the other skeleton. It was the same. He turned and looked at Enoch who was busy studying the writings.

"These are members of your race."

Enoch nodded, still focused on the writings.

Susie moved her torch back over one of the skeletons. "My father says that these people were the parents of the Anasazi. The old ones say that they were the first ones buried here. They were considered gods because of their nature and their knowledge. The burial grounds were built here because of them."

Enoch had not taken his eyes off of the wall. Father knew he was studying the writings but the sadness on his face said a lot about their content.

"Enoch, what does it say?"

Enoch raised his torch to the top of the writings. He read: "With hope gone we seal this tomb. Only two of us remain. Behind this wall lie the remains of our comrades. We have gone to live with the people here. What the future holds for us is unsure. Our mission has failed and we are aliens in a strange and primitive land." Enoch moved his torch lower down the wall. "If you can read this, then you are Atlancho. To recover your brothers remove the large stone to the right of this message. Stand back from the wall. Our regret is not being here to welcome you. Know that our hearts long for our country of Atlantis."

Everyone stood in silence, trying to digest the message. They understood that the two sets of remains that lay before them were the ones who had written the message. They had sealed the wall and then departed to live with the people in the area. Apparently, when they died the people had brought their remains back here. History had proven that their influence in the area was tremendous. The achievements of the Anasazi remain both a mystery and a testimony even to modern man.

Father looked to the right of the markings at the stone that seemed to protrude from the wall. Anyone could tell that the stone had been worked or milled. It was smooth with about eighteen inches exposed to view. He looked at Enoch. "What do you think?"

"It is my opinion that the stone is an activator for some type of mechanism that opens the tomb. I think it must be activated but we need to get everyone back away from the wall."

Enoch handed his torch to the Chief. "I'll stay here with Father. You and Susie get the others back until we give the okay."

The Chief nodded then looked at Father. "Don't take any chances."

"Don't worry," Father answered. He waited until the Chief and the ladies had moved back from the wall about thirty feet then he looked at Enoch. "Why don't you do the honors?"

Father held the torch as Enoch reached up and took a grip on the stone. With one swift motion he pulled it completely out of the wall. They could hear what sounded like loud thumps coming from behind the wall. They hurriedly made their way back to the others and waited. The sounds seemed to increase and change in intensity until the wall suddenly blew out toward them. Denise screamed as the debris hurled toward them. They all put up their hands to protect their faces from the fragments of flying stone. The dust cloud caused them to cough and wipe their eyes.

"Look," Susie screamed, pointing to where the wall used to be.

Through the cloud they could see an opening in the wall.

Removing the stone had released some type of mechanism that had acted like an internal battering ram. They could still see the head of the ram hanging in the opening. It was illuminated by light coming forth from inside the tomb. Father was the first one to venture forward. He waved his hand in the air ahead of him to clear the dust. Carefully approaching the opening, he peered in.

"Unbelievable." He turned and motioned for the others. "You guys need to see this."

The rest of the group joined him at the opening then followed as he entered the tomb. It was huge. Gasps and expressions of awe echoed off the walls as each one surveyed the room's contents. Somehow the stone had not only released the ram but also plugs in the ceiling that allowed both air and light to enter. On both sides of the room were stone slabs on which lay a total of six bodies. They were enclosed in a suit much like a modern day space suit. Enoch walked over and looked down into the helmet of one of the bodies.

"Atlancho," he said softly.

The others walked around the room as if they were in the Smithsonian. Strange machines and metallic objects rested against the wall at different places. Two empty suits lay spread out on one corner of the room. The matching helmets sat neatly on the neck of each suit. Two large billboard-like murals were located on the walls of the tomb opposite each other. They had a white background like a large sheet of notebook paper and each mural was covered with more strange lettering. It was obvious that a large amount of time had been spent on their fabrication.

Father walked the entire room several times, taking in each piece of equipment and inspecting each body. The suits must have been outfitted with some type of environmental protection equipment. The visors on the helmets were translucent and afforded a clear view of the men inside. They seemed to be asleep.

Their bodies appeared to be perfectly preserved. Each one bore a resemblance to Enoch. They were most certainly his countrymen.

The group finally assembled around Enoch who stood studying one of the large murals. Everyone was anxious to know what it said. With reverence Enoch began to read.

"We came seeking Enoch the Tongue Master."

"What's a tongue master?" Father asked, quickly interrupting his reading.

"On Atlantis I was one who studied different languages. I am fluent in many different tongues, hence the name Tongue Master. That is one of the reasons I was selected for this mission. Who and what I would make contact with was unknown. But my understanding of different tongues made me more qualified to communicate with whoever found the coufre."

"That is how you picked up so easily on our language," Angela added. "I was amazed at how fast you learned."

Enoch put his attention back on the mural. He continued his reading. "We spent many days searching for the place they had hid him. Lord Anakicrey commanded us to not return without the Tongue Master. It was imperative that we not fail. After three full moons morale became very weak. Everyone realized that without a successful search we would never see our families again. During the time of the fourth full moon, six of the Atlancho seized the aircraft and attempted to leave their post and abandon the search. The craft crashed and killed all on board. We salvaged what we could from the wrecked craft and brought it here. Our hope was that others would come from Atlantis to rescue us. No one came."

Enoch took a deep breath and turned to face Father. "Elwa said they would try to stop me. Here is the proof."

"Anakicrey knew God saved you from Atlantis for a reason. Apparently he wasn't going to take any chances."

"Who is Anakicrey?" Denise asked.

Father looked at Enoch, waiting for him to answer. "Anakicrey," Enoch explained, "was the ruler of Atlantis. His name means dark angel."

"Today we call him the devil," Father added.

All stood silent, studying Father's comment. The Chief was the first to speak. "You know this is really beginning to make sense now. The Bible says that before the flood the thoughts of men's hearts were evil continually. If Satan was in charge of the place no wonder it was evil. The greed, the killing of the babies, the genetic altering, the deviant sexual practices with the Monstrobi, the entire place was exuding Satan's character. God was obligated to sink the place because there was no hope for change. Noah and his ark became the salvation of the genetic code for mankind and all the animals on the earth. But, Satan's nature never changes and God knew that Beelzebub would try the same diabolical thing again at a later time in history. So, God encouraged His followers through dreams and visions to use their technology and send a messenger or prophet to that future generation when Satan would once again make his move. The messenger would share his story and his people's plight and thus, prevent mankind from undergoing the same fate as Atlantis. Enoch is that messenger, but he really doesn't have a right to be here. This is God's mercy in action. The fact that we see him and we know his message is true obligates us to believe and to act accordingly. This is not Enoch's fight with Satan. This is ours, the people of *this* generation." He pointed around the room. "Here we see the magnitude of Satan's hatred for mankind. These bodies represent, once again, Satan's attempt to foil God's plan. Praise God, he failed in that attempt, but if we don't succeed in our proclaiming of the message then all of this will be for naught and he will have succeeded."

"I don't understand," Denise frowned, "How did Satan get control of Atlantis in the first place?"

"Adam gave it to him," Father replied. "When Adam fell, he gave the leadership of the earth over to Satan. If you think about it, the Chief is right. We really don't know a lot about what happened from the time of the Garden to the time of the Flood except that evil grew to critical mass and God had to stop it. We now know what caused that evil to become so powerful. Satan or Anakicrey, as Enoch calls him, was in charge. The more despicable and deviant that man becomes the better Satan likes it because man then takes on his nature. In essence, man is formed in *his* image and he becomes their god."

Denise shook her head in disgust. "That is really sickening, but what's to keep him from doing it again? I don't think I can carry this message by myself. This is a tremendous responsibility. I need some help."

Father understood her feeling of inadequacy. "The Lord has given it to you." He looked around at the group. "He's given it to all of us. When we accepted Jesus, He gave us His Holy Spirit and with Him we can get this job done. Look at Enoch. He was nearly dead when we started on this trip but now he is not only alive, he is full of the glory of God. It radiates from his face. The same Spirit that is in Enoch is in us. We have that same life and power."

"Amen," the old Chief agreed. "The responsibility is not ours, it belongs to the Lord. All we have to do is trust Him and be obedient to what He tells us."

The small group stood weighing the words of the Chief. Enoch walked across the room to the other mural. The others slowly followed. Every eye was focused on the strange letters as he began to read. "We have run out of supplies. It has been two cycles of the sun since we came here. No one has come to look for us. We now know that all hope of return to our country is lost. Our bodies have now become more accustomed to this new climate but it is causing us to age much faster. We have made contact with a primitive group of humans. They honor us highly. We have decided to join them for now. We have no choice. Our lives as Atlancho have come to an end. We are taking only what we can use in this new world. We have left markers, and if you are reading this, it means they were successful. Take our brothers back to the homeland. Our hearts go with you."

Denise groaned. "That is so sad."

"Being marooned is a sad fate for anyone," Father agreed. "They must have built the ram, sealed the entrance then left the cave."

"Then joined the natives and became a part of their history," Susie added. "The stories of Atlantis and the Atlancho have been with us all these years and we never realized it."

Father looked at the Chief. "We now know who the people are on the Holy Ghost panel in Chaco Canyon."

They were still studying the mural when they suddenly heard a great commotion behind them. Turning they saw men dressed in fatigues and carrying guns coming through the entrance opening. The first man through lowered a pistol toward the group.

"I'm Major John Walcott with the United States Rangers and all of you are under arrest for theft of government property. I must demand that all of you stand still and do not make any sudden moves."

As the major was speaking the other men formed a circle around the group. No one said anything. Father thought his heart was going to beat out of his chest.

"Trust the Lord," he heard the Chief whisper to the group.

The major took out a hand-held radio and put it up to his mouth. "Alpha Team chopper, this is Alpha Team leader. Come in."

The radio blared back. "Go ahead, Team Leader."

"We have Project Atlantis in tow. Find a place for pickup."

"Roger, Team Leader."

As the major put the radio away, Enoch stepped out from the group and started toward him. Every gun in the room clicked its readiness.

"I must warn you, sir," the major said loudly, "that I have orders to shoot anyone who puts this mission in jeopardy. I will not hesitate to follow that order. Please stop and step back with the others."

Enoch was now to the center of the room, but he showed no signs of following the major's commands.

The major raised his pistol and pointed it directly at Enoch. "Sir, this is my last warning. I will shoot you."

Suddenly a ray of bright light seemed to shoot out of the ceiling and engulf Enoch.

"Ahhh!" All the soldiers cried in unison, dropping their weapons and covering their eyes.

Father watched as each of the soldiers fell to their knees in severe agony, rubbing and tearing at their eyes.

The column of light around Enoch began to expand and increase in intensity. Father looked around at the others in the group. Every eye was trained on Enoch. As he turned back to the light, another being appeared in the light and stood by Enoch. Father watched as the figures embraced. Tears came to his eyes. He knew who the being was. It was the Lord. Enoch had finally come home. The anointing in the room was tremendous. Tears were flowing from everyone in the group. In his spirit Father heard the Lord say to Enoch, "Well done, my good and faithful servant."

Almost with one heart the entire group fell to their knees.

Suddenly through the tears, Father saw three other beings appear in the light. He could tell that two were male and one was a female.

Jesus looked at the small group on their knees. He bowed, then held out his hands toward them. Susie was the first one to get up, followed by the old Chief who slowly walked toward one of the male figures. Denise quickly followed their lead but went straight to the female figure. Angela was last. Slowly she pulled herself to her feet not taking her eyes off of the last male figure in the light. Father watched as she walked into the light and practically fell into his arms. Father could see his friends hugging and talking with the figures. The love radiating from the light was tremendous. Deep down in his heart he heard a familiar Voice. "My son, come to Me."

Father Macon slowly stood and walked toward the Lord. Enoch's face was all smiles. The closer Father got to the Lord the faster he walked. "My Lord," he cried as they embraced. The feeling was more than he had ever imagined. He knew that one day he would meet the Lord, and it would be wonderful. It was better than wonderful. He held on to the Lord for a long time. Finally he pulled away.

Jesus smiled and patted his shoulder. "You have done well."

Enoch nodded then held out his arms. "Thank you," he said, as they too, embraced. "I'll be waiting for you."

Father pulled away and looked at Jesus. The Lord knew his question.

"Not now. There is much to be done. If you love me, feed my sheep."

Father smiled. "Lord, there is none I love more."

Jesus smiled and nodded. "I know. Go in My Name and finish

the mission."

Father stood, looking at his Savior. He knew what the three apostles had felt on the Mount of Transfiguration. Like them, he did not want to leave.

Slowly the strength of the light began to diminish. "Good-bye, my friend," Enoch said, as Father took a step backwards.

Just as suddenly as it had come, the light was gone. The anointing in the room was still strong as everyone in the group looked around. Enoch was gone. The soldiers were still in various states of disarray. It was apparent that none of them could see. Father's heart went out to them. He walked over to the major and knelt down.

"Major, are you okay?"

"Yes, but I can't see. What happened? Where are my men?"

Father scanned the room. "Your men are fine."

He felt a hand on his shoulder. He turned and looked at the old Chief.

"Father, we need to get these men out of here as soon as possible."

Father turned back to the major. "Major, we have to get you and your men out of here. What do I need to do?"

The major reached down to his belt then looked back up toward Father. "Help me find my radio."

Father and the Chief looked around the room, scanning the floor.

"There it is," the Chief shouted, running over and picking up the radio. He took it back to the major and placed it in his hand.

The major quickly activated the radio. "Alpha Team chopper, this is Alpha team leader requesting your twenty."

The radio came alive. "Alpha Team leader, we are seventy-five yards downstream from the cave opening, in the river. I repeat, we are in the river."

Father looked at the Chief then at the others who had gathered around. "Each one of you take one of the soldiers and help him to the chopper. As soon as we get them loaded we'll come back and help the others."

The group quickly dispersed and each picked one of the soldiers. When everyone was ready, Father helped the major to his feet.

"Major, we are leading you and your men out of the cave to the chopper. Just hang on to my arm."

The major did as he was told and fastened himself to Father's arm. Father grabbed one of the torches from its resting place and headed toward the entrance. "Let's go," he shouted. "Everyone stay close."

It was very cumbersome and awkward but the group managed to get around the ram and out of the room. Father could see the tiny hole of light at the end of the tunnel. With a torch in one hand and the major attached to the other, he slowly led the group to the entrance.

"We're at the opening," he shouted. "Everybody needs to duck their heads."

The last forty feet was the roughest. It was hard enough for one person, but dragging a blinded soldier along raised the difficulty exponentially.

"Praise the Lord," Father shouted as he and the major met sunlight. Immediately he looked downstream. The chopper had found a wide enough spot in the canyon to set down but only if it landed in the river. Father led the major toward the chopper as the others followed directly behind.

The river was shallow where the chopper had landed, the water covering about a fourth of the landing gear. As they got to the chopper the co-pilot met Father at the bank. The rotors were spinning but they were remarkably quiet for a helicopter. The co-pilot removed his headset.

"What happened to them?"

"They can't see," Father shouted. "Help us get them onto the helicopter. There's still some left in the cave."

The co-pilot took the major and led him through the water to the chopper. Father turned and helped the others do the same. As soon as the men were safely on board, the small group headed back toward the cave.

It took them awhile to make their way to the tomb. They found the men huddled in different spots along the wall. Each one adopted one of the soldiers and carefully explained the situation. When they had assembled near the opening of the tomb, Father gave the order and they started once again out of the cave.

"Everyone okay?" Father shouted as they came to the narrow entrance hall.

Each one of the group responded so Father reminded everyone to duck down before entering the small tunnel. He was the first to make it out so he turned and waited on the others.

The Chief was last to exit and as he made contact with Father he said, "Rex, we need to hurry. Something in my spirit says we need to get out of here as quickly as possible."

Father nodded his head in agreement. "I know. I can feel it, too."

They hurried everyone along until once again they made contact with the co-pilot who helped them load the rest of the soldiers. The Chief helped each one of the group to board the chopper then turned to Father. "Wait just a minute."

Father watched as the Chief ran back to where Susie had tied the horses. As he brought them out of the overhang they were jumping and pulling against him because of the chopper. Once outside, he let go of the reins, raised his hands in the air and began yelling. The horses didn't need much encouragement. They took off down the river bank like a stampede. The Chief ran back to the chopper. Father reached out and pulled him on board then looked up front to the co-pilot.

"Let's get out of here."

The co-pilot made a salute motion with his hand then reached over and tapped the pilot on the side of the helmet. Immediately the engines began to increase and the chopper started to rise. Father looked out and watched the canyon wall as it seemed to move with them. As soon as they cleared the canyon a huge explosion sounded below them. The chopper moved away but not before it was pounded by the shock wave from the blast. It pitched back and forth momentarily then continued on away from the canyon. Looking back through the door opening Father could see a small mushroom-like cloud rising from where they had just been. He knew it was the sacred burial grounds. All proof of their journey was now gone. Father looked across the chopper at the old Chief. As their eyes met, he knew that they were both thinking the same thing. All that was left of this adventure was their testimony. The mission would have to be accomplished through their witness and by their faith. They no longer had any evidence to prove that Enoch ever existed.

Father looked around the interior of the helicopter. Angela had her arms around two of the soldiers giving them comfort. Susie was giving one of the soldiers a drink from a canteen. One of the young men was using Denise's shoulder as a support. She offered it gracefully. The Chief had his hand on two of the young soldiers and was praying for them in the Spirit. There was no longer any fear among any of them. Something not of this world had touched every one of their lives and he knew that none of them in that helicopter would ever be the same. He wondered how long their blindness would continue. He started to pray for them but felt a check in his spirit. He was suddenly interrupted by the young co-pilot.

"We will be landing shortly."

Father looked at the young man and nodded. He watched out through the door opening as the chopper began its decent. Suddenly he could see out over tents and portable buildings. He knew they were landing on the military's temporary base.

Closer to the ground the view changed. He could see many vehicles with their red lights flashing. The pilot had apparently called ahead and told them that emergency medical care was needed for the soldiers.

As soon as the chopper touched down it was surrounded by medical and military personnel. Father watched as each one of the soldiers was taken from the craft and placed on a gurney then wheeled to an ambulance. The ambulance would then speed away from the area.

As the last soldier was removed only the small group was left on board. They looked around at each other, each one anticipating their fate. A lone soldier appeared at the door opening.

"My name is General Sears. All of you are under house arrest until further notice. We have vehicles waiting which will take you to your quarters. We hope you will allow this transfer to take place as peaceably as possible."

Father recognized the general as the top official at the news briefing they had attended in Albuquerque. Father could tell from the look on the man's face that he was not happy about what had occurred. The general took a step backwards which allowed two other soldiers with rifles to appear at the opening.

"Ladies and gentlemen," one said sharply, "I demand that you disembark and come with us."

Father made the first move. He led the small band out of the chopper and onto the runway area. Another soldier stood directing each one of them to a separate car. As Father was led to the car he turned and looked toward the old Chief. The Chief nodded then smiled.

"Acts 16," he yelled.

The young soldier guarding the Chief gave him a stern look and shook his head. The meaning was clear: no more talking. The old Chief obeyed and was quickly placed into the back seat of the vehicle.

Father underwent the same fate. He was placed in the back seat of another vehicle, the military guard seated at his side. A wire frame separated him from the driver's seat. As soon as they were inside, the car pulled away. Neither of the young soldiers said a thing as they drove their prisoner toward the main part of the military base. Father prayed quietly in the Spirit, thinking about the Chief's words.

The ride was not very long. The driver pulled the vehicle to a stop in front of a long portable building. The guard opened his door, stepped out, and then slammed the door shut. Father waited. Suddenly his door opened.

"Please step out, sir," the young soldier in the front seat said.

Father obeyed, and was greeted again by the other guard. Together they walked to the door of the building.

Once inside, Father was taken to a room with no windows. An old cafeteria-type chair was the only item in the room. The guard ushered Father inside then closed the door. Father looked around at the four blank walls then took a seat in the chair. He sat with his eyes shut, praying. He smiled as he remembered Jesus' embrace. He had never experienced anything so wonderful. The smile on Enoch's face would forever be etched in his mind. After thousands of years Enoch finally was allowed to come home and he had been blessed to be part of the reunion party. Only his own reunion could be better.

His concentration was suddenly broken by the sound of the door knob.

CHAPTER ELEVEN

The Mission

Father opened his eyes to see a young officer enter the room. He was familiar with the bars on the young man's shoulders but was unfamiliar with the accompanying insignia. That was quickly explained as the young man closed the door and introduced himself.

"I am Captain Michael Jarvis with the United States JAG corp. And you are?"

"My name is Rex Anthony Macon."

"Are you aware, Mr. Macon, that you are in serious trouble?"

"For what?"

Father's question caught the soldier off guard. He laughed nervously. "What for? For theft of United States property, highly secret property."

"What secret property would that be?"

The captain cleared his throat, obviously frustrated with Father's response. "You know!"

Father shook his head. "I was on a horse back riding trip with my friends when your men barged into our lives and invaded our privacy. I didn't steal anything."

The interrogation was not going at all like the captain had planned.

Before he could speak again, Father said, "Your men found us and if something had been stolen then they would have surely recovered it. I would like to see what I am being accused of stealing."

The captain looked at Father. He exhaled his frustration and in a much calmer tone, he asked, "Mr. Macon, what do you do?"

Father smiled. "I am a Catholic priest from the Diocese of Little Rock, Arkansas."

The captain's jaw dropped and his eyes widened. He looked like a cat caught in headlights. He quickly turned and left the room.

Father sat quietly for a long time. He praised God for putting words in his mouth. He knew they had no proof because God had taken Enoch and destroyed the cave. To admit that Enoch was the secret governmental property would open Enoch and the Chaco Canyon cave contents to the public. He didn't think they were willing to do that. It was just like fighting demons, all they had was a bluff.

After about two hours, the door opened and Captain Jarvis re-entered. He was accompanied by General Sears who was carrying a telephone. The scowl on the general's face revealed his disgust for the priest sitting before him. He walked over to the wall, bent down and plugged the phone into an outlet, then turned and shoved it toward Father.

"Someone wants to talk to you."

Father took the phone, picked up the receiver and put it to his ear. "Hello."

"Anthony," the person said, "what have you gotten yourself into?"

Father quickly recognized the voice as that of the Bishop. Father could tell from his question and the tone of his voice that he was deeply concerned.

"Bishop, I am about the Lord's business."

There was a long silence. "Anthony, are you sure? General Sears says that you and a group of others are accused of stealing government property."

He looked up into the face of the general. "Bishop, that is not true. I assure you we have stolen nothing."

Again there was a long silence. "Anthony, do you want me to send you a lawyer?"

Father looked at Captain Jarvis, "Just a minute, Bishop." He put his hand over the receiver. "Captain, do I need a lawyer?"

The captain looked at the general, then back at Father. "I don't think so. All we want is cooperation."

Father still had his hand over the phone. "I will cooperate fully if it's the truth you want to hear. But, I will not play games."

The captain again looked to the general. The general nodded. He looked back at Father, "Fair enough."

Father put the phone back to his mouth. "Bishop, it's okay; don't worry. I am here on the Lord's business and I will be fine."

"Okay, Anthony, if you are sure. I trust your judgment. Let me know if I can help in any way. I'll be praying for you."

"Thank you, Bishop. I appreciate that; the more the better."

Father hung up the phone and handed it back to Captain Jarvis. The captain took it and walked over and set it down on the floor under the outlet. He turned back to Father Macon. "Would you like something to eat or drink?"

Father smiled. "That would be wonderful, thank you."

The captain opened the door and held it as the general and Father walked into the hallway. "This way," he said, motioning for them to follow.

He led them down to the end of the long hallway and into a large room that served as the cafeteria. The walls were lined with food and drink machines and there were many tables but they were all empty.

"Coffee or soda?" the captain asked, motioning with his hand for Father to sit down.

"Cola would be fine."

The captain nodded, "General, how about you?"

"Cola sounds good."

The general sat across the table from Father. The scowl was gone. Captain Jarvis returned with the soft drinks and put them down on the table. He sat next to Father. Each one of them silently sipped their sodas. After several minutes, Captain Jarvis finally turned to Father.

"What can you tell us about Enoch?"

"Enoch was a messenger from God."

"Oh, really?"

Father didn't like the tone of the captain's response. He looked across the table at the general. "Your scientists have been working on a longevity serum at Los Alamos and they have been sacrificing innocent life to gain the needed enzymes. To God that is an abomination. Enoch was sent here to warn us that if we didn't stop, our country would suffer the same fate as his. You know he was from Atlantis and he told you he was sent here in a *coufre,* as he called it. He didn't know why until he ran into us, then his mission became clear. He ran off because he did not want your scientists killing any more babies to keep him alive." He looked at the captain. "Do you have a Bible here?"

The captain's eyes grew big as he looked at the general. "Yeah, there should be one around here somewhere." He scooted his chair back, then got up and left the room.

Father looked across the room at the general. "I serve a God of truth and I will not lie. Everything I am saying is the truth. You have the rank and the power to change things. For the sake of this country, you must stop killing those babies."

The general only nodded.

"Here's one," the captain announced as he walked into the room and over to the table. He handed it to Father Macon. Father took the Bible and thumbed through it. He found the passage then pushed it back over to the captain, keeping his finger on the verse. "You read it."

The captain put his finger under Father's. "So all the days of Enoch were three hundred sixty-five years and Enoch walked with God and was not for God took him."

Father pulled the Bible back to him, thumbed through it again then pushed it back to the captain.

"By faith Enoch was taken away so that he did not see death, and was not found, because God had taken him. For before he was taken he had this testimony, that he pleased God." The captain looked up at Father and frowned. "You're saying that this Enoch," he tapped the Bible with his finger, "and our Enoch are the same?"

"Exactly."

"But that's impossible."

Father again pulled the Bible away. He searched through the pages then handed it back to the captain. "One more."

The captain again read where Father pointed. "Then the Lord saw that the wickedness of man was great in the earth and that every intent of the thoughts of his heart was only evil continuously. And the Lord was sorry that He had made man on the earth and He was grieved in His heart. So the Lord said, 'I will destroy man whom I have created from the face of the earth, both man and beast, creeping thing and birds of the air, for I am sorry that I have made them.'" He looked back up at Father.

"Ask the others," Father said, "they'll tell you the same thing." He looked over at the general. "Dr. LePage was one of yours, ask her."

"We have," the general replied. "None of them will talk. They say that they will talk but only if you give them permission."

Father pushed his chair back and stood up. "Let's go."

The captain stood up. "If what you say is true, then you won't mind us talking to each one of them individually?"

"Not at all."

The captain looked across at the general who again gave a nod of okay. He turned to Father and smiled. "They're down at the other end of the hall." He again led the way as they left the cafeteria and started down the long hallway.

"How are the soldiers?" Father asked as they walked together.

"I don't know; I haven't heard. Last report they were still suffering from shock and blindness."

Their journey brought them to a door which the captain opened. Inside, in a solitary chair sat the Chief. When he saw Father Macon a huge smile came to his face. He stood up. Father walked to him and they embraced. The old Chief patted Father on the back.

"Good to see you."

Father turned back toward the officers. "Chief, this is Captain Jarvis and General Sears."

"We've met."

The old Chief's tone conveyed that it was not a good meeting.

"I've told them about Enoch's mission and they don't believe me. Tell them everything you know."

The Chief walked back over to the chair, sat down, and folded his arms. "I will be glad to, but not in these surroundings. I will speak words of truth but I will not be interrogated like a criminal."

Father looked at the captain.

"I'll see to it. I'll call and find each of you a nice place to stay."

"Thank you."

The captain told the Chief to sit tight as they left the room. The three men then visited three more rooms, each room containing one of the group. The ladies were relieved to see Father and cried as he embraced them. He told each of them to share their story and to remember as much as they could when questioned. They agreed, but each of their conversations quickly changed to their experience while in the light. Father assured them that there would be plenty of time to share later.

Back in the hallway, the three men walked the long corridor again to an office adjacent to the cafeteria. The captain offered Father a chair while he walked behind a large desk and picked up the phone. The general took a seat across from Father.

"You know, Mr. Macon, I've known Dr. LePage for over two years and that woman we just now talked to was not Dr. LePage." His eyes narrowed. "It looks like her but it is not the same woman I knew."

"She is a very brave woman. She was the instrument God used for this whole thing. If it had not been for her courage, we would have never known Enoch's purpose for being here."

The captain had been trying to talk on the phone and listen to the men's conversation at the same time. As he hung the phone back on the receiver he looked at Father.

"What did they all mean by 'the light.'"

Father smiled, remembering the experience. "I don't mean to be lock jawed, but wait and let them tell you. It will be more convincing."

The captain laughed. "I guess I deserve that." He walked back around to the front of the desk. "Each of you has a room over at the officer's quarters. I have transportation coming to take each of you there. It will be here in just a few minutes. I ask that you not speak with each other, however, until after we have had the chance to interview each of you."

Father smiled. "I understand."

Father stood in the shower, praising God as the hot water bounced off of his chest. He had never had a shower feel so good. He laughed as he found himself thanking God for the man who invented the hot water heater.

Each of the group had been taken individually to eat then brought to the officer's quarters. They had been confined to their room with a sentry posted at each door. Father didn't mind. He looked forward to a good night's sleep in a soft bed. The thin bedrolls had not offered much padding against the hard rocky ground. It had been well worth it, however. He would do it a thousand times if each time it ended with the same experience. As he crawled into bed, he remembered the wonderful feeling of being embraced by the Lord. His prayer life would never be the same. He put his hands behind his head, allowing his mind to drift. None of the group would ever be the same. Even General Sears had noticed the profound change in Dr. LePage.

Suddenly Father is standing in a desert. He looks out over the rolling sand dunes. Standing on one of the distant dunes is the five year old Doris LePage. Slowly the desert begins to change and transform into a lush garden with copious vegetation and a huge water fall. The small girl begins to walk toward him and as she does she changes into Dr. Angela LePage. Two young girls come from another path in the garden and join Angela. They continue to walk toward Father hand in hand. As they reach him, he can see that they are filled with joy and exuberance. The young girls look up at him and smile as Angela softly speaks.

"Thank you for helping me."

Father smiles but says nothing. Angela and the two girls turn and start walking away. One of the small girls suddenly stops, turns, and runs back to Father.

"Mommy says the vampire is gone." She giggles, then turns and runs back to Angela.

Father opened his eyes. The light coming in from the window indicated that the day was well on its way. He thought about the dream. Doris had changed to Angela. Who were the two young girls? He smiled as he remembered how beautiful they were and how much joy radiated from them. He was glad that the vampire was gone even though he had no idea what it meant.

He turned over and looked at the clock on the night stand. What was going to happen was a big question but he knew that those on military time usually started early. He pulled the covers back and put his feet on the floor. He decided to get dressed and spend time in prayer until he found out the plan for the day.

He had almost finished his time of meditation and prayer when he heard someone knock. It was Captain Jarvis. He informed Father that they would go have breakfast then come back to his room for the interview. Everything would be recorded and later transcribed. The entire group would then come together for what Captain Jarvis called a grand session.

The way Captain Jarvis treated him gave Father the impression that the government was not going to press charges, but that they wanted to accumulate as much information as they could about Enoch's last days. Besides, Enoch was not governmental property, he was a person. Father knew the government could not present a case against him or any of the group that would stand up in court, and that Captain Jarvis realized it, too. They walked to the officer's mess, a small dining area inside the building. The place was alive with military personnel starting their day. Captain Jarvis led the way through the serving line then found a small table over in the corner of the room.

"Father, why don't you say the blessing this morning?"

Father smiled. "I would be glad to."

The prayer was more than a blessing of the meal, it was an invitation for the Holy Spirit to take charge and direct the day's proceedings. He also prayed for each of the group and that truth would prevail in every situation.

"You guys are going to spoil me if you keep feeding me like this," Father said, spreading jelly on his toast. "The fine meal last night and now a great breakfast, I could get used to this."

"It's all a part of the Army life," Captain Jarvis laughed. "We could always use a good Chaplain."

"Right now, that doesn't sound that bad."

They laughed and talked about life in the military. Father found out that the captain had only been in the service for three years. He had graduated from law school in Illinois and immediately joined the military. A proud look came on his face as he pulled out his billfold and showed Father his wife and two small sons. Father's heart rejoiced when he shared that he was a Christian.

"Did you ever meet Enoch?" Father asked, as he put his napkin on his plate and pushed his chair back.

"No, I only became involved when he was found missing along with Dr. LePage."

"So you know nothing of the babies being sacrificed or of Enoch's reason for leaving Atlantis?"

"I know very little. I asked General Sears yesterday, after you mentioned Enoch being from Atlantis, if there were indeed babies being killed. He said the information was too classified to discuss."

Father frowned. "So what do they want from us?"

"They want to know what happened to Enoch, what happened in the cave, and why fifteen soldiers out of our top notched Special Forces section are blind and your group is not."

"Everything we all share is going to sound crazy and made up unless they understand that Enoch was sent here by God for a specific mission. He passed that mission on to our group and then was caught up to be with the Lord."

Captain Jarvis shook his head. "Father Macon, my job is not to judge the content of your deposition. It is only to make sure that it is taken in an atmosphere free of influence or bias. It is the same for every member of your group."

Father rubbed his stomach and smiled. "I'm as ready as I'll ever be."

"Good, let's go back to your quarters and we'll get started."

The two men went back to Father's room and set up the recording equipment. Captain Jarvis performed a sound check and when everything was ready Father began telling his story. He started from the time he met Enoch at the mine shaft. At times the captain would stop him to ask a question but most of time was content just to let Father talk. Father included every detail he could remember, realizing that those who would listen to his deposition would have the power to shut down the experiments at Los Alamos.

When he came to the part about 'the light' he shared about the figures he saw in the light but only that he recognized Enoch and Jesus. Captain Jarvis frowned when Father described his encounter with the Lord. To Father that was the most important part and he didn't care what they thought. He wasn't going to leave it out in fear that it would scandalize the deposition. He knew that others in the group had also seen Jesus in the light and they would validate his claim. When he shared about carrying the soldiers to safety just as the cave exploded Captain Jarvis asked him who blew up the cave.

"I'm going to say that it was the Lord. There were things in that cave that could add proof to our story, but that is not the Lord's way. All we have is our words. Either you believe what we are saying and stop the experiments at Los Alamos or you conjure up some logical explanation to satisfy your mind and continue with the sacrificing of the babies until God puts a stop to it. Either way, I promise it will end."

Father pulled his finger across his throat indicating that he was finished, prompting Captain Jarvis to shut off the recorder.

"Pretty amazing story," he said, as he wrapped up the microphone cord and put it away.

"I know," Father laughed. "It sounds amazing to me too, but every word is true."

Captain Jarvis looked at his watch. "Do you mind waiting here until I run this tape and equipment back over to the office? Then I'll come back and take you to lunch."

"I don't mind at all. Any idea when I can talk with the others?"

"I'm not sure. As soon as they finish their depositions it should be okay. But I'll have to check on that and make sure." He looked at his watch again. "I'll see you in about an hour and fifteen minutes."

"I'll be waiting."

Captain Jarvis bundled up the recording equipment and left. Father wondered how the others were doing. He prayed that each one would remember every important detail. He lay back on the bed and thought about the time in the light. Suddenly he heard the Voice.

"Bring all the young soldiers together in the room with the

group and I will heal them. Have them share what is in their hearts and what I have shown them. They will assist you in the mission."

Father waited, wondering if there would be more. He prayed and listened until the captain returned. There was no more.

They again went to the officer's mess for lunch. Father said nothing of the message. After the meal the captain rode with Father back to the building where the group had first been taken. They walked to the cafeteria. As they entered they were greeted by the rest of the group. There were hugs and handshakes. They talked and shared until Captain Jarvis reluctantly asked them to be seated. As they did General Sears entered the room accompanied by two men that Father recognized as Dr. Melvin Laird and Dr. Bernard Tobin from the press conference in Albuquerque. He looked over at Angela as the two men were introduced. She showed no sign of fear or intimidation.

General Sears explained that they would listen to the deposition tapes and compare stories. He had called this meeting to give the group the opportunity to hear each other's experience and maybe add to their content. The discussion would focus only on what happened in the cave. The entire meeting would be recorded. After the equipment was in place the old Chief was called on to begin.

He started his story with Susie leading the group to the two burial sites that they determined were men similar to Enoch. He shared what he could remember of the writing describing the fate of the men and how the tomb could be entered. Others in the room nodded in agreement as he shared how the wall exploded by using a battering ram somehow encased within the tomb. Father sat remembering every detail of his story until the Chief got to the part about the light.

"When the shaft of light suddenly appeared I saw every one of the soldiers drop their weapons and grab their eyes as if they were on fire. I wanted to go help but I could not move. Suddenly the light became brighter and inside the light with Enoch was Jesus." He laughed. "I have never seen Jesus before but I knew it was Him. A sense of extreme peace came over me. The love was so overwhelming that I had difficulty keeping my composure. Then I heard Gabe Running Deer's voice. He invited me into the light. I had no trouble moving toward him. I noticed that to my right, Susie was walking toward him also. We both made it to him about the same time. He smiled and hugged us both. He looked wonderful. He told us that he was proud of us for being obedient to the Lord's calling, and how being true to the mission was vital to the destiny of many souls. He thanked me for leading him to the Lord and that both Susie and I needed to be a..." He looked at Susie. "What was the word?"

"A conscience for the red man."

"Yes, that's right. And that God would soon open a door for the conversion of many of our native brethren. He said something to Susie but I'll let her tell you."

Susie stood up. Tears were running down her cheeks. She looked at the general and the two scientists. "He told me to forgive the men who had meant him harm." She stood, wiping her eyes then sat down.

The old Chief continued his story of how they had helped the soldiers to the chopper and how he had felt the urgency in his spirit to get out of the cave as soon as possible. He recounted the explosion and how it had rocked the helicopter.

"The rest is really uneventful. We flew to here." He looked at Captain Jarvis who nodded his appreciation. The Chief smiled then sat down.

Captain Jarvis then looked at Susie. "Miss Running Deer?"

Susie shook her head as she stood again. "I have nothing to add.

Everything was just as George described it except that I now know we have much work to do. No one should miss what we experienced. My brother's face shone like the sun. There is no need for my father to morn." She looked at General Sears. "If it is immortality you seek, find the light of Jesus. It is there that your quest will end."

Father looked at the old Chief and smiled. At least one powerful witness had been born in the cave. Considering the joy radiating from the faces of Angela and Denise as Susie sat down, he knew there were two more.

Captain Jarvis seemed unmoved by Susie's remarks. He looked over at Denise. "Miss Cameron, anything you want to add?"

Denise quickly stood. "I have nothing to add up to the time the light came into the cave. As soon as the light engulfed Enoch the soldiers went blind. It was the light that blinded them but it did not harm us." She looked at the old Chief. "I did not see Gabe Running Deer. I did, however, see Jesus standing with Enoch. I, too, knew it was Jesus even though I have never seen Him, except in pictures. As I focused on Him the peace that filled me was awesome. It was then that I heard my Aunt May's voice. She invited me to come to her. As I walked into the light, I remember my necklace falling off."

General Sears interrupted. "Miss Cameron, what kind of necklace was it?"

"It was a black braided cord with a small medallion about the size of a quarter. On one of its surfaces was the symbol for the yin and the yang."

General Sears nodded that he understood. "Please continue."

"In the light I met Aunt May. She was beautiful. She was so excited that I had made Jesus my Lord. Her prayer, she said, had been answered. She told me to make the mission a top priority."

Denise wiped her eyes as she looked at Father. "Right before Aunt May departed she told me to leave there, go forth and write her a headliner." Denise removed a napkin from the table and wiped her eyes. She looked up at Captain Jarvis. "Because of what happened to me I am not afraid of anything on this earth. I know that God loves us so much and He wants the best for all of us. When we begin to play God and use our power and status to misuse and abuse innocent life, He is obligated to intervene. What you found in that cave in Chaco Canyon was God's mercy. Enoch was preserved for thousands of years as a testimony to God's mercy to this generation. We can either heed the call or continue to play god ourselves. Now you can shoot me or lock me away, but I will do all that I can to open the eyes of the people and let them know that we can no longer treat innocent life as nothing, just because we have the opportunity and the capability. As I shared in my deposition, Enoch said that Atlantis was destroyed because the people became drunk on the blood of the innocents." She looked at Dr. Laird. "You men are trying to give birth to that same drunkenness. I beg you to leave it alone."

Dr. Laird looked down, breaking eye contact with Denise. She knew he was the one in charge of the program and he had the power to end it. She continued to stand and stare at Dr. Laird until Captain Jarvis asked her to be seated. Father could feel the tension building in the room. Before the captain could say anything else Dr. LePage stood and faced the general and her former colleagues.

"What all these people are saying is the truth. I am the reason they are here. No, let me rephrase that. God is the reason they are here. Science is a wonderful thing but I have found that it must have boundaries. We cannot become demented and barbaric under its banner. You were becoming that way and I along with you. But something happened years ago that gave birth to a voice, a voice crying in the wilderness. I had an abortion. I was told by the scientists and medical people that it was just a piece of tissue. It was not really alive. But that was a lie. It was alive and it had an immortal soul. And that soul had a voice, too. Every time we took the life of one of those babies I could hear that voice crying out to me. At first I paid it no attention, but the more we sacrificed, the louder the voice became until I could stand it no longer. When Enoch told me of Atlantis and how the scientists of his day were doing the same thing and it had resulted in the destruction of his country, I knew I could no longer be a part of the madness. When he asked me to help him get away, I agreed. And I would do it over again a thousand times over." She looked across the table at Father Macon. "On the journey to the cave, you told me to name the baby I had aborted and I did. I named him Nathan because, just like you said, I asked the Holy Spirit and He told me it was a boy. When the light came into the cave, I too saw Jesus. I saw Enoch and Jesus embrace. But then I saw Enoch smile and point to a young man also standing in the light. As I walked into the light I came face to face with the soul I had aborted. I was ashamed and he knew it but he embraced me and held me for a long time. I could not stop crying." She paused to wipe her eyes and gather her composure. "He was such a handsome young man. He was not a blob of tissue or a mistake. He was a living soul that I had refused to let live out his life." She continued to cry. "But do you know what? He did not hate me or hold one ounce of bitterness toward me. Right before he left he said two things to me: 'Mom, I love you,' and 'Mom, thanks for giving me life.'" She broke down and began to sob.

"I recommend that we take a thirty minute recess then conclude with Father Macon."

The general and the scientists quickly left the room. Father Macon and the others crowded around Dr. LePage who continued

269

to sob. Now they all knew what God had used to bring them together. Angela had heard Nathan's voice every time she had assisted in ending another innocent life and it had finally become overpowering. It had not ended, however, in sadness but in ultimate joy. God had rewarded her by reuniting her with the voice of the one crying in the wilderness, her son, Nathan.

After a few minutes she apologized and wiped her eyes. "Thank you. I don't know what I would have done without all of you. I love you all."

It was obvious that the group had grown together and had become bound together by the light and the mission.

Captain Jarvis opened one of the coolers and issued everyone a soft drink. Father placed one in front of Angela then sat down across the table.

"Angela, I've been wondering. Who is Doris LePage?"

Angela's eyes grew wide as she smiled. "The Holy Spirit told you?"

"I've had two dreams about a little girl named Doris LePage."

"I was born Doris Ann LePage."

The others gathered around her as she continued. "When I was a small girl I loved my dollies. I wanted to be a mother so badly. When I became pregnant, my parents had a fit. They were high up on the social ladder and an unwed pregnant daughter meant instant ridicule and alienation for them and me. I wanted to keep the baby, but my father demanded that I have an abortion. After the abortion I felt terrible. I hated Doris LePage and I think I started hating my father and all men. I changed from wanting to be a mother to wanting to be something equal with men. I became a scientist. How manly can you get? When I left home I dropped the Doris and added to the Ann. I became Angela LePage and I've been Angela until the cave. Now I know that Doris has been there all the time. She has just wanted to be free."

"Do you have any sisters?" Father asked, thinking about his recent dream.

Angela laughed. "No, I was an only child." She looked at Father and frowned. "Why?"

"In my second dream I saw two beautiful young girls hanging on to you and referring to you as mom."

"What does that mean?"

Father shrugged his shoulders. "I don't know. I was hoping you might."

Their conversation was suddenly interrupted by the captain calling everyone back to order.

Everyone found their seats as the general and the two scientists entered the room. Captain Jarvis quickly took the lead and announced that Father Macon would be the last to share. The recording equipment was restarted and Father was given the cue. He stood and looked at the group.

"I would like each of you to know that I am very proud of all of you. God rewarded us with a great gift and gave us a mission. We were privileged to meet and get to know a man who came from a previous time and age, but a man who loved and served the same God. We observed this love as he gave his life to save the life of our young children. But we also saw his wisdom. It was above and beyond anything I had ever witnessed and that wisdom proclaimed a dire warning to this generation: God will not allow the sacrificing of innocent lives to go unpunished. A time of retribution will come." He looked at Dr. Laird. "Dr. Laird, I know that you are the one in charge of this program and that you are a man of science. What you have heard from all of us is not science but it is the truth. You could accuse us of lying or you could say that the tomb contained some rare chemical and we were all delusional. But God wants you and all of your companions to know the severity of your work and the condemnation you are bringing to this world. General Sears, the doctors have examined the soldiers and have found nothing pathologically wrong with them. Am I correct?"

The general nodded reluctantly. "That is correct."

"The Lord has told me that if you will bring those soldiers here and line them up around us, when we pray for them, they will be healed and receive their sight. But, the Lord also wants you to hear what they have to say."

The general stood. "Mr. Macon, we have flown in medical specialists from across this land and none have been able to diagnose or solve the problem. Do you expect me to believe that a simple prayer will restore these men to normal?"

Father shook his head. "General, these men will never be 'normal' again as *you* define normal. They have stood in the presence of the Prince of Peace and even though they never saw Him, they felt His presence. They will no longer have a heart of hate and war. You have already witnessed it but you define it as shock because the men no longer behave like soldiers. While in the cave, they also received a gift, the peace that surpasses all understanding. They are all still soldiers, but from now on they'll be fighting for a different Kingdom."

The general looked at Captain Jarvis. "Captain, this is highly irregular. While we have gathered here to discern the facts it is very obvious that Mr. Macon wants to keep us on this roller coaster of fantasy. I think it would be best if we called a halt to this meeting. We have heard their testimony and now we will need time to study their depositions and correlate the facts."

Captain Jarvis started to speak but Father interrupted. "General, what did you find in the cave?"

The general frowned. "We had a team scour the cave. Whatever exploded in there was like a mini atomic bomb. Everything was destroyed. The heat was so strong that even the walls of the cave were turned to glass."

"And what did you find?"

The general stood in silence in defiance to Father's question.

"General, what did you find?"

The general reached into his pocket and pulled out a small yellow envelope. He opened it and poured the contents out on the table.

Denise gasped. "It's my necklace!"

The general took the necklace and held it up. "This, Mr. Macon, is all we found."

"General, don't you see?" Father asked, almost shouting. "Isn't it interesting that the heat destroyed the soldier's weapons, the bodies of Enoch's countrymen, the ram device, everything in the cave but that necklace? When Denise entered the light that thing fell off because only the truth is allowed in the light. That necklace represents a lie but it is the lie that you have sworn allegiance to. That is why your heart is hardened to the truth that stands before you today. God protected that necklace to give you a choice. You can receive what God is saying through Enoch and through us and stop this infanticide or you can put that thing around your neck and live the lie the rest of your life. But if you choose to wear that thing, may God have mercy on your soul."

"General," the captain interrupted, "we don't have anything to lose. I can have the men here in less than thirty minutes. After all, they are a part of this. It would not be right to exclude their testimony."

Every eye in the room was on the general. He looked at the captain then at Father Macon.

"Mr. Macon, I've never believed much in prayer or in God, but I am a just man. What Captain Jarvis said is true. These men are part of the equation and they need to be heard. But sir, I am their commander and I am damn proud of my men. I refuse to allow any of them to be subjected to some carnival type prayer meeting. I will, however, allow for you to pray for them. If your God can heal them He can do it without a lot of fanfare and hullabaloo."

Father smiled. "I will be as respectful to these men as if they were my brothers."

"Fair enough. Captain Jarvis, you may call the infirmary and have them escort Major Walcott and his men to this cafeteria."

The captain quickly left the room. Father sat down and looked at the old Chief then at the others. "Everyone just be quiet and pray."

CHAPTER TWELVE

The Power of Love

Captain Jarvis was true to his word. Within thirty minutes four vans pulled up to the front of the building. All fifteen of the soldiers were on board along with eight attendants assigned to assist the men. Father was amazed at how the men handled themselves even in their blindness. The pride of who they were was still very apparent in their demeanor. Under the direction of the captain the soldiers were escorted to the cafeteria then the attendants were asked to go back to the vans. The soldiers stood at parade rest around the group. Not one could see but they all stood like stone. They were not dressed in military garb, but in suits similar to jogging outfits. It was apparent that they knew nothing of why they had been summoned. Captain Jarvis closed the door, turned on the recording equipment and then looked at Father Macon.

"Father Macon, it's all yours."

Father stood and looked around at the men. "Rangers, can all of you hear me?"

"Yes, sir," they repeated in one voice.

"Good. This morning the Lord Jesus Christ told me that if I would bring you here, He would heal your blindness. I believe that you were blinded in the cave because you were not prepared for what the Lord was doing. I know since that time each of you have heard the Voice of the Lord along with other visions and voices. I believe that your being in the cave was no accident. Like us, you were there for a purpose. As I pray I hope that each of you will come to understand that purpose. Let's pray." Father held his arms up toward the men. "Lord Jesus, you are the God who heals and makes whole. Nothing on, below or above this earth can withstand the power of Your Name. These men are Your creation, the work of Your hand. And so in the Name of Jesus Christ I speak to the blindness that has each man bound and command that the blindness cease and that each and every eye be opened."

The soldiers stood still for a few seconds but suddenly all of them began to rub their eyes. Laughter began to break out among them. Each one began to blink then turn and look around at each other.

General Sears and the scientists stared in amazement. They looked around the room as each soldier gained his eyesight and began to rejoice. Suddenly Dr. Laird removed his eyeglasses and also began to blink and look around the room.

"Ha," he laughed. "My eyes are healed too."

Father laughed out loud as the room broke out in spontaneous rejoicing. The soldiers began to clap their hands then hug each other. Major Walcott walked over to Father and hugged him. Tears were flowing down the major's cheeks.

"Thank you."

"The thanks belong to Jesus," Father said quietly. "His love for you has set you free."

Soon the entire room was aglow with the love of God. The old Chief and the ladies joined the fellowship. They hugged and encouraged each of the young soldiers. Even General Sears and Dr. Tobin realized that they were witnessing something beyond their understanding. Suddenly the door swung open and the hospital attendants and others from the building stood wide-eyed, gazing at the spectacle. The power of God was so strong, however, that soon they too became part of the celebration. One big, heavy attendant was crying like a baby as Denise hugged him and gave him comfort. Soon every person in the entire building was in the cafeteria and caught up in the presence of God and the power of His love. Father laughed as he watched people come to the door, look in, then become "zapped" by the anointing. For over an hour people laughed, cried, confessed their sins, prayed, and several ended up on the floor, slain in the Spirit. Several times the room would erupt in shouting as someone realized that their eyes had been healed. Father counted at least six pairs of eye glasses held in the air in witness to their healing. Suddenly he felt a tap on his shoulder. He turned to find Dr. Laird. Tears filled his eyes.

"What do I have to do to gain forgiveness for the terrible things I have done?"

Father smiled. "Just tell Jesus you're sorry and that you will change. Then ask Him to forgive you."

Dr. Laird shut his eyes and began to pray. Father put his hand on the doctor's shoulder and prayed for him. He wondered if it was the first time the man had ever prayed. He knew it would not be the last. As Dr. Laird opened his eyes, a huge grin came to his face.

"What love," he said, excitedly.

"Amen," Father laughed, as the two men embraced.

The excitement in the room continued for over an hour. As it began to wane the atmosphere changed from exuberance to reverence. People began to take a seat around the cafeteria and quietly pray. What started with fifteen soldiers had grown to almost a hundred people, all who had no desire to leave. Father allowed the silence to continue for a little longer then he stood up and faced the general.

"General Sears, you are the commander of this base and you

rule over all those who are stationed here. What we have just experienced is the Ruler of the universe. You stated that you didn't want your men subjected to a carnival type prayer meeting. With all due respect, sir, I believe you were overruled. I believe with all my heart that God has spoken very profoundly to us." Father looked around the room. "The soldiers were temporarily blinded and they were healed. But, many others in the room also received an increase in vision. God is saying, 'Don't be blind. Open your eyes to the truth. I uphold the universe with the Words of My mouth and I will not allow you to destroy innocent life." He turned and looked for Major Walcott. Finding him, Father motioned for him to stand. "Major, I believe that you and your men were given something during your period of blindness. Would you please share that with us?"

Major Walcott stood and faced the General. "Sir, let me say that I am still not sure what has happened to me, but I am no longer the man that walked into that cave. I have talked with every one of my men and they bear witness to what I am saying. During our period of blindness we were given a vision. That's the best way I can describe it. It was like watching a movie on a huge TV screen. In this vision, my men and I were standing in full gear, ready for whatever comes, when suddenly we were surrounded by thousands of babies. They were too young to be able to walk and talk but they somehow could, and they were pulling on the legs of our trousers and shouting at us. 'You're killing us. You're killing us.' They were shouting! Their shouts became so loud that it sounded like a great waterfall. As the sound became so deafening we all dropped our weapons and covered our ears. Suddenly the yelling stopped and we heard a voice say, 'Love one another. Each of you has been given a great gift. Learn to look out for one another and to respect and nurture the life you have been given. Cease in your blindness and your dedication to your own selfishness and desires. The future of the world is in your hands and in your hearts.' I turned to see where the voice was coming from. On a platform above us, all the children were now changed into a single man. He didn't look like any man I have ever seen. His facial features were odd. I asked him, 'Who are you, sir?' And he answered, 'I am Enoch, the Tongue Master, the messenger of the Living God.'"

The major paused and looked strongly at the general. "General, you know me. I am the holder of the Bronze and Silver Stars. I am not a quitter. But, something has happened to me, and to my men, that I can't explain." He turned and looked around the room and as he did, his men began to stand. "General, my men and I have all talked. We can no longer be soldiers. We have lost the desire to fight and kill."

Silence filled the room. Father looked at the major and smiled. How awesome it is, he thought, to fall into the hands of the Living God.

The general stood and motioned for everyone to be seated. Father, the major and his men took their seats. "Any good leader recognizes when he had been out maneuvered. I have always done what I thought was best for the people I command and my country. I, too, realize that in some areas I have been blind. I promise that I will, along with Dr. Laird and Dr. Tobin, study everything associated with this matter. I understand the responsibility that we have and the consequences that could result if we fail to understand what favor has been granted to us." He looked at Father Macon. "Father, would you mind dismissing us with prayer?"

Father stood and had everyone stand. He prayed that those in authority would have the grace and wisdom to make the right decisions. He thanked the Lord for all that had happened and for sending Enoch into their lives. Then he had everyone say the

Lord's Prayer together. As they finished, the entire room broken into spontaneous applause.

The Chief looked at Father. "As Aunt May would say, the Lord is good."

Father and the group spent the next couple of days waiting on orders from the general. They were given the freedom of the base. The group spent most of their time together, talking and sharing about the experience and about what the future held for them. They were all together in Father's room in one such discussion when someone knocked on the door. As Father opened it, he was surprised to see Dr. Melvin Laird. Everyone greeted him warmly as he entered and took a seat on the side of the bed.

"I came by because I wanted you to know that we have stopped the research on the anti-aging enzymes."

The group cheered and applauded.

"Realize, however, that there was strong opposition to our decision. I refused to carry on with the work, but there are others who do not have our understanding and they are unrelenting in their determination."

"So our mission is not really over," Denise stately sadly.

"It is for now. But long term, I'm afraid not. General Sears was very forceful in his sharing of what has transpired, but for many it seemed too outlandish. Dr. LePage and I know the people who have worked on this project and they are very strong-willed. Enoch only proved to them that anti-aging was possible. They will stop at nothing to achieve their goal."

"So, Father, where does that leave us?" Susie asked. "Was all this for nothing?"

Father shook his head. "No, Susie, we were successful. It is stopped for now, but it *is* stopped. The only way we can make sure that it never starts again is to share Enoch's message with everyone who will listen. Enoch's message really must become our message. If we do nothing, it will return for sure. But, if we tell the story of God's special visitor some people will listen and they will believe. When enough believe, it will stop forever."

The old Chief agreed. "That is really all we can do. We were chosen for this mission. We have come from many paths, but our path has become one. We must all believe that. And we must believe that we are not alone. The Great Spirit will always be the wind beneath our wings. If we trust Him, we cannot fail."

The group knew he was right. For some reason God had selected them from different walks of life to bear witness to a great event in time. If they would be bold and share the story, He would honor their efforts.

Dr. Laird stood and extended his hand to Father. "I came by to tell you the good news and to tell you that all of you are free to go."

Father smiled as he shook hands. "That is good news."

"They'll have transportation for you in about an hour. They will take you wherever you want to go."

Dr. Laird shook hands with the group. When he got to Susie he laughed. "Miss Running Deer, General Sears wanted me to tell you that your horses were recovered and taken back to your father."

"Oh my gosh," she laughed. "I forgot about them. Thank you."

Father walked with Dr. Laird out into the hallway. "Dr. Laird, what about Major Walcott and his men?"

"They have asked for an early out and General Sears has agreed to sign their papers. That is all I know."

"Thank you, and tell the general thanks for his help and understanding."

"I will. He said to tell all of you good-bye and good luck. He also said to tell you that if he ever really gets in a jam he may call you for another carnival prayer meeting."

"Tell him, anytime."

The men again shook hands.

Father walked back into the room. The others were waiting silently. He could sense the sadness. They all knew that their journey together was coming to an end. It had been exciting and rewarding but it seemed almost like a fairy tale. The silence was broken by another knock on the door. Father turned and opened the door. He was greeted by Captain Jarvis.

"You guys doing okay?"

Father smiled. "We're facing the reality that we're all going to have to go home." He stepped aside and motioned with his hand. "Come on in."

The captain entered and looked around at the others. "I want you to know that for the last two days my phone has not quit ringing. This base is abuzz with what happened in the cafeteria." He looked at Father. "Every chaplain stationed here has called me. My vocabulary was very inadequate in describing what we all witnessed. They have apparently been swamped with calls that caught them completely off guard. I want you to know that I have never experienced anything like that. Many of the people who were in that room had miraculous things happen and they need some answers. I must admit that my own faith was stretched beyond its limit. This type of stuff is kind of hard to explain when you've been a pew sitter all your life."

"Captain Jarvis, we told the truth in our depositions and God was simply backing up our stories. When He shows up miracles happen because what is miraculous for us is normal to Him."

"I still don't understand it but I do owe each of you an apology. When I first heard your depositions I thought all of you had been smoking some peyote. Since the cafeteria, however, I must admit that my opinion of you has changed. I don't know if you're interested, but there is an open door for any or all of you who would like to stay and share with the different churches here on base. All of the chaplains said to give you an invitation."

Father looked around the room. "Well gang, what do you think?"

"I don't think we've got an option," Denise quickly replied. "When Aunt May spoke to me in the light, she said to write her a headliner. She would not have told me that if this thing was over this easily. I'm convinced that Dr. Laird is right. It may be a dead issue now, but if we don't inform the people, this thing will try to return. Enoch handed the mission on to us. If God opens the doors we have to be ready to walk through them."

Everyone in the room agreed. Father looked at Captain Jarvis. "Well, Captain, I guess the answer is yes. I for one, however, would like about a week to make contact with the people in my parish and let the bishop know that I'm okay."

The captain smiled and walked toward the door. "That should be about right. I'll talk to the various chaplains and get times and dates set up."

The old Chief walked over and took the captain by the arm. "Does this mean that you are going to be our manager?"

The entire group laughed.

The captain laughed too but his face suddenly became solemn. "Chief, I'm not sure. But, I do know that I'll never be satisfied to just be a pew sitter again. I know that somewhere in the Bible Jesus talked of 'living water.' I now have a better idea of what He was talking about. I, too, would like to know more. I will be glad to help in any way I can."

The group again broke into laughter and applause. Everyone

was excited about the opportunities that the Lord was providing for them all. Father gave the captain a business card.

"Keep me informed. I should be back within the week."

The captain agreed, wished everyone well, and then left the room.

Everyone decided to take the week and make necessary arrangements. As they stood in the parking lot, their good-byes were not nearly as hard as they first thought they would be. They would all be back together in a week. That made departure so much easier.

Denise was taken back to her hotel. Dr. LePage was already living on the base. She stood and waved as Father, Susie and the Chief drove away. They rode together as far as Susie's house then the driver chauffeured them to the old Chief's. The journey had come full circle. As they pulled up in the yard, another car was already parked there.

"Whose car is that?" Father asked.

"Beats me. I've never seen it before."

The two men thanked the young driver then said good-bye. They walked to the house and opened the door. There at the dining table sat Bill Staples. A huge smile covered his face as he stood to greet the two men.

"Gentlemen," he said, sticking out his hand to greet them. "Miss Cameron has informed me that you had a most excellent adventure."

"With an emphasis on 'most,'" Father laughed. "How are you doing?"

"I am fine. I was so glad to see Denise back at the hotel. She told me a lot of what happened. I wanted you to know that you're truck is in town. When I drove it back after we left, they intercepted me. I tried not to talk but they started threatening me, my business, and my family. After a while I finally gave in and told them where I had last seen you and the man from Atlantis. I prayed that they wouldn't find you but I guess it was part of God's plan that they did."

Father and the old Chief told Bill the entire story including the part in the cafeteria. It was getting very late when Bill finally ran out of questions. Father called the airlines and made reservations for a flight the next day to Little Rock. Bill decided to stay the night then run the old Chief to town and Father to the airport. Bill was so excited to hear the story of their adventure that he didn't want to go to bed. Father laughed as he asked, 'one more question.'

"I still haven't figured out how the crash of the UFO at Roswell fits in. Is it a part of all this?"

Father frowned. "You know, Bill, I've thought a lot about that this past week. I've wondered the same thing. I've come up with two scenarios. One, the aliens are time skippers as you call them and they were looking for Enoch to make sure he was okay until the appropriate time. If they were, that would make them good guys and part of God's plan. Unfortunately they met with an uncalculated disaster much like the Atlancho. But, what if they were from a future where Satan has a strong influence and they were sent to destroy Enoch, and prevent his message. They would then be bad guys. Maybe God intervened and destroyed them before they could destroy Enoch. We'll probably never know. But think about this. The description of the 'men' in that UFO was not a good indication of the future of the earth, if they are time skippers."

The frown on both Bill's and the old chief's face told Father that they did not understand.

"Think about their description. The body was hairless, grey-colored skin and large eyes and long fingers. All species are designed for maximum efficiency for their environment. Every characteristic indicates that they dwell in caves or holes in the earth, the large eyes, the tough grey skin, the long fingers, and the lack of hair."

"Just like the Dropa," Bill exclaimed.

"Exactly. Now what type of condition would drive men to live in caves or holes in the earth?"

The old Chief was first to answer. "Nuclear fallout."

Bill shook his head in disgust. "Man! That would explain their interest in the past. If they could change it, they could change their future."

The old Chief stood up and yawned. "Plenty of food for thought, but right now, we have a mission that can definitely affect the future of many souls. I can shut my eyes and still see the smile on Enoch's face as he stood in the light. Jesus Himself met Enoch to escort him to his reward. The power of that love is something that others must come to know. With enough love maybe the earth won't need any more visitors."

EPILOGUE

Father returned home to the excitement of his parishioners and to the comfort of the bishop. The bishop was glad that one of his priests was not going to have to serve time in a federal pen.

The time back at the base was exciting. The churches were full and attentive as the group shared about Enoch and his message. There were some who scoffed and walked out in disbelief. But in nearly every service, there was someone who testified that they had been healed that day in the cafeteria.

Captain Jarvis became a good friend to the group and embraced the spreading of the message. In all, ten days were spent sharing on the base and in churches around the area. Holy Spirit rock in Chaco Canyon became quite a tourist attraction.

Denise stayed with the paper, but also became very involved in ministry, as did Susie and the old Chief.

Angela moved to West Texas where she entered a theological school.

Major Walcott eventually became the senior pastor of a thriving church in Northern California.

Father went back to Arkansas and continued to share the story whenever the opportunity arose. He found himself much more involved with the anti-abortion platform and worked hard at teaching others the sanctity of life. One day he was surprised to find a letter on his desk. The return address read: Doris Ann Foster. He opened the letter.

The Visitor

Dear Father Macon,

It has been some time since I have heard from you but there is not a day goes by that I don't think about you and the others. About half way through theological school I met a wonderful man. We were married and after graduation he was assigned a church in Colorado. We live there now and the church is doing very well. Recently I found out I was pregnant. Today we had our second ultrasound. The doctor says that we are having twins and that they are both girls. I immediately thought of your dream. I know now who those two little girls were. God is so good. Now I will get to experience motherhood.

We would love for you to come and see us. Denise has been to see us several times and always asks about you. What would you think about a reunion with the group? I pray for every one of the group every day and it makes me miss all of you so much. I heard that Susie and the Chief are heavily involved with ministry to the Indians in New Mexico and Arizona. Susie wrote me and told me that she had prayed with her dad for salvation. Enoch is still touching our lives after all this time. I can't wait to see him again. Let me hear from you. I can't wait to see you. God bless,

Doris Ann (LePage) Foster

Father laid the letter back on the desk. His mind went back to the dream of Angela and the two little girls. Even though years had passed, God had been faithful to the dream. But that was no surprise; God has always been faithful. Thousands of years ago when different civilizations covered the earth, God had taken a messenger from that time and used him to confront the same growing evil of our time. That was definitely above and beyond all anyone could ask or think. A smile came to his face as he realized how fortunate he had been to be among only a select few who had met and come to know the Visitor.

Other Books by Dr. Dennis Holt

Presented by
CORNELIUS' HOUSE MINISTRIES

Available online at: www.corneliushouse.com

Handbook to Heaven – Reclaiming the Kingdom

The Kingdom of God

The Covenant

The Principality – A Novel*

The Manitou – A Novel*

The Anakim – A Novel

The Sorcerer – A Novel*

The Witch – A Novel

The Living Presence – Why the Eucharist is Alive

Living a Life in the Spirit Manual: A Seven Week Course

The Levitical Principle – God's Way of Financing the Kingdom of God On the Earth

It's Not Global Warming. It's Global WARNING!!!
Why the Earth Is Rebelling Against Man

The Gift of Tongues: The Fire of God

All books available from Cornelius' House Ministries
3115 Pyburn Extended, Pocahontas Arkansas 72455
Or go on-line at: www.corneliushouse.com

*Available as E-Books on Amazon.com or Barnes&Noble.com

The Visitor

The Visitor

The Visitor

The Visitor